ANGI

C000000803

Jennifer
Brown
To The Manner
Born

Riverside Publishing Solutions

I dedicate this book to Maurice Stevens

1931–2019

Acknowledgements

B ooks are not written in a void.

Writers need inspiration, encouragement and support and that comes from other people. The response to *Jennifer Brown's Journey* and *Jennifer Brown Moving On* has been so overwhelmingly positive from my many thousands of readers that it's made writing *Jennifer Brown To The Manner Born* both pleasurable and painful.

Pleasurable because it's been so much fun to dive into Jennifer's world again and take her on a new journey. But painful because the plan was always to stop after book three. So now I have to let her go.

But writing this book has been painful for other reasons. During the course of writing, we lost the wonderful Maurice Stevens, the hugely talented illustrator and graphic artist whose cover designs have contributed so much to the widespread appeal Jennifer Brown has enjoyed.

But the biggest blow came with the loss of my endlessly supportive husband, Brian, to pancreatic cancer. More than anyone, it was Brian who made me believe I could be a writer. Carrying on without him has been the toughest challenge of my life.

I was able to rise to the challenge with the help of my freelance editor, Howard Sargeant. Without him, Jennifer Brown just wouldn't be the same.

And, finally, *Riverside Publishing Solutions*. Their support and professionalism have helped me steer a steady course.

Thank you all. I hope you've enjoyed the ride as much as I have.

Contents

*You never notice how much space someone fills
in your life until the space is empty*

1

The Long Road Back

'Get a move on, you dozy cow!'

The cocky little sod buzzed his window back up and floored the gas in his BMW, throbbing away into the distance at a speed I imagine is *de rigueur* at Silverstone but rarely seen on this stretch of the A40.

I looked at my speedometer. Fifty-seven. A mere three miles an hour short of the limit. Not exactly pootling.

'Idiot!', I screamed, pointlessly, as his batmobile disappeared from view, leaving my little rental Kia Picanto in its dust.

Why was everyone in such a bloody hurry? Especially in the middle of winter. Who the hell knows what might be around the next slippy bend!

I was driving into the unknown in more ways than one, my life every bit as unpredictable as these winding Oxfordshire roads.

Just a few years ago, the old Jennifer Brown had marched out of the shitshow of a failed long-term relationship armed with nothing but a couple of suitcases and a clapped-out old Peugeot. And now, after a fair few twists and turns and the odd hairpin bend, here was the new Jennifer, on her way, via some lightning bolt of inheritance, to the Elizabethan manor house of which she was now mistress. The house and all its seventeen acres.

To say it had taken an effort of will for this to sink in is like saying Attila The Hun could be a bit testy.

After Camilla Winstanley had passed away, I'd been summoned to the oak-panelled offices of Montague and Maybole expecting to find I'd been left the oil painting that had been the treasured possession of Camilla's late husband and my ex-employer, George Winstanley. I'd been George's estate manager at Thornhill Hall and I knew how impressed he'd been that I'd managed to turn the crumbling estate into a profitable commercial enterprise.

When I'd admired the portrait that hung in the library, he'd told me it was of Arabella, his first wife. That I reminded him of her. We had the same spirit, he'd said. And he'd seen from my reaction that his words had only made me admire the painting even more. I'd felt sure, when Patrick Maybole had invited me to his office and poured me a sherry, that it was the painting I'd be inheriting.

What I didn't know was that, three weeks before his death, George had instructed his solicitors that, as there were no children to inherit, once Camilla has been laid to rest beside him, ownership of the estate was to pass to me.

Me. The woman who'd once been the worst typist on the planet.

Me. The erstwhile housekeeper to a saucy sexagenarian fisherman.

Me. The woman who'd been secretly groomed for the high life by the sophisticated and glamorous Cécile, George's not-so-secret lover and CEO of Artisan Wines, a high-end merchant supplying the finest of wines to the highest of high-net-worth individuals.

My role as client manager with Cécile's company had all been part of George's elaborate plan to prepare me for what now lay ahead.

My biggest adventure yet.

At the next set of lights, the BMW buffoon was revving his engine with delusions of Formula One grandeur. I pulled alongside, glanced over, and gave him my best *See how far that got you, you pillock* stare before the lights turned to green and he roared away to intimidate some other poor sod further up the road.

I checked the ETA on the Picanto's satnav. At this rate, I'd be reaching Thornhill in a short thirty-four minutes. Suddenly, all the old insecurities gathered on my shoulders like demons.

What if I wasn't up to this? What if my past successes had all been flukes? What if my old workmates and friends at Thornhill would resent me now I was lady of the manor?

This last one was the biggest demon of all. After a rocky first few days in my time as estate manager, we'd quickly become a solid team of mutually supportive colleagues and (in my mind, at least) pretty close friends.

But had I been kidding myself? Had they always thought of me as an uppity Jenny-Come-Lately parachuting in to take all the glory? And if that's how they'd thought of me as estate manage how would they think of me now as estate *owner*?

I tried to focus on George's description of me, relayed by Patrick Maybole. In me, George had told him, Thornhill had found 'the perfect custodian.'

Dear George. I could still see his beetling eyebrows, his shock of white hair and his steady gaze, that day of our first meeting. I liked him immediately and I think the feeling was mutual.

'I'm a crusty old bugger. But I've a feeling you can handle me and we'll get along.'

'I'm confident we will, Mr Winstanley.'

A series of strokes had made George's wheelchair a necessity but not a way of life – simply another challenge in a long life that was to test his spirit, not least in relation to affairs of the heart.

Arabella had died in a skiing accident at the tender age of twenty-eight. The grief-addled George had sprinted headlong into a rebound marriage with Camilla, a former fashion model who moved in 60s celebrity circles, had the Jean Shrimpton cheekbones and figure but, he would soon discover, lacked the spark and the polish of his first love.

And poor Camilla had then spent the following five decades of their marriage trying to make him love her but knowing all along he didn't. Knowing she didn't have his heart. Knowing his heart had been quietly won by another woman, an elegant sophisticate much more in the mould of his first wife. Cécile, the widow of his good friend, Charles. Cécile, whom George had supported through her grief. Cécile, to whom he'd slowly but completely given himself.

As I had to my lovely David. The man with the hazel eyes and the velvet vowels, David Harwood had been a constant presence on the edge of my mind for so long. And now he was finally mine to love.

I'd hoped he'd have been here at my side on this important day. But work commitments had dragged him to an office in New York where trouble had been brewing for months. And now, for the foreseeable future, he'd be bouncing back and forth across the Pond like a tennis ball across a Wimbledon net.

And anyway, this – pitching up at Thornhill as lady of the manor – was something he thought I should be doing very much on my own, rather than with a boyfriend in tow. I knew he had a point. But I'd have given all the bacon rolls in Billingsgate to have him by my side as I took on the mantle of mistress of Thornhill Hall, family seat of the Winstanley's, one of England's oldest families, with a direct line to John of Gaunt. What a name to conjure with!

Jennifer Brown. Not quite the same ring.

Brown. Mousy. Fawn. Dun.

Drab words with drab associations.

Jennifer Harwood-Brown. Hm. Now that sounds so much finer.

I was missing the warmth of David's smile, his quietly wicked sense of humour and, above all, the way he made me feel about life and about myself.

Being in love with him had renewed my faith in both, a position I could never have imagined reaching again after the devastation of my break-up with the treacherous Pete. Although my and David's long-distance relationship was bringing its own challenges, leaving some chinks in my newfound armour through which all the old insecurities could land their arrows. Skype and FaceTime were a help, of course, but the cameras on my devices had a knack of capturing images of my face that suggested a close resemblance to a steak-and-kidney pudding.

When David did manage to fly home for the odd weekend – currently averaging once every three months – I was a teenager all over again: hours in front of the mirror, half a dozen outfits tried on, butterflies waiting in Arrivals.

Then the very adult main event of a lazy weekend feasting on each other's company in a smart city hotel or a cosy lakeside retreat.

Our time together was precious. And we didn't waste a single second.

They say opposites attract. Our backgrounds could hardly have been more opposite. Cut from very different cloth, as my mum would have said.

David had come from a very affluent niche of a very well-heeled corner of Surrey. Top-notch prep school had fed into high-achieving private school which, in turn, had paved the way to Oxford.

By contrast, I'd been born a garter's throw from Portsmouth dockyard and the only thing I'd ever prepped were the ingredients for my mum's cakes. My five years at Brookhill High (largely spent bunking off with my partner in crime, Nat) had very much *not* been covered in academic glory. And while David had been cramming for his finals in PPE at Oxford, I'd been sinking vodka shots at Tiger Tiger before shaming myself on the dancefloor to the strains of *Relight My Fire*.

I glanced at the time. Still on track to arrive at noon. Suddenly, pitching up at Thornhill around lunchtime seemed like a bad move. I didn't want Rosemary to feel she had to feed me, delicious though her cooking always was. A neutral time in the middle of the afternoon would be a much safer option.

I pulled off the A40 at Burford, gateway to the Cotswolds, a chocolate-box vision of English gentility, a rural idyll heaving with teashops, antiques emporiums and retired colonels.

The pub just off the high street looked as unassuming as anything does in this part of the world. Its inglenook fireplace and heavy oak tables radiated cosy luxury, a luxury matched by the prices on the menu, a list of lunch options that was light on cheese-and-ham toasties and heavy on pigs cheek with samphire puree (*What the hell is samphire?*).

The waiter rattled off a litany of practised assertions about 'locally sourced ingredients' for dishes 'freshly cooked to order', a speech intended to make the prices more palatable.

I decided I was due a big-day treat so I relaxed into the opulence of the place and, an hour or so later, tried not to look sweaty as I swiped my card and swallowed a fifteen percent service charge the cheeky buggers slipped in under the radar, designed to squeeze as much blood as possible out of their standard clientele of Japanese and American tourists.

By the time my little rental Picanto buzzed through Thornhill's ancient and imposing wrought-iron gates, a watery January sun had burned through the cloud. Seemed like a good omen.

Then, from nowhere, a boy on a bike shot across the road in front of me, inches from my bonnet. My tyres bit into the gravel and my heart crashed into my back teeth. The boy continued to pedal on up the road, apparently unfazed by this nearest of misses. Then he skidded his machine to a halt twenty yards away, turned to fix me with an impudent gaze, and slowly and defiantly raised a middle finger in my direction, before pulling off the road and pedalling away over the grass towards the lake.

Who was this cheeky little sod? And what was he doing on my land?

You'll never get used to saying stuff like that, you daft cow. So don't even think it.

Veronica and Rosemary were walking down the steps to greet me as I climbed out of my little car.

Rosemary took my hand in both of hers.

'You look like you could murder a cuppa.'

2

Pecking Order

As we three sat around the old pine refectory table in the kitchen, slugging tea and tucking into Rosemary's world-beating scones, the familiarity of the scene was calming most of the nerves that had been fluttering around inside me.

Most, but not all.

Rosemary and Veronica were doing their best to radiate ease and warmth but it was clear they felt every bit as uneasy as I did about this new and very different dynamic. It was down to me to break the ice.

'So I was thinking I'd change my name to Henrietta de Quincey-Trumpington. What d'you reckon?'

Rosemary spat out her scone. 'They'd never fit that lot on a credit card.'

'Plus,' said Veronica, 'we'd call you Trumpers.'

It was good to hear their laughter.

'Seriously, though. This is really weird for me. When I got the call from George's solicitor, I thought I might be inheriting the painting. Of Arabella. Because I'd always admired it. And Camilla had always hated it. But when they told me … well, it still hasn't sunk in.'

Rosemary gave me her maternal smile. 'I can imagine, love.'

'I just want you both to know that, for me, this changes nothing. Between us. We're a team. Of equals. A bunch of people doing their best to keep this place going. For George. And a bit for Camilla.'

Rosemary put her hand on mine.

After an evening of laughter and wine and one of Rosemary's finest lamb roasts, Veronica helped me carry my bags up the stairs, past all the portraits of Winstanley ancestors glaring down unsmilingly at this low-class interloper.

It occurred to me, for half a second, that I should consider having myself immortalised in oils and hung up beside them.

Strung up more like, you daft cow.

As we walked along the corridor towards my old room, I noticed how threadbare the rug looked. What had always seemed like character was now looking like neglect.

We reached the room that had been Camilla's, its door firmly closed. Veronica saw me hesitate. 'We haven't had the stomach for it yet. It's up to you now, of course.'

'Let's find the right time to do it together.'

We got to my door. I hugged her. 'Good night.' She pulled me in tight. 'Night. Nice to have you back.'

The nervous energy that had fuelled me all day suddenly drained away and I flopped down onto the huge familiar bed and stared at the ceiling, memories of the place flooding in.

I'd come to Thornhill as estate manager on the back of a job as housekeeper to Gerald Fisher, a saucy old Hampshire fisherman who'd initially imagined my services might have extended into the bedroom. I'd very quickly and firmly quashed that notion and we'd settled into a relationship that had worked fairly well all round and in which my domestic management skills had developed apace. It had only been when his bombshell Russian mail-order bride, Tatty Anna, made it clear she was set on undermining my influence at every turn that I'd seen the writing on the wall and moved on.

But my rural Hampshire interlude had done its job. It had given me the chance and the space to rebuild myself, to climb out of the

depths I'd plunged headlong into after my relationship with Pete
and his Performing Pecker had come to a spectacularly messy end.

After Hampshire, Thornhill had felt right. The next logical step.
I was a person who knew her own flaws but also knew her own
strengths. I had the confidence I could do a good job. And others
seemed to believe that, too. It was a novel feeling. And one I enjoyed.

I glanced over at the elegant little walnut writing desk that
overlooked the garden and I remembered the first time I'd sat there.
You're exactly where you should be, I'd thought then.

I tried to recapture that feeling now.

I woke with a start, fully clothed. My mobile was buzzing on the
bedside table. David, calling from New York. Midnight his time.
5am mine.

'You said you'd call me. Is everything okay?'

'I'm sorry. I dropped off. Slept all night in my clothes.'

'How did it go?'

'Pretty well. I think. I've said my piece. Been honest. It's early
days, but I think it's going to work. Once we all adjust.'

'It's always tricky when a co-worker becomes the boss. I've been
there. It takes time. But I'm sure you'll handle it.'

'Thanks. It's really nice to hear you say that. But …'

'But what?'

'But I can't really think straight. It's five in the morning.'

'God! Of course. I'm sorry. I was just worried.'

'I know. I'm sorry for making you worry.'

'Get some sleep, my love.'

But my body had had its standard seven hours and now decided
it was time to be awake. I plugged my earphones in and tuned my
phone to the BBC World Service – my standard back-to-sleep
wonder drug – but after forty minutes of a report on human rights
in Angola (Africa's seventh largest country, since you ask), I needed
to get up. I blinked and looked at the ceiling.

Had that crack in the cornice always been there?

It was still a little too early for the rest of the household to be up and about. I decided to take advantage of the solitude, so I showered quickly and headed downstairs to have a proper look at the old place.

I pushed open the heavy oak door to the sitting room, which was clothed in darkness, as it had been, I suspected, since Camilla's death. It took most of my strength to heave open the heavy jacquard curtains. It wouldn't be properly light for another half hour but a silvery dawn revealed a little of the room's elegant interior: the Afghan rug, all swirling reds and golds; the deep four-seater feather-stuffed couches; the massive mahogany grandfather clock ticking away slowly and dependably in the corner.

Two rival feelings jockeyed for position. The first: *All this belongs to you. How exciting!* The second: *All this belongs to you. Don't bugger it up.*

In search of a lighter mood, I made my way through the house to the Orangery, Camilla's favourite spot in the whole house and the room where she'd hosted her afternoon tea parties, famous with the county's most affluent and well-connected ladies.

I remembered it from her funeral reception. Remembered toasting her with Rosemary and Veronica and Robbie and Kate (I was looking forward to seeing these last two again). Remembered Rosemary calling Camilla 'a bloody good egg.'

In the gathering dawn, the room's Italian mosaic floor looked sad and a bit shabby. My slippered footsteps echoed all the way up to the glass ceiling as I padded across the room's cavernous space, stroking the pineapple plants from which Robbie had, for years, tried to coax fruit.

'Lush in here, isn't it?'

I spun round to see, standing at the doorway into the hall, a middle-aged woman clutching a whole battery of cleaning equipment.

'Yes. It's very peaceful.'

She must have noticed the quizzical furrow in my brow and she dropped one of her buckets and stepped forward with her hand outstretched.

'Delyth. Pleased to meet you, ma'am.'

'Hi. Are you …?'

'The cleaning lady.'

'Right.'

'Veronica hired me. You know, after the previous woman … left.'

So Kate's gone. No, I didn't know. 'Right. Of course.'

'Well, I'd best get busy.'

'Yes. Sure.'

'See you later, ma'am.'

'Please. Call me Jennifer.'

'Right. Jennifer.'

An hour later, I buttonholed Rosemary in the kitchen.

'Kate decided to do the beauty thing full time. I miss having her around but, to be honest, Delyth does the work of five Kates. She's a whirlwind.'

'Do you get on okay with her?'

'She's fine. Sounds like her homelife's a bit of a challenge. Her husband's a lazy loser. So she does a full eight hours here, six days a week, and works evenings behind the bar at the golf club in Longrove. I have to drag her away from the hoover for a cup of tea.'

'Sounds like she's a very good worker. But are we paying her enough?'

'I think Veronica would like to pay her more. But …'

'But what?'

'Things are pretty tight.'

Veronica and I sat at the long library table and looked at the figures on her laptop. I could tell just by looking at the bottom lines that things had slipped quite a bit in the last two years.

When I'd left, there'd been a healthy diary of corporate events, all year round, averaging six or seven gigs a month: clay-pigeon shooting, quad-biking, the odd conference. I'd seen that as a solid foundation on which Veronica could build the business even more, expanding the portfolio of services, beefing up the hospitality side to include weddings and parties.

But it seemed that, with George's death, the enterprise had lost its direction and its drive. Companies were tightening their belts, Veronica said, and a lot of the clients that had briefly been regulars had now fallen away.

'Feedback has been consistently high, so it seems we're doing things right. We're just not doing them often enough.' She looked sheepish.

'Times definitely seem to be harder than they used to be. But there *is* still money out there. I know that from my time at Artisan Wines. Lots of money. I guess we just have to be more creative in how we find it. Look at other sources of income.'

'I'm sorry.'

'Oh, god. Don't apologise. It's business. It's a challenge. But we're up to it.'

I tried to sound confident and upbeat, but the figures on the screen were putting the fear of god in me. I owned this place. But I didn't have any private wealth to plough into it (contrary to appearances, neither had George). And it was clearly not self-sustaining at this point.

In addition, I discovered we were being chased for payments by Windrush House.

George's impossibly frail but redoubtable father, Edmund, now in his nineties, had been living in a private nursing home since his various health conditions had become impossible to manage in the apartment at the back of Thornhill Hall where he'd lived for a couple of decades.

The care he now needed didn't come cheap. But for the last couple of months it had come free. And they were now on the warpath.

On top of all this, I learned we had unwanted (and unpaying) tenants occupying Woodman's Cottage, on the lakeside edge of the estate.

Malcolm Clapp had been engaged by Camilla (in a rare moment of household rein-taking) to fix the badly weathered north-facing section of the ancient clay-tiled roof. In return for carrying out this work, Malcolm and his family would be allowed to live in the cottage rent free until the work was completed, a period Malcolm estimated at three months.

Everyone, Veronica included, had warned Camilla against this arrangement, not least because it was to be entered into on a handshake, with nothing written down, because Malcolm seemed like 'a nice man.' But in a final of show of independence in her final months, Camilla ignored everyone's advice and overruled all objections.

Predictably, Malcolm Clapp had never got round to fixing the roof, citing the onset of a back injury that would involve 'a few weeks' of recovery. After Camilla's death, and with Malcolm never having offered a penny in rent despite never having fixed a single tile, when Veronica challenged him he'd mentioned sitting tenants' rights and given her a mouthful of abuse.

All of which solved the mystery of the cheeky little sod on the bike.

The Clapps were yet another challenge I'd have to face. The words of my old boss at Intext, the effortlessly suave Jonathan Dashwood-Silk, leapt into my head.

It can be tough at the top.

3

Clapps And Some Applause

I'd cleared the air with my friends, clocked that the house's interior could use a bit of work, and established that, as a commercial enterprise, Thornhill was not quite driving over a cliff into the abyss but was nevertheless in a car park quite close to the cliff edge. And with no money for the meter.

I decided a wander round the grounds would clear my head and give me a chance to catch up with Robbie, the gardener and all-round handyman whose quiet good humour always made me feel just fine.

I pulled on my Aran jumper and a faux astrakhan coat I'd bagged for a song at Leather Lane market after a healthy autumn sale of Haut Médoc.

The air was cold enough to freeze your brain and I marched across the driveway like Mussolini at a military parade, the pace intended to get some heat into my body, feeling like a cosseted softie too used to the centrally heated confines of the capital.

You're a country girl now. Woman up!

Striding out in the fresh crisp air soon felt good. I'd forgotten the joy of walking on a bright and frosty morning, grass glistening in the sunlight and frozen leaves crunching under your feet like sugar.

I walked through the formal gardens, past the neatly boxed lavender beds sleeping quietly until the warmth of spring sunshine came to breathe new life into them. I stroked the sundial on the terrace where George and I had often sat to discuss affairs of estate. I passed through the stone arch and into the walled kitchen garden that had always supplied the house with freshly grown produce.

It looked bare and neglected.

Robbie's vegetable beds, always thick with luscious crops even in winter – kale, sprouts, leeks, winter cabbage – now lay empty. The paths, normally clear and well raked, were clumpy and weedy.

One of the venerable glasshouses looked ripped apart, victim of the cruel December storm Rosemary had told me about.

This wasn't Robbie's fault. I'd seen enough of the state of the house to know that indoor maintenance jobs would be keeping him out of the garden more than he would like.

But people – clients – saw the grounds before they saw the house. They could forgive the odd cracked cornice and worn Persian rug if the grounds were elegant and imposing. Right now, however, the grounds were anything but.

Over by the henhouse, Robbie was mending a fence. From twenty yards away, I stood and watched him work, quietly, steadily, just getting on with what needed to be done.

He had a passion for motorbikes and Motörhead tattoos, but gardening was his first love. He'd originally been hired as gardener and gamekeeper but he'd been forced to morph into a jack of all trades. Now that there was always a leak to plug, an electrical fault to trace, or a fence to repair, plant husbandry was shoved to the bottom of the list.

He heard my footsteps crunch on the gravel and turned his head. His face broke into a broad smile and he stepped forward with his arms outstretched, taking me into a warm embrace.

'I cannot tell you how pleased I was to hear your good news. Which is good news for all of us.' It was the longest sentence I'd ever heard him utter and I had to choke back tears.

'That is so very kind.'

'I mean it.'

'I know. Thank you.'

He glanced around. 'I'm sorry. About the state of the place.'

'The place asks too much of you. Always has.'

'There just aren't enough hours.'

'I know. It'll be a challenge, but we'll get there.'

Maybe if I say it often enough, I'll start to believe it.

'At least we've still got fresh eggs,' he said, and nodded towards the hen run.

'Yes. How are they?'

He pointed to the strutting cock. 'Mick Jagger still can't leave the young females alone. I have to watch him like a hawk.'

Every creature in the run was named after one of his musical heroes: Blondie, Tina, Amy, Chrissie, Patti … I didn't know how he kept track of them all.

'It's good to know some things never change.'

'Do you want to stay and feed them?'

'Some other time. I've got something to attend to over at Woodman's Cottage.'

Robbie's brow darkened. 'Want me to come with you?'

'Thanks, but I think I need to deal with it on my own.'

I heard the dogs barking before I saw the cottage. In the yard, a flat-bed truck was stacked with a tangle of old washing-machines and other bits of assorted machinery. The dogs making the noise were tied to one of the cottage's ornate Victorian cast-iron clothes poles. A couple of yards away from the dogs, an old fridge was lying on its side, door open.

The place looked a scrapyard. Or a scene from *Shameless*.

I took a deep breath. *You've got to do this.*

I looked at the sky. The day's earlier brightness was being erased by gathering cloud. Then something sharp hit me in the face, just above my eye. 'Ow! What the hell …?'

The boy dropped out of a tree and raced towards the yard, a catapult dangling from his hand. The same urchin who'd nearly got himself mopped up by my car was now using me for target practice.

No. I'm not having this.

I stepped over the rubbish, all the while glaring at the dogs, whose barking had now reached a maniacally shrill fever pitch. I marched right up to the door and knocked. Three short but firm blows with the knuckles of my right hand.

The door was yanked open.

Malcolm Clapp looked to be early forties. He was at least a foot taller than me and looked down at me with the smug self-assurance of someone who thinks no situation is beyond his control. He leaned on a walking stick I guessed he kept by the door, a convenient prop used for the benefit of visitors.

'Hello, Mr Clapp.'

'Who are you?'

'I'm someone your son just nearly blinded with his catapult. I'm someone whose car nearly crashed into your son just yesterday.'

'Sounds like you're quite accident-prone. You ought to be more careful.'

My blood boiled but I managed to smile. 'I'm always very careful, Mr Clapp. You, on the other hand, have been very care*less*. You've been sloppy. You've believed it was in your interest not to have your little arrangement with the previous owner written down. But you didn't do your homework. In fact, a verbal agreement was your biggest mistake.'

'I don't think so.' Malcolm Clapp tried to look calm but I could see my words had ruffled him.

I had no idea if what I was saying was true but I was determined to say it with enough conviction to get the wind right up him. 'It's a little late for thinking, Mr Clapp. You should have done your thinking a few months ago. I do hope you can afford a good lawyer. You will soon be hearing from mine. Very soon. If I were you, I'd get a head start on the packing.'

I turned on my heel and strode across the yard and past the hellhounds.

Malcolm Clapp bawled after me. 'Piss off!'

Verbal abuse. Good. He's properly rattled.

I headed for the lake and the little chapel at its far end. As I rounded the dogleg, a new sight greeted my eyes. The tall, overgrown bank of dogwood that had once formed a screen between graveyard and lake had all been cleared away – by Robbie, no doubt – and the stone wall that had stood at head height at Camilla's funeral was now no taller than my waist and had been sandblasted and treated to a crisp new coping.

My eyes filled with tears. Of all the vistas this gorgeous estate offered, the lake had been Camilla's favourite. Now there was a clear view of this small but elegant body of water from her final resting place. I imagined the hundreds of hours of work Robbie must have put in – quietly, perhaps even secretly – as a posthumous gift to his old mistress.

The white marble headstones marking the resting place of George and Camilla had begun to weather but they still looked like shockingly recent additions to the ranks of the Winstanley departed.

I knelt down beside them and brushed away two or three handfuls of dead leaves. Perhaps if I spent a few minutes in the company of George and Camilla, I'd get some inspiration on how to handle the enormity of the legacy they'd bestowed on me.

I looked up at the door to the little chapel and, as it had always done, it beckoned me in and, once inside, I enjoyed its particular smell of stone and damp fabric and the deep silence it was always clothed in. I sat on the front pew and remembered George's funeral, so quickly followed by Camilla's. The heavy cream altar cloth carried a biblical verse, picked out in gold thread: *Therefore do not be anxious about tomorrow, for tomorrow will be anxious for itself. Sufficient for the day is its own trouble.*

Over coffee and scones, I talked to Rosemary about my encounter with Malcolm Clapp.

'Can you kick him out, just like that?'

'I have no idea. But I enjoyed firing a warning shot over his bows.'

'Yes. Well done.'

'I've made an appointment with Patrick Maybole for next week. I'll see what he says.'

'Let's hope he can help.'

'One more challenge to face before bedtime.'

'What's that?'

Veronica and Rosemary stood back. I was to be the one to open the door.

The first thing I saw was Camilla's nightgown, folded neatly on the bed with, draped alongside it, her long silk dressing gown. We hadn't crossed the threshold but already this felt like an intrusion. But who else was going to do it?

Camilla's dressing table was still laden with the expensive creams and lotions she'd spent a fortune on over the years, in the hope they had the power to win her George's heart. Veronica's arms were firmly folded but Rosemary stroked the pale pink cashmere cardigan draped across a chair.

I picked up a crystal perfume bottle. Its glass stopper squeaked as I turned it, releasing the unmistakable aroma of Chanel that had always followed Camilla round the house.

I looked at Veronica and her eyes filled with tears.

The hardest thing, a little harder for being unspoken, was not the absence of Camilla but the sense that, had we all made more of an effort, we might have coaxed the real, natural, warm Camilla out from behind the veneer of porcelain face powder and lacquered bouffant hair. The woman I'd shared an hour with, on my last visit to Thornhill, had been strangely but charmingly affectionate, clutching my hand and occasionally squeezing it as we talked and, at one moment, lifting her own weightless hand, with its paper-thin skin, to stroke my hair with maternal care.

She'd kissed me goodbye and (the first time I'd ever heard her use an endearment) called me 'darling.'

That was the last time I saw her in this world.

4

I Think This Chalice Might Be Poisoned

I wasn't looking forward to my meeting with the Thornhill accountants. I was no financial wizard but you didn't need to be one to see the whole enterprise was in deep doo-doo.

And a four-way set of temporary traffic lights just outside Stow wasn't doing much to calm my fevered brow. The clown who'd set up the sequence seemed to have fixed it so the guy at the head of our queue had just enough time to slip his handbrake off before the green light sprinted back through amber to a resolute red. After fifteen minutes of going nowhere very slowly, we were all getting a bit tetchy. And a middle-aged man in an ill-fitting suit had now climbed out of his Audi to glare up the road, in the hope (presumably) that the power of his glare would fix the problem.

I dipped my hand into the emergency Maltesers in the Picanto's glove compartment (cocoa butter being one of your five a day), checked my slightly sagging chin in the mirror, and attempted to dislodge a handful of dead flies with a burst of screenwash.

Audi Man had now abandoned the superpower glare in favour of the more earthbound but considerably more confrontational solution of walking to the front of the queue and stabbing his finger at a workman in a high-vis vest.

There was a loud rap on my window. I buzzed it down to see a cyclist with a damp face wearing an expression of barely contained rage.

'I think your jets need adjusting.'

'Sorry?'

'I'd already had a shower this morning. And now I've had a second one. Thanks to your screenwash. Which I imagine hit everyone between me and the International Space Station.'

'Oh god! I'm really sorry!'

I reached past the Maltesers for a packet of tissues. Then, suddenly, in response to a miracle worked by Audi Man, the traffic ahead of me started to move and, desperate not to be any later for my meeting, I ended up not really passing the sodden cyclist a tissue so much as dropping it at his feet before squealing off to beat the buggering lights.

Stow-on-the-Wold is very, very pretty. It makes the gorgeous Burford look like an East German labour camp.

In a considerable flap about the time, I was hugely relieved to see a Picanto-sized parking spot on its pretty high street, about fifty yards from the offices of Hutton and Frimley. As I was expertly backing the little motor into the space, a man with a paint-spattered overall waved both his arms at me in a way that suggested I'd breached some fundamental tenet of the Human Rights Act.

'You can't park here, love.'

'Why not?'

'Trust me.' And off he marched, presumably to decorate his clothing with more paint.

Right. Cue another fifteen minutes circling the whole place for a kerbside spot, the only actual car park in the town consisting of about twelve spaces, each of them occupied by SUVs of eye-watering size and glamour.

After about the fourth circuit, I had no option but to ignore my mysterious prophet of doom, stick the Picanto back into the forbidden space, and leg it.

Matthew Frimley confirmed what I'd already gleaned from my chat with Veronica. Things at Thornhill had been bad for some time. The list of unpaid bills was getting longer and, he revealed, some suppliers had actually been in touch with *him*, asking what the hell was going on, a particularly shameful state of affairs for any business.

It was looking like we'd need a few quid short of £15,000 a year just to keep the house from falling down. That's before anyone had been paid.

And with Windrush House on the verge of wheeling Edmund into the street and leaving him there, it was not a time for optimism.

'Is there any private income you'd be happy to dip into as a stop-gap?'

'There's a few thousand left from the sale of my mum's house in Hampshire.'

'But that's not money you'd want to eat into?'

'Oh, I don't mind eating into it. I'm just not sure it'll make a very substantial meal. Might only do us until lunch time.'

Matthew didn't smile at what I thought was quite a clever little development of his metaphor.

'Right.' Eyes back on the books. 'Then we're looking at generating increased income from the estate itself, to help cover costs. There are five other properties on the estate. Which could theoretically be sold or leased.'

Yes. The operative word being 'theoretically.'

'That's right. But two of the staff live in the Coachman's Lodge, as part of their employment package. And Gamekeeper's Cottage is occupied by another member of staff and his elderly mother, again as part of the deal.'

'I see. And the other three properties?'

'We might be onto something with a couple of those, but one of them is problematic.' And I rehearsed the history of the Clapps' disgraceful occupancy of Woodman's Cottage. 'I'm speaking to my solicitor this week. To establish where we stand legally. Apart from that one, the Pavilion is a substantial building that was renovated a few years ago and used to be used as accommodation for overnight events. I'd like to keep the potential for that function alive. The Shooting Lodge was once used as a sort of hub for corporate parties on hunting events. It's rather fallen into disrepair now but could have a commercial use, if it doesn't need too much work to make it viable. I could arrange a survey.'

'Good. I don't wish to be apocalyptic, but these properties may be the only way to, as it were, save your bacon.'

Back on the high street, I was greeted by an icy January drizzle. Good job the car was nearby.

As I looked up the road, a man in a black Victorian tailcoat and a stovepipe hat was standing in the street with his hands on his hips, glaring at my Picanto and shaking his head, while, in the middle of the road, two of his colleagues were holding up the traffic with the coffin they were carrying across from the hearse they'd been forced to park at a bus stop. The coffin-bearers were, I could see now, making their way towards a narrow passageway. The one blocked by my car.

The passageway hadn't been there when I'd parked.

But it was making its presence very obvious now. As was the brass plaque on the wall that announced Hillsmore Funeral Directors. And the 'Polite Notice' asking for the entrance to be kept clear.

I glanced through the narrow passage to see a wide courtyard where two other hearses were parked. Then I dipped my eyes pavementward and marched past the Picanto with, I hoped, a convincing *Nothing to do with me* demeanour. As I passed him, I heard Hands-On-Hips Guy mutter, 'Bloody tourists.'

After the morning's assault and battery, I felt in need of a very friendly face, so I Skyped Will.

My outrageous best friend for as long as I can remember had helped me through every bleak episode in the last crisis-laden five years. And, at times – usually involving some major break-up with a guy Will had been convinced was 'the one' – I'd been a shoulder for him, too.

But Will had, for the last three years, been firmly settled in a rock-solid relationship with his gorgeous Kavi. They'd met when Kavi, then a waiter at Will's favourite Indian restaurant in Portsmouth, had spilled a chicken biryani all over Will's white satin shirt. Their eyes had met over the turmeric stains and Will had immediately stopped being a dangerously promiscuous trouser-hound and had morphed into Mr Steady.

That didn't stop him being a scandalous purveyor of verbal indecency. But beneath all his smutty repartee are always buried nuggets of genuine wisdom.

'You could go on the game.'

Okay. Deeply buried. 'Be serious.'

'I *am* being serious! With those legs and that cleavage, you could charge a fortune. A lot of men like a more mature woman. And would be happy to pay a premium.'

'What do you know about what heterosexual men like?'

'Enough to know you're a valuable asset. With valuable assets.'

'Pack it in.'

'Sorry. Back in the room.'

'Well?'

'Well. Rosemary and Veronica and Robbie are on your side. Right?'

'They seem to be.'

'Right. And, like you, they want what's best for the place. And they want to keep their jobs. Right?'

'Okay.'

'So it seems to me they'll be willing to make some changes. To keep you all afloat.'

'Such as?'

'Such as moving out of these places that could be rented. Or sold. And moving into the big house. Which is where you live. Right?'

'Hmm. I can't ask Robbie to move – his mum's far too elderly and infirm to be upping sticks. And I don't know about Rosemary and Veronica. That's not the way it's always been.'

'Come on, Jen. If you've learned anything these past five years, it's that things don't stay the way they've always been. They can't. If you're going to survive. All of you. I'm sure Rosemary and Veronica will understand.'

'Maybe.'

'Trust me. You need to have the talk.'

As usual, the ridiculously randy Priscilla, Queen Of The Desert was spot on. He'd seen right through my dancing round the problem and forced me to look at tackling it head on.

But I just couldn't face having that talk now.

I'd only been back at the place for a few days and I didn't want to risk upsetting what still felt like a delicately poised applecart by suggesting a major change to the lives of three of my friends. That conversation would have to wait.

Besides, my head was full of David. That evening, he'd flown in from New York and pitched up at Thornhill, delightfully unannounced. When I opened the door, he was standing there cradling a box of Jacques Torres chocolates the size of a dustbin lid.

The last time David had been at Thornhill was during my stint as estate manager, when he was with a party of businessmen booked in for an afternoon's quad biking, another occasion when the stars seemed to have aligned to bring us together.

We stood in the sitting room with glasses of champagne, another of his treats.

'It's a gorgeous place, Jen. Very *To The Manor Born*. Although you're far more attractive than Penelope Keith.'

'Liar.'

'Any man would say the same. Not just one who loves you as much as I do.'

'Stop it. I'm blushing.'

He looked around the room. 'Although I can see what you mean about the place needing some work.'

'I'm afraid the lady-of-the-manor routine is not quite as glamorous at it might look from the outside.' I pointed to the fireplace where a log fire was crackling. 'For example, we've agreed this can only happen when we have posh company. It's too wasteful to burn logs all the time in every room.'

'No money for luxuries like heating?'

'That's just about where we are.'

David looked up at the portrait of Arabella, now reinstated in its traditional spot above the fireplace.

'Well, she seems to have plenty of confidence in you.'

George's first wife smiled down at the room with her soft eyes. I told David all about her – the tragic early death, how second wife Camilla had never really measured up to her, how the painting had mysteriously disappeared after George had died and we'd all assumed Camilla had taken a knife to it, then how, the last time I'd seen her alive, Camilla had been at pains to show me that she'd had it restored.

'I know what you mean about her eyes,' David said. 'And they're exactly the same colour as yours.'

I looked up at Arabella and felt like I was seeing her for the first time. He was right. Taking the eyes alone, it was a bit like looking in the mirror. A lot like it, actually.

Maybe that's why I'd been drawn to the painting in the first place. Maybe that's why George had taken an instant shine to me. Maybe that's why he'd bequeathed me the entire estate.

I was starting to feel like I was in an episode of *The Twilight Zone*. Then David took my hands in his.

'We need to talk.'

My heart collided with the back of my teeth. 'Oh god. You're dumping me.'

'Good god, no!'

'Because that's what that phrase means.'

'I did not know that.'

'Didn't you ever watch *Falcon Crest*?'

'It was never on my radar, I'm afraid.'

'What do we need to talk about? Now that my heart is back in my chest.'

'I've been asked to head this thing in New York.'

'You're already doing that.'

'True. But they want me on a more permanent basis.'

My heart began making its way back up to my oesophagus. 'How permanent?'

'There's talk of two years.'

'Two YEARS?'

'The timing's terrible.'

'You can say that again.'

'But if I take this, that's it. The icing on the cake. Then I shut down. Pack it in.'

'Pack what in?'

'Work.'

'Retire? You're not even fifty.'

'I know.' He pulled me in closer. 'But I've found what I want to do with the rest of my life. I just need a little more time before the rest of my life can properly begin.'

I must have looked vacant.

'*You. You* are what I want to do with the rest of my life.'

'Oh.' I smiled. 'Right. Great.'

'But if we're going to be comfortable, financially, for the long decades to come, I need these two years. Can you agree to that?'

Decades. Had he just said that?

'Yes. Yes, I can. But I'll miss you.'

'And I'll miss you. Tremendously. But it's a price I'm willing to pay for a lifetime of happiness.'

'Me too.'

'Thank you.' He picked up the champagne glasses and handed me one and we clinked. And kissed.

'How are you feeling about the party?'

Vacant again. 'Party?'

'My grandson's first birthday party. Day after tomorrow. You've forgotten.'

It wasn't so much that I'd forgotten as that I hadn't remembered.

'Of course I haven't. Got my dress all picked out.'

You can be such a bullshitter, Jennifer Brown.

5

A Family Affair

I hoped I wasn't showing it, but I was ridiculously nervous about the Harwood gathering.

Meeting family had never been part of the equation with Pete. He was an only child and both his parents had passed away a few years before I'd met him.

David, on the other hand, came with an elderly mother and two grown-up children.

David's son, Mark, lived in Canada and only came over to the UK once a year. But his daughter, Charlotte ('Lottie'), lived in Kensington. Although married and now with a child of her own, she was still (I'd gleaned this much from the numerous one-sided phone conversations I'd earwigged on) very much a Daddy's Girl. And, judging by the photographs, a catwalk model.

Brilliant.

Notwithstanding the fact that my eyes were (by common consent, it seemed) quite nice, the rest of my face was not inspiring me with confidence for the important meeting ahead. My eyes were baggy, my skin looked as puffy as the pastry on Rosemary's chicken and bacon pie, and my roots were beginning to creep through.

I shared my concerns with Veronica.

'Give Kate a call. She's very good and she'd be delighted to pop over and see you. Save you trailing into town.'

Hmm.

I'd always liked Kate. Something relentlessly good and nice about her made her impossible to dislike. But there was no getting away from the fact that, as a cleaner, she'd been about as much use as a handbrake on a canoe. And although the realm of Beauty seemed much more up her street, I wasn't convinced she'd be any more focused or professional in a salon environment than she'd been with a bucket and a mop.

'I'll think about it.'

But I'd have to think fast. The buggering party was tomorrow. Dismissing the notion of making a one-hundred-and-seventy-mile round trip to Southsea to see Gareth, my stylist of the last ten years, I called a few places in Burford, Stow and the greater Poshster area.

Only one place – Placebo Hair, in Heythrop – offered to 'fit me in', but not until the following week, so no use. Mind you, even if they'd had an appointment there and then, I wasn't sure I had any more confidence in a place with 'placebo' in the name than I did in Kate.

What was their MO? Did a stylist with invisible tools move his hands around your head and make scissor noises with his teeth?

So, getting David out of the way for a few hours with a not-entirely-bogus request that he cast a professional eye over the grounds, I called Kate and explained my predicament.

Inside half an hour, her Barbie-pink campervan was crunching over the Thornhill gravel.

She certainly hadn't stinted on mobile advertising. You could barely see the van's bodywork for all the saucy slogans she'd had printed on it: *Treat Yourself To Something For The Weekend, Just Lie Back And Let Me Work My Magic, Whatever Your Length I Can Handle It.*

This was starting to feel like a bad idea.

She tumbled her gorgeous size-8 frame out of the van and sprinted up the steps to hug me.

'Oh, it's so good to see you! And you're lady of the manor now! That's bloody brilliant! I am so pleased!'

'Thanks. It's all a bit bonkers but I'm hoping we can make it work.'

She looked me squarely in the eyes. 'I believe in you. There's nothing you can't do.'

See what I mean? Impossible to dislike.

Kate soon had my roots under control.

'So what now?'

'I don't know.'

'You look a bit pale. How about a spray tan?'

'You can do that? In this van?' I glanced at Kate's orange glow.

'Sure.'

'Hm. It's not really me.'

'Okay. Well, these eyebrows could do with a bit of emphasis.'

'I was thinking they needed thinning out a bit.'

'Right.'

I wanted to help Kate's new business but I didn't fancy leaving the van looking like the love child of Kim Kardashian and Groucho Marx.

Then Kate got a twinkle in her eye.

'This is a romantic weekend, right?'

'I'm hoping there'll be time for romance, yes.'

'I've got the perfect thing. Trust me.'

Two hours later, Kate handed me a mirror.

The hair colour was perfect. And the cut was every bit as stylish as Gareth's normal handiwork. I was pleased and impressed.

Then I moved the mirror down to my groin.

Seeing my garden not only stripped of its natural vegetation but also decorated with shiny plastic gewgaws was going to take some getting used to.

'The GlitterGram should do you for a month. Depending on how ... erm ... active you are.'

My pubic panel was already beginning to itch when David strolled back into the kitchen, tapping a final few notes into his phone.

'The estate is basically in very good shape. I've made a couple of dozen notes and recommendations – I'll ping you a PDF – but I think the overall picture is fairly rosy, actually. What's needed is, in my view, mostly cosmetic rather than structural. And fairly affordable, I'd imagine.'

I resisted the urge to scratch my nethers. 'Right.'

'Which is great news.'

'Yes.'

'Isn't it?'

'Yes. Great news.'

'Is everything okay?'

My groin is on fire. And not in a good way. 'Yes. I'm just a bit tired.'

***

Even on a dreary Sunday in dreary January, the traffic on Kensington High Street was impossibly heavy.

David glanced across at me from the driver's seat. 'Have I told you you look gorgeous?'

'You have. Several times.'

'Sorry.'

'Don't apologise. I like to hear it.'

He, of course, was looking as handsome as ever, in green tweed jacket, crisp white shirt, and dove grey trousers.

He squeezed my hand. 'It'll be fine. They'll love you. Because I do.'

'I hope so.' *I also hope there'll be a pot of Greek yogurt somewhere so I can plaster a handful over my bits.*

Lottie and husband Alexander ('Sandy') lived on the ground floor of a very grand building that, with the addition of a couple of flags, could have easily passed for an embassy. Its high black-and-gold railings looked a lot like the ones Hugh Grant climbs over to catch the eye of Julia Roberts in *Notting Hill*.

David saw I was impressed. 'Lottie's a lucky girl. Sandy's doing very well in the City.'

'Right.'

The last time I'd seen railings this tall was round the Army Surplus Store in Fratton.

Inside, the spacious apartment was all Persian rugs, original art, and people with skin the colour of money.

Huddles of confident, well-heeled guests were gathered in every room, at ease with themselves, with each other, and with the occasion, a hundred smiling faces of people I'd never met, the women preened to casual perfection, the men the epitome of merchant-bank self-mastery, the toddlers gussied up in the latest kiddie fashions imported from Paris and Milan.

I hoped nobody would notice that my outfit was the same one Twiggy was wearing in the M&S advert on the bus stop by the Albert Hall.

I felt a burning need to tend my garden.

'I'm sorry, David, but where's the loo?'

'Just there.' He pointed to a wide, brass-handled door guarded by a grandfather clock about three feet taller than the one in the Thornhill sitting room. 'Is everything …?'

Before he could finish the sentence, a rakish-looking man grabbed him by the arm and dragged him into a group assembled in front of a photographer clutching the kind of camera David Bailey uses when he's taking pictures of Mick Jagger.

I turned and headed for the bathroom, on the way lifting a handful of ice from a bucket dumped on a side table.

Every inch of my bikini line had broken out in painful little bumps. Whatever Kate had used to stick the glittery little buggers on was reacting very badly with my lowland plain. The ice brought a few moments of sweet relief but I knew they wouldn't last.

Bollocks!

I'd hoped for a weekend straight out of *An Affair To Remember*. Instead, my downstairs looked like *The Rocky Horror Picture Show*.

David Bailey was still doing his stuff when I tiptoed into the fray.

'He makes a lovely grandfather to darling Hugo.'

I turned to see an elegant woman in her late sixties standing at my side. I assumed the remark had been addressed to me, although she had her eyes firmly fixed on the family tableau in front of the lens, so I wasn't sure.

'Yes.' She was right. David looked very comfortable cradling the little blighter (if there'd been a sweepstake, I might have plumped for Algernon, but Hugo wasn't far off). The very pretty and beamingly proud young woman standing next to him I took to be Lottie.

'Do you have children?' Still eyes front.

'No.' Not for the first time, I was being defined not by what I *was*, but by what I *wasn't*. I felt my hackles rise.

'I have two sons. Of one of whom I am inordinately fond and proud.'

'And the other?'

'Well, let's just say he lacks David's integrity.'

Right. So you're David's mother.

I wondered if Patricia, the matriarch, was being wilfully rude in not introducing herself. If she knew exactly who I was but was pretending not to. It seemed like the kind of mind-game a staunchly upper-middle-class matron would play.

She beckoned a waiter over, lifted a glass of champagne from his tray with one hand and a smoked salmon canapé with the other, dismissed the waiter without pausing to consider whether I might also like either, and picked up the conversation again.

'He has a new ... partner.' The modern word was clearly causing her some pain.

'Which one? The son with integrity, or the other one?'

'David.'

'Right. Is she nice?'

'I have no idea. We have yet to be introduced.'

I could have remedied that situation, of course, but I was keen to see what path she would take the conversation down.

'Well, if your son is all you say he is, I'm sure he's made an excellent choice.'

'He *is* a man, though. Their choices in some respects are driven, are they not, less by their head than by their trousers. And David's made some very poor choices. His last wife – there have been two so far – lasted a mere matter of months. I liked the girl. Exactly the right sort. But they were not, it seems, compatible.'

She practically snorted that last word, as if the notion that people in a relationship might actually expect to get along was a quaint and irrelevant (and distinctly lower-class) frivolity.

'So how long has this latest relationship been going?'

'Oh, I think it's still very much in the embryonic phase.' *Do you, now?* 'She's inherited a country estate, apparently.'

'How fabulous.'

'But, from what I hear, she might not be ... suited ... to that sort of life.' She took another bite of her canapé.

I was wondering who she'd heard that assessment from when David broke away from the tableau and made straight for me and his mother. He slipped his arm round my waist and addressed Patricia.

'I see you've met Jennifer.'

The first response was wide-eyed alarm. That was swiftly followed by a choking sound, a purple face, and a frantic scan for water.

I grabbed a glass from the side table and handed it to her. 'My old mum used to have the same problem. She was forever getting food stuck in her dentures.'

Patricia managed to splutter an 'Excuse me' before scurrying off to the bathroom that my vajazzle and I had not long vacated.

She was replaced by the rakish guy who'd dragged David over for the family photography session. He held out his hand.

'I'm Giles. And you're Jennifer.'

'Yes, I am. Hello.'

'David's told me all about you. And about the estate. It sounds like quite a project.'

'Project. Yes. That's one word for it.'

'Will you be in need of a financial advisor?'

'Er, I …'

David stepped in. 'Excuse us, Giles. Jennifer's hardly met anyone here.' And he pulled me away towards the kitchen.

'I love my brother. But I could heave him out of a window when he gets that look in his eye.'

'What look?'

'Dollar signs. Giles is good fun to be around. But, as a businessman, he walks a very fine line between taking risks and taking the law into his own hands.'

And he told me a long story. Of a nice, respectable accountant who'd been offered a chance to work as a business consultant in a company with shadowy connections and an open-minded approach to morality. One dodgy deal too many had resulted in a referral to the Financial Ombudsman which had in turn resulted in court proceedings when the company's affiliations were probed. Giles claimed he'd been thrown under the bus by his colleagues, although, David said, it had been pretty clear he'd crossed the line willingly. Leapt across it, in fact.

'As I say, I love him. But he'd swap the lot of us for a winning lottery ticket.'

The very pretty young woman from earlier was walking towards us, smiling warmly.

'Now, this one,' said David, looking at his beautiful daughter, 'I would trust with my life.'

Lottie would not have been out of place on the cover of *Vogue*. In fact, she was easily the most beautiful woman I'd ever seen in the flesh. But, if she was aware of her beauty, she wore the knowledge very lightly. This was the encounter I'd been dreading but, I have to say, I liked her immediately.

I held out a hand and she took it firmly then leaned down from Mount Olympus to kiss me on the cheek.

'Please forgive me for not coming over earlier. We only had the photographer for an hour – his charges are ridiculous – so I wanted to make good use of his time.'

'It's fine.'

'I'm so very pleased to meet you at last.'

'It's very kind of you to invite me.'

'Oh, please. Don't wait for an invitation next time. There is an open invitation to visit. With or without Dad. Who is abandoning you, the swine. So please do come and see us. Without …' she took in the busy room with a sweep of her hand '… all this. Come anytime. I'll give you my number. And please use it. If you come to London and you don't stay here with us, I shall be offended.'

'That's really kind.'

'Not at all. Hotels in London are ridiculously expensive, and awful unless you're at the sheikh end of the spectrum, so consider this your *pied à terre*. And now it is my duty to circulate, so forgive me once again. But promise me we will have some time together soon.'

'I promise.'

'Good.' She kissed me again and glided away.

God. Tall, impossibly gorgeous, and nice. I should hate you. But I don't.

6

Like Something Out Of A Film

'Call me the minute you land.'
   'I will.'
'And thank you for such a lovely weekend.'
'I'm sorry about my mother.'
'It's fine. I'm sure we'll have the chance to properly hit it off.'
'Lottie really likes you.'
'I think she's fabulous. I hardly know her but I know enough to know we're going to get on. That's too many *knows*, but you know what I mean.'
'I know what you mean.'
'And I'm sorry about the … body art.'
David threw his head back and laughed all the way up from his shoes. 'It was quite a surprise.'
'To me, too.'
'I hope it … you know … clears up.'
'So do I. I promise I *won't* keep you posted.'
'I love you, Jennifer Brown.'
'It's probably a good job.'
'It's the best job I've ever had.'

I tried to drown my sorrows in paperwork.

Veronica and I sat at the long library table and worked slowly through a hefty pile of brown envelopes, Veronica wielding a calculator.

My priorities were twofold: keep everyone paid, and keep Windrush House happy so Edmund could continue to receive the care he needed.

By my reckoning, we could do that for three months, maybe four, if we held off doing all other work that wasn't absolutely essential while we figured out how to generate more income. By then, we'd be well into Spring and, with a bit of money behind us, could begin to properly spruce the place up. And, between us, Veronica and I could go like the clappers with marketing and begin to build a portfolio of bookings we could fulfil, with luck, by mid-summer.

It was a gamble. But with hard work, good faith, and a heavy dose of smoke and mirrors, I thought we stood a good chance of being well on the way to recovery within twelve months.

Then Veronica hit me with a sledgehammer.

'I'm leaving.'

'What?'

'I've been thinking about it since we heard the news about the inheritance.'

'Oh god, Veronica. I hope you don't think …'

'It's only natural you'll want to take the reins again. And you're much better at this than me. Any fool can see that.'

'That's not true. It's just the ups and downs of business.'

'And the downs have all been on my watch.'

'We can bring things back up together.'

'I've been offered a job. Housekeeper and companion to an elderly lady. Not too far away. Posh house. Good salary. It's what I do best. Caring for people.'

'Please don't think I'm pushing you out. All this talk of belt-tightening … it doesn't mean …'

'Come on, Jennifer. It makes sound business sense.'

'Sod business. We're friends.'

'There's no role for me here.' She looked me in the eye. 'I'm redundant. You know I am.' I opened my mouth to protest but she stopped me. 'Please don't say anything. It'll just make it harder. Okay?'

'Okay.'

'You're lovely. And you'll say lovely things. But this is best. For everyone. And it's not some heroic Captain Oates thing. I'll be fine. Very fine indeed. And it'll give you a bit more breathing space here. And I can work as short a notice period as you like. She can start me right away.' I could feel my eyes filling up but Veronica gave me a glare of comic steeliness. 'Stop it, now. You'll just get me going.'

'I'll miss you.'

'Don't say nice things.'

'Okay.'

'Anyway. Back to business.' She opened a browser window on her laptop. 'I came across this lot the other day. I think it's worth speaking to them.'

Lexington Locations was an agency that matched film companies with properties they needed for filming. It was a glossy site with images of fabulous houses and ranches and castles, with the world's biggest film stars standing in them – people like Ryan Gosling, Scarlett Johansson and Ben Affleck.

A few key sentences caught my eye. *The industry rate is generally between £1000 and £5000 a day.* And *In some cases, the fee paid to the homeowner is tax-free.* And *More often than not, filmmakers leave the location in even better condition than before.*

This was an extremely attractive prospect. I turned to smile at Veronica.

'See. You're priceless.'

Over the next few days, I made a long list of all the Thornhill features I thought would appeal: space, light, fine furniture, oak panelling, historic facade, plentiful accommodation, extensive grounds, lake, chapel …

Then, one evening, with a glass of Rioja at my elbow, my notes to hand, and 67 photos sitting on the SD card from my Canon EOS 250, I clicked the List Your Location tab and uploaded the lot.

And allowed my mind to explore an image of Colin Firth striding out of our lake in a sopping wet shirt.

Delyth was up a stepladder vigorously polishing the huge hall mirror when I told her about this latest idea.

'Be great for all them period shows. *Harlots*, *Belgravia*, *Outlander*.' Then a lightbulb went on in her head and she paused, shammy in mid-air. 'Ooh. *Poldark*. Now that *would* be lush.' She wrapped herself in some forbidden image. 'That Aidan Turner. He could buff my bedknobs any time.'

Then she was back in the room. She nodded at the mirror.

'Looks like you've got a visitor.'

I turned to see a plump, middle-aged woman stepping out of a green Range Rover. I recognised her immediately as one of Camilla's cronies from the afternoon-tea circus.

Anthea Orchard-Lyons tiptoed over the gravel drive in patent heels that belonged on a woman half her age, a string of pearls bouncing off her capacious bosom.

It was clear from the sneer on Delyth's face that she wasn't a fan.

'Carries on like the bloody Duchess of Cornwall. Just because her husband's something big in cardboard. Makes a fortune supplying them on-line companies. He's just as big a snob as she is. Bloody Maurice Minor.'

'Maurice Minor?'

Delyth chuckled and dangled her little finger in front of her face. 'Hung like a wasp, I'm told.'

Anthea swept into the hallway in a cloud of Estée Lauder Youth Dew. 'Lovely to see you again, Jessica.'

'Jennifer.'

Anthea ignored my correction and pressed on. 'As a tribute to darling Camilla, we want to continue the tradition of the afternoon tea party, which I will now be hosting at Orchard House.' *I bet you were rubbing your hands together when you heard Camilla had died.* 'We're switching to a monthly schedule, beginning in April. And, as the new mistress of Thornhill, you would of course be very welcome to join our little coterie.'

Coterie? Cabal is more like it. Or coven. 'That's very kind.'

'Oh, not at all, Jessica, dear.'

She moved away from me to survey the hallway, with a proprietorial air that immediately got my back up.

'It must have been quite a shock, discovering you'd inherited all this?'

'It was very unexpected, yes. A very pleasant surprise.'

She wandered through to the sitting room, her eyes settling with alarm on the *Kiss My Cracker* sweatshirt I'd draped over an armchair (a typically smutty Christmas present from the incorrigible Will).

'How *are* things here?'

'Things are fine.' *If you like being up shit creek with only half a paddle.*

'Excellent. Of course, you're blessed with first-class staff. That wonderful cook of yours is the envy of the county.' She turned a probing eye on me. 'It must be difficult for you, adapting to all of this when you were once staff here yourself.'

And there it is. You poisonous bitch.

'It's been very easy, actually.' I held her gaze. 'The secret, I've learned in my years of experience of household management, is to treat people with respect.' I lingered, unblinkingly, on that last word.

'Very commendable.'

'I think it's only natural.'

'Of course. Well, I must dash. Will we see you at Orchard House on the second?'

'Oh, I wouldn't miss it for the world.'

7

Two For One

February hobbled into March.

I was still coming to terms both with my new role at Thornhill and with the bombshell of Veronica's imminent departure.

And the issue with the Clapps was still unresolved. My meeting with Thornhill solicitor, Patrick Maybole, had had to be postponed when Patrick had suddenly been taken ill with crippling stomach pains two days before I was due to see him. He was now, his secretary said, awaiting a date for exploratory surgery and would be off work indefinitely. So Malcolm Clapp was spared, for now.

Unless I could find a discreet and affordable hit man.

I was finding long dark evenings in the house a little unsettling. Rosemary and (for the next couple of weeks) Veronica weren't far away at the lodge, and Robbie's cottage was only a five-minute dash away in nightie and slippers if a marauding serial killer took it upon himself to pop round.

But I still felt fearfully alone.

Evening FaceTime chats with Will became much more frequent.

'Get a dog. You love dogs. Plus you've got enough space for a small zoo.'

'I don't know.'

Any mention of dogs was apt to bring a lump to my throat the size of a plastic bone. Throughout my time with Pete, even before the turbulent months of our messy breakup, my two little dogs had been my constant companions: Betty, the Jack Russell with the gentle eyes, and Eric, the terrier-cross rescue dog who gave so much love even after a previous life of unimaginable cruelty. Our long morning walks in the fields behind Pete's house had been my favourite time of the day.

And leaving them behind when I walked out of Pete's life had made the upheaval so much harder to bear. Four years on, I didn't even know if they were still alive. In order to keep my heart from breaking a second time, I'd kept my thoughts of, and feelings for, my erstwhile sweet companions locked away in a little compartment in my head. This was the first time I'd unlocked it.

Will knew it was a sensitive subject. 'Look, I know you. I know another dog would feel like a betrayal. But, trust me, they're dogs. They live for the next bowl of food. They'll have moved on. And so should you.'

'I'll think about it.'

'Not good enough.'

'If I just knew they were okay – happy, healthy – that would help me move on, dogwise. But I can't know, can I?'

'Right. Here's the deal. I get you news of the little buggers. Then you get yourself down to the Dogs' Trust.'

'How the hell are you going to do that?'

'That is not your concern. Do we have a deal?'

'But …'

'Ah ah. Deal or no deal?'

'Deal.'

I was in the Orangery with Robbie, discussing alternatives to the pineapples, when my phone pinged – a message from Will with a photo of my two long-lost sweethearts, smiling for the camera, both of them looking fine and dandy.

Major lump in the throat.

I excused myself with Robbie and called Will.

'How did you manage that?'

'Just went round to his house and knocked on the door. I reckoned, if he answered, I'd figure something out.'

'You didn't have a plan?'

'I work best when I'm winging it.'

'And precisely how did you wing it?'

'I told him my granny had lived there in the sixties. That I'd spent a lot of time in the garden as a kid. That she'd just died. That I had very fond memories of the place. And could I take a few minutes in the garden to remember her.'

'That's some story.'

'I even managed a tear. So, basically, I'm George Clooney. But better looking.'

'You don't even *have* a granny.'

'He doesn't know that. And, trust me, with that performance, even my mother would have believed me.'

'They look just as I remember them.'

'They're doing fine. Him, not so good.'

'How d'you mean?'

'Well, he looks a lot different to the heartthrob you showed me pictures of. He's packed the beef on a bit.'

'He was always really slim. Thirty-inch waist. He lifted weights.'

'Well, he's been lifting pies. And stuffing them in his face.'

What struck me about this news about Pete was that I felt neither delight nor sorrow. What I felt was nothing. At all. Which was interesting. And strangely comforting.

'There was some woman in the garden, playing with them. Slim, thirtyish.'

'Bronwyn, I assume. The woman he was playing away with. Blonde?'

'Hm. Fairish, anyway.'

'Yeah, that's her. Oh, well. They're still together. Good for them.'

'Do you mean that?'

I took a deep breath and investigated my feelings. 'On the whole, yes. I do.'

'So?'

'So?'

'So when are you going to the Dogs' Trust?'

The last time I'd been to a rescue centre was about ten years ago, when I'd come home with Eric. The stories I'd heard about the litany of abuse he'd suffered at the hands of his previous owner had made me mad and sad in equal measure.

I've always been a total softie where animals are concerned, so this experience was going to challenge me in all sorts of ways.

Care Assistant Lucy walked me round the centre.

'We are almost entirely dependent on the generosity of members of the public. There are five permanent members of staff here, and sixteen volunteers. People don't just give their money. They give their time.'

This was clearly a sales pitch. But, with everything going on at Thornhill, I had enough on my plate.

'Yes. It's good that some people have so much time to spare. Which dogs should I be looking at?'

Lucy smiled, then glanced at the form we'd filled in back at the office. 'Well, you have a lot of space at your house, so a dog that needs a fair bit of exercise shouldn't be a problem. Unless time is an issue.'

'One long walk before the working day will be fine. And perhaps another shorter walk in the evening. And a lot of outdoor living will be possible – we have a walled garden that can be closed off for safety. I've had dogs before and I like to keep them fit. It'll help me to keep fit, too.' I patted my buttocks.

'Oh, I know. Me, too. You'd think running around after dogs all day would keep the weight off, but somehow I manage to put it on.' Lucy patted her tiny belly. She looked about seven and a half stone.

Cow.

'I had a smallish dog in mind. One that would fit on my lap in the evenings, or at least beside me on the couch. Something spanielish.'

'Hm. You won't want Luther, then. Which is a shame, because he's lovely. Very friendly. Very well behaved. Loves women *and* men – some of our dogs don't take kindly to men – and also loves a good run-around.'

She lingered by the enclosure of a skinny black lurcher with big eyes. When I stopped to look at him, he pricked up his ears. His tail started to beat the ground. Then he walked over and pressed his long wet nose against the window. A major charm offensive.

Lucy could see I was charmed.

'We always advise potential foster families to take their chosen dog for a little walk. That's the only way to feel if the dog is right for you.'

Luther came up to my hip. He looked like a black wolf. But, on the lead, he was a paragon of cool. He didn't pull, or bark, and when a snappy little bugger someone else was taking for a spin had a go at him, he just raised one eyebrow and trotted on past.

I was smitten.

Lucy turned a sheepish eye towards me as she closed the door on Luther's enclosure.

'There's just one thing. Luther has a companion. And we're looking to re-home both dogs as a package.'

Woodbine was a small white terrier with a brown head. He was never going to win any rosettes at Crufts but, like his mate, he was a total charmer. I stroked his wiry head and he licked my hand with enthusiasm.

When reason and emotion collide, you can bet your bottom dollar emotion will win. I'd imagined I'd find the task of choosing one dog from forty an impossible one. But the choice had been made for me. And I was walking away not with one dog, but with two.

Lucy had stitched me up good and proper.

Luther took his role of protector very seriously. In the days that followed, he barely left my side. When I got up from my desk, he sprang to attention, and followed me until I reached the kitchen or the library or the sitting room, then, destination established, he dropped down at my feet and scanned the new room for potential threats, like a hairy James Bond.

Woodbine, on the other hand, took a little longer to get used to his new life. For several days, he was suspicious of anyone who wasn't me, took an instant dislike to Delyth, charged around the walled garden like Genghis Khan on speed, and was unnervingly aggressive when eating, guarding the bowl like he was never going to see food again.

But the three of us eventually settled into a routine that suited us all.

At night, both dogs slept in the hallway, in the huge basket under the stairs that had belonged to George's faithful old retriever, Benson, Luther sleeping on his back with his legs at an unseemly angle, and Woodbine curled in a tight ball beside him.

In the mornings, I took them for an hour-long walk round the grounds, rain or shine. In the evenings, we all took turns taking them for a quick spin round the garden. They liked Robbie and Rosemary a lot but they were (ironically) particularly fond of Veronica.

How was I going to break it to them?

8

One Out, One In

We said goodbye to Veronica on March 21st.

The first day of Spring.

The planets were aligning to wring as much emotion out of me as possible. Veronica was holding it together much better.

'Come on, now. We said we wouldn't do this.'

Rosemary wiped her eyes. Even the phlegmatic Robbie looked a bit misty. I was on my fifth tissue.

'You will be sorely missed. Very, very sorely.'

'I'm only twenty miles away. I'll be popping back all the time for a scone. You'll be sick of me.'

'Take great care.'

'And you lot. I look forward to hearing about all your wonderful successes.'

That evening, I was curled up in the sitting room, watching the dying embers of an illicit log fire and (although it was only 8.30) thinking about taking myself and the dogs off to bed, when there was a loud rap at the door. Luther raised one eyebrow and Woodbine hared off to greet the intruder with bared teeth and fists at the ready.

'Jonathan!'

He leant forward and kissed me on both cheeks. I straightened the *Kiss My Cracker* sweatshirt that had become my default evening wear and clocked my flushed, fire-warmed complexion in the hall mirror. The ever-handsome, ever-cultivated Jonathan Dashwood-Silk, my old boss at Intext Software, handed me a bunch of freesias, remembering (of course he would) that they'd always been my favourite flower.

'Sorry for springing a visit on you. I was on my way back from a conference in Warwick – boring as hell – and saw on the satnav just how close you are to the A34. It felt rude not to call in. But I should have phoned. Forgive me.'

He'd said all this with Woodbine's teeth buried in his trouser leg. 'Feisty little chap.' He leaned down to stroke Woodbine's wiry head and the dog immediately released his grip and licked Jonathan's hand.

The phrase *charm the birds from the trees* popped into my head.

I ushered Jonathan through to the sitting room and threw another couple of logs on the fire and stirred it back into life while he settled his athletic and well-tailored frame into an armchair.

In leggings and sweatshirt, with my hair all ratty and my face bright red from the fire, I must have looked like Nora Batty's knackered older sister. If Jonathan noticed, he was far too polite to say anything, instead sweeping his eyes round the sitting room.

'This is a gorgeous place.'

'It could be. And will be.'

'I'm sure. What's the plan?'

'It's a little up in the air.'

And, over a bottle of Montrachet from the case Cécile had given me as a leaving present, I told him all about the Clapps, the shifting domestic arrangements, my meeting with the accountant, and my various plans and hopes for commercial ventures, including the film location angle.

'It sounds like you have everything in hand.'

'Not yet. But, with luck, we'll get there.'

'You know, Jennifer Brown, you inspire confidence and affection in everyone you meet.'

'I'm not sure that's true.'

'I know it is. And, in the spirit of friendship, please allow me to contribute, in a small way, to the good luck you have every right to expect will come your way.'

He pulled a cheque from his jacket pocket and laid it on the coffee table. The figure he'd written on it was eye-watering.

'No, Jonathan.'

'If you prefer, think of it as a loan. I'll even work out a payment plan. With a commercial rate of interest.'

'It's very kind. But, no. I can't accept.'

He gave me the soft eyes that have been reducing grown women to a quivering mess for a couple of decades. 'Then I will be very hurt.'

'I don't want to offend you. But I have to do this on my own.'

'I understand and respect that. But I hate the thought of you struggling to make ends meet.'

'There are challenges ahead. I can't deny that. But I'm up to them.'

'I don't doubt it.'

'Thanks.'

'Can we agree on a compromise?' He slid the cheque towards me again. 'You put this in a drawer for now. And you think of it as a safety net. A shelter if things get stormy.'

'I won't need it.'

'But promise me you'll use it in the unlikely event that you might. I am regarding it as money spent. And money that is spent in support of a very good friend, a very good person, is money very well spent.'

'You're such a flatterer.'

'I'm serious. The charmer bullshit works on a lot of women but I know it doesn't work on you. And that's not what this is.'

'I know.'

'Please. Put it in a drawer. For a very rainy day.' He held my gaze with his intensely blue eyes.

I took a deep breath. 'Okay. Thank you. You're very kind.'

'And we will never speak of it again.'

'Agreed.'

***

I've never been one for fate and karma and horoscopes and universal forces.

And when people say stuff like 'Good things happen to good people' it makes me want to slap them. I know a lot of good people whose life is a cruel struggle.

But Veronica's stumbling across a potential lifeline with Lexington Locations, followed closely by Jonathan's impromptu white-knight social call, was beginning to feel like a pattern.

They say things come in threes.

But when my phone buzzed with a call from Miranda, my frantic former landlady from Wood Green, I didn't immediately see it as part of the pattern.

'Your old room's been empty for a couple of months but now I've found someone. I'm telling you in case you thought I was keeping it empty as some sort of shrine.'

'Very funny. I bet Sarah Millican's sweating.'

'I miss you, you snotty cow.'

'I miss you too. But I don't miss the drippy tap in your bathroom. Has your new lodger complained about it yet?' A lot of things about life with Miranda had driven me round the bend – the drippy tap, the 'upcycled' (ie knackered) bedroom mirror that made applying makeup only slightly less of a challenge than the assault course on *The Krypton Factor*, and the fact that her mother, Mad Mary, might pop in at any time for a spot of casual faith-healing and bible-bashing.

But hearing Miranda's voice again made me think how easy and comfortable that episode of my life had been. Compared to now.

'No, she's too nice to complain. A lot nicer than you. She's some kind of researcher at the LSE. She's teetotal. And she plays the flugelhorn in the Sally Army band.'

'What's a flugelhorn?'

'Looks like a cross between a trumpet and a yard of ale.'

'Sally Army. She'll get on well with your mum, then.'

'Actually, Mad Mary's not that keen. Says she's too opinionated.'

I laughed out loud. 'That is *the* perfect example of pot and kettle.'

'You're telling me.'

'How's she getting on? Mary.'

'No worse than usual. She's not been arrested this week. That's something.'

'It's only Wednesday. Give her time.'

Mary was something of an activist. In later years, a lot of people lose their inhibitions and, perhaps sensing that life's too short to be lived sensibly, let their hair down in ways their younger selves would never have entertained. These days, Mary's hair was never up. And she liked nothing better than a public brawl with a burly police officer or five. This recreational activity had earned her a criminal record so long Al Capone would have been proud, as well the odd TV appearance on *Look London*, much to Miranda's annoyance and embarrassment.

'How's the romance of the century?'

'The fires are still burning bright. But we don't get to light them very often.' And I explained about New York and two years and the reality of one weekend every few months. 'How about you?'

'Well, there was this plumber. Kev. Very fit. In every sense. He came to fix the leaky tap.'

'You've got it fixed?! Finally!'

'Shut up. I'm telling a story.'

'Sorry.'

'And we hit it off. Went on several dates. Had numerous nights in. Steamy ones. Then I got him to rip out the bath and fit a walk-in shower.'

'So you wait for me to move out then you spend thousands remodelling the bloody bathroom!'

'Will you shut up!'

'Sorry. Pray continue.'

'And it was a big job so he brought a young apprentice. And the pair of them slaved away for days on their hands and knees, under floorboards, behind walls, going great guns. And then it all went pear-shaped.'

'What did you do?'

'How d'you know it was something *I* did?'

'I just know. What was it?'

'Well, Kev was on his knees with his head under the bathroom sink.'

'Right.'

'And the view from behind was very … appetising. His thighs. The curve of his buttocks. The hint of a package hanging down. And I just … fancied a squeeze.'

'Which he didn't appreciate?'

'He didn't know. He'd gone out to the van to fetch something. The package I squeezed belonged to the apprentice. Who didn't take kindly to being groped by an old woman. And is threatening to take some sort of action. And has fallen out massively with Kev. Who has fallen out with me.'

'Seems a bit over the top.'

'That's what I think.'

'So it's back to the dating apps.'

'Oh, I can't be arsed. I've done the sodding lot: *Tinder*, *Match. com*, *eHarmony*. And that's just the mainstream ones. I've even done *Gluten-Free Singles*, *Ready To Tumble* and *Tindog*.

'Tindog? Sounds like something you do in a car park at night.'

'It's for dog owners, not doggers.'

'You don't have a dog. You have a cat.'

'I could borrow one.'

'You're nuts.'

'D'you know there's even an app called *Bristlr*. It matches men with beards with women – or men – who like to stroke beards. No dinner or sex or walks on the beach. Just beard-stroking.'

'Can you see me shaking my head in disbelief?'

'I know. Young people run the world. And they're all bonkers.'

'Speaking of young people, how are things at the college?'

Miranda had been teaching Catering to bored students at a less-than-salubrious Further Education place in Hornsey ever since her bistro in Crouch End had folded when her (now ex) husband, Patrick, had gambled away their profits.

'My career's like my love life. Going nowhere. I have daydreams about running a cookery school. River Cottage, that sort of thing. Then I look at the commercial rent costs in North London and reach for the gin bottle.'

The Earth's rotation slowed for three seconds.

'Jen? You still there?'

'Yeah. I'm here.'

'What is it?'

'I was just thinking it's a shame you don't know someone with a nice big property you could run a cookery school from.'

'And it's a shame I can't win the lottery.'

'For a very clever woman, Miranda, you can be very stupid.'

'Why?'

'*Nestled in the heart of the beautiful Cotswolds, in the Elizabethan splendour of the historic Thornhill estate, lies one of the country's foremost cookery schools.*'

Silence.

Then Miranda's warmest, softest voice.

'You are an absolute bloody genius.'

9

Passing Muster

Miranda and I sat in the library and devised a cunning plan. The division of labour, cost and responsibility was honed to perfection: I'd engage a surveyor to establish if the Shooting Lodge was a workable location and (at Miranda's insistence) we'd split the cost of his work; I'd pay for the structural work and the basic refurbishment, while Miranda would source and pay for all the kitchen equipment needed to furnish each cooking station; we'd share company costs such as a brand, a logo, and company registrations; I'd do admin and marketing; Miranda would take charge of all licences and inspections and she'd devise the courses and menus and run the classes; I'd handle the accommodation side of things.

This was going to work.

Peter Potter laid his cycle helmet on Rosemary's kitchen table and held out his hand.

'I feel like we've met before.'

I know exactly where we met. In a traffic jam on my way to Stow. I gave you your second shower of the day with my screenwash.

'No, I'm confident we haven't. And I'm very good with faces.'

'Hm. So am I. And I just know I've seen yours before. Don't worry. It'll come to me.'

I really hope it doesn't.

The surveyor looked around. 'So ...?'

'The Shooting Lodge. I'll take you across.'

We walked the hundred yards or so from the house's east wing to the building that would, I really hoped, prove viable as a site for this new venture.

It was a bright morning in late March and, even in its current rather shabby condition, the estate was jaw-droopingly lovely. I imagined a clutch of six exuberant paying guests admiring the view as, after a satisfying dish of breakfast delights, including Robbie's delicious eggs and Rosemary's freshly baked wheaten bread, they prepared themselves for the first exciting day of their premium residential cookery course.

I went to open the main door but Peter Potter stood back and lifted his eyes towards the roof.

'I'll do the exterior inspection first.'

'Right you are.'

He swung his backpack onto the ground and, like a modern-day Mary Poppins, unpacked an array of equipment that looked far too bulky for the modest bag that had contained it all. Some items he looked through, some he shone light from ('It's a line laser.' 'Right.'), and some he attached to a telescopic tripod.

After about twenty minutes and a couple of pages of notes, he gestured for me to open the door and we moved inside.

More kit was unpacked. He got particularly busy with something that looked a lot like the gizmo Mr Spock uses when he and Kirk land on a new planet and they want to know if there are monsters behind that rock. ('Moisture meter.' ' Okay.')

Then he walked around for two or three minutes scouring the floor, like I do when I've dropped an earring. Then he said 'Aha!', hunkered down, and lifted a loose floorboard. Then another couple. Then he strapped a little torch to his head and, as Houdini might have done, folded his body into the hole and disappeared.

After two or three minutes of silence, I heard a knocking noise from somewhere below the fireplace, thirty feet away.'

Then more silence.

Then his head, still torched, popped out of the floor and he pulled himself up to a standing position, scribbled another page or two of notes, then turned his attention to the ceiling.

'Is there a hatch?'

'Erm ...'

'Don't worry. I'll find it.'

And he was off again, through a door that led to one of the Lodge's anterooms.

'Found it!'

'Okay!'

Then I heard him walking around above my head. Then it sounded like he was doing a spot of practice for his Cossack line-dancing class.

Then, five minutes later, he was back. With more notes.

He grinned.

'Days like this, I love this job. They just don't build them like this anymore.'

'Is that good?'

'I'll send you my full report by the end of the week, but would you like the edited highlights now?'

'Yes, please.'

'Structurally, there's nothing to worry about.'

I resisted the urge to kiss him.

'Although the roof needs a bit of work, the previous owners had it felted at some point – I'm guessing twenty or so years ago – so the roof timbers are bone dry and the structure sound. You're talking about twenty or thirty slates and some repairs to the chimney flashing. Basic stuff.'

'Sounds good.'

'There's some rising damp ...' *Oh shit.* '... but that's normal for a building of this age and a chemicure treatment is both affordable and efficient. If you don't do it, the place won't fall down – it's been here for pushing three hundred years – but I'd recommend it. And that dampness has got into some of your joist ends, so the floor's a bit springy in places, but a qualified builder can bolt fresh joist ends on and wrap them in DPC so they stay fresh.'

'That sounds like a lot of work.'

'It's not. As I say, it's basic stuff. This is a fine building. If you get these few basic jobs done, the rest of what you see is just cosmetic stuff, really. She'll be good for another three hundred years.' He began squirrelling his gear back into the rucksack. 'I'll email you the full report by Friday. I'm not allowed to recommend a specific builder but … ' He fished around in his pocket and pulled out four cards. '… any of these guys will do you a good job. Do a bit of online research, see which one you fancy, and pick one.'

Back in the kitchen, he strapped on his cycle helmet.

'Lovely to see you. Again. And thank you for not dousing me with screenwash this time.'

My mouth fell open.

'I told you it'd come to me.'

This very good start to the week was followed swiftly by an encouraging email from Lexington Locations. My submission had caught their eye and they'd like to send a portfolio manager to 'do a full recce.' And would I phone them to arrange it.

'When were you thinking?'

'Is tomorrow too soon?'

Barry was about six feet five and probably a stone or two lighter than me. If you put grey denims and a quilted gilet on a giant stick insect, you'd get Barry. The row of gelled-up spikes on his head only added to the general arthropod vibe. A fifty-year-old who'd found a style in 1979 and stuck with it.

We sat in the kitchen and I poured him tea and, clocking how loosely his jeans hung on his skinny thighs, slid a plate of Rosemary's scones towards him.

He pulled a tablet out of a battered leather shoulder bag and tapped at the screen.

'None at all.'

'And you're six miles from the A34, so I'm guessing not much in the way of traffic noise?'

'Nothing. It really is blissfully quiet.'

'Terrific. Can we take a look at the principal interiors?'

'Sure. Bring your mug.'

I showed him the sitting room, the library, the dining room, and the Orangery.

'Just gorgeous. I can think of a couple of productions just off the top of my head that would be *very* interested. Can we see upstairs?'

I showed him the guest bedrooms. He pointed at the door to Camilla's room. 'How about that one?'

'Not available, I'm afraid. And neither is the one at the end – that's where I sleep.'

'How open are you to cast or senior crew using these excellent rooms as accommodation?'

'They'd want to *live* here?'

'In a place as lovely as this, some might. And, frankly, even if they paid you a generous day rate for the use of the room, it would still be cheaper for them than housing a Hollywood A-lister in a top hotel and sending a car for them every day.'

I didn't hear much after *generous day rate*.

'Then let's say I'm at least open to discussion.'

'Perfect.' Barry tapped a note into his tablet. 'Can we look around outside?'

I ushered him back downstairs and out through the main hall onto the gravel drive.

'Forgive the condition of the gardens. We're just about to embark on a regeneration programme.' *God! When did I become such a bullshitter?*

'Oh, please. Don't worry. Filmmakers don't care about weeds. They care about space and privacy and a general look. The general look is excellent, you've got acres of space …'

'Seventeen acres.'

'Seventeen. Terrific.' More tapping on the tablet. 'And you've got a controlled space. No public. No fans. No journalists. No people walking past the camera with bags of shopping.'

'No. None of the above.'

'How cool would you be with the idea of a production company operating a base on your grounds?'

'A base?'

'It's where they set up all their vehicles. The trailers where the actors hang out during the day's shoot. The trucks that wardrobe and makeup and props operate out of. Catering vans. Panalux trucks full of massive lights. Holding stations for extras.'

'Wow.'

'Having all that on site is a massive saving in time and money for a production. You don't have to ferry people back and forth from a place three or four miles away. And they're happy to pay a premium for that.'

'Then I'm sure I could be very cool with that idea.'

'Perfect.' Another couple of taps. Then a serious face. 'I need to say this. Having a film crew in what is essentially your home is a major intrusion. People think the world of film and television is glamorous, but a set can be a busy, noisy, messy, chaotic environment full of people very much on a schedule. Throw a few egos into that mix and you've got a very heady brew. It can make you a lot of money. But how acceptable you'll find the experience depends on what you expect and how good you are at taking the rough with the smooth.'

I smiled. 'I've taken quite a lot of rough in my time. Nothing you've said puts me off. I'm sure we can make it work.'

'Excellent.' Barry drained his mug and passed it to me. 'Thanks for the tea. I'm sure it won't be long before you hear from us again.'

'I look forward to it.'

10

The Lavender Mob

I was feeling buoyant until I looked at my diary.

We were now in April. That fact normally fills me with anticipation – a sense that winter is nearly over and spring will soon be gearing up to put on its breathtaking show.

But, this year, the first of April was merely the day before the second of April, the date of my first foray into the blue-rinse world of afternoon teas with the county's most distinguished ladies.

You have got to become better at saying No.

I was getting used to my little rental Picanto but the satnav could be a bit iffy.

On this particular morning, when Sally with the sexy satnav voice announced I'd arrived at my destination, she must have been doing her nails or something. She certainly didn't have her eyes on the road and had sweet-talked me down a single-track lane and brought me nose-to-nose with a FedEx delivery truck.

Maybe he had the same satnav as me.

Either way, he wasn't for backing up. Which was fair enough. I was driving something the size of a Dinky toy and he was steering a vehicle only slightly smaller than the Queen Mary.

To say my reversing skills could do with a little work is a bit like saying the Visigoths could be a bit boisterous.

After a halting ten yards or so (during which my armpits had taken on the humidity level of downtown Kuala Lumpur), I heard a familiar crunch. My heart sank.

Freddie FedEx hopped down from his cab in the sky and trotted over.

'Bugger. Sorry. I should have given it a go but there's a tractor behind me pulling a year's worth of straw.'

I climbed out and surveyed the damage. I'd backed into a concrete post too short to be visible in my rearview mirror but tall enough to put an ugly crack in the plastic bumper and a serious-looking dent in the bodywork.

'It looks worse than it is. I reckon about two-fifty. What's your excess?'

I had no bloody idea.

'I'll sort it out.'

'Hang on. I'll get this clown in the tractor to back up then I'll shift and you can get on your way.'

I pulled up at Orchard House in a hire car that would now need to be repaired with money I could do without spending. I wasn't in the best of moods.

I was led into a small and imperfectly formed sitting room by a forty-year-old maid dressed in black who looked like she was having a worse day than me.

Anthea stood. 'Thank you, Theresa.' The maid held her gaze for an insubordinate second or two then wheeled out of the room. 'How lovely to see you again, Jessica.'

'It's Jennifer. My name is Jennifer.'

There was a faint crack in the veneer of Anthea's smile. 'Forgive me. Jennifer. You remember Sylvia.' She waved towards a woman who looked like she'd studied Laura Bush at the height of the Dubya presidency and seen a style she'd wanted to copy down to the last pearl button.

I nodded. 'Hello.'

'And Erica, of course.' A Falklands-era Margaret Thatcher and wife of local MP Claude Dickens. She'd always been Camilla's lady-in-waiting at the Thornhill gatherings and must have been inwardly seething at Anthea's Machiavellian mantle-grabbing. 'And Deirdra.' A smiling seventy-year-old with a fabulous figure who looked about as close to human warmth as you could get in this kind of crowd.

'Yes. Hello, again.'

I was introduced to another handful of horsey types whose names I immediately forgot then Deidra smiled and patted the seat next to her and I plonked myself down on a sofa newly covered with a William Morris fabric I'd seen online a few weeks before at nearly two hundred quid a metre.

It was all a long way from *Jam and Jerusalem* and much closer to the Girls in Pearls set I used to see in the copies of *Country Life* my dad's sister, Auntie Brenda, used to leave lying around the house to impress my mum when we went over for a visit. Brenda was an absolute darling but couldn't hide the very middle-class aspirations of a very working-class girl. I wondered what she'd have said if she could have seen me in this company.

After ten minutes of small talk, Theresa materialised again to tell Anthea that tea was ready. 'In the library.' The maid managed to say the words with just enough mockery to make a point but not quite enough for it to be an out-and-out sacking offence. I wondered how long this disharmonious domestic dynamic had existed.

The lavender ladies stood up and wandered through. Deidra held me back.

'Anthea's told me about Thornhill Hall. Well done, you.' She squeezed my hand. 'What's the plan?'

I talked (in very general terms – this wasn't an occasion for opening up) about domestic renovation and commercial development and she seemed genuinely impressed. 'Well, I wish you much success. I'm sure you'll make a fabulous go of everything.'

'Thank you.'

'I wish I'd had your drive at your age. I started modelling at eighteen. My mother modelled for Dior and it was always understood I'd have the same life. And I didn't have the brains or the gumption to make my own choices.'

'Didn't you enjoy it?'

'I don't know. Really I don't. I'm not sure I know what enjoyment is.' She cracked a wry smile at this sentence, which was possibly the saddest I'd ever heard anyone utter. I felt the need to say something nice.

'I'm sure you were very good at it. You have a figure that would be the envy of, if I may say so, most women half your age.'

'I inherited my mother's genes.' Deirdra ushered me towards the library. 'And her resistance to sugar. And she gave me good advice – everything in moderation, stay out of the sun, and choose your men carefully. Ideally with lots of cash in the bank.'

Anthea's 'library' had a couple of bookshelves and a desk that practically filled what would have been a perfectly nice room in the hands of someone with a few tons less pretention. I suddenly understood her earlier cattiness at Thornhill.

The ladies were already tucking into sandwiches and pastries. I observed Deirdra weighing her options with the care of someone for whom watching her figure had been a lifetime's occupation. She lifted a couple of crackers with what looked like salmon paté and I followed suit. She chastised me. 'Eat what you want. Don't be polite. Life's too short. I wish I'd learned that lesson fifty years ago.'

Anthea tapped her teaspoon against her china cup and the buzz of conversation died down.

'Welcome everyone, friends old and new.'

All eyes on me. *Smile like you mean it.*

'We have a busy year ahead. And let's make this year a fitting tribute to darling Camilla, whom we miss terribly.' Grim faces pasted on. Nods of concurrence. 'So let's get cracking.' *Back to business. That didn't last long.*

Anthea steered us through the agenda at breakneck speed then slammed the anchors on at what seemed to be the destination.

'The summer charity fair in July.' Smiles and eager eyes. 'We have a problem.' Grim faces pasted on again. 'Our usual venue, the fabulous hall in Nether Brompton, is closed for refurbishment until October.' Groans. 'But let's try to see this as an opportunity. I've always thought the summer fair a rather modest …' Anthea struggled for a word that didn't sound like *fair*. She failed. '… affair. I've always thought we could, and should, be more ambitious. I've always thought (*Do you begin* every *sentence with that?*) we should have not simply a fair, but a GALA!'

There were *ooh*s and *aah*s from the assembled company. All I could think of was bingo.

'A proper outdoor country gathering with stalls and events. And a huge MARQUEE!'

Wide eyes. Mutterings of approval.

'But, of course, we'd need a venue with plenty of space. But where might we find a generous benefactor with an expansive area of ground they'd be willing to donate for a weekend? For a very good cause.'

All eyes on me. Again.

You have got *to become better at saying No.*

11

Holy Rock 'n' Roller

I walked away from Orchard House feeling a little like the victim of a cruel experiment.

In the face of my own better judgment and something of a pep talk from Anthea's pal Deirdra, I'd allowed myself to be talked into offering Thornhill as the site for the summer gala and into organising some sort of 'entertainment' for the primetime Saturday night spot.

It seemed the best person to approach for access to top performers was the vicar at St Mark's in Great Farrington. He'd helped out a lot with Camilla's previous charity efforts and was distantly related to a girl who'd come third on *Britain's Got Talent* a couple of years before.

He seemed like an unlikely shout for a direct line to Gary Barlow or Cher but I promised I'd give him a bell.

Rosemary thought I was a mug for agreeing. 'You're just too nice. You have to learn to be a bit more of a cow.' She wasn't wrong.

And I got it in the neck again later from Will.

'Organising events is a major pain in the arse, you dozy sod.'

'I know. I could kick myself.'

'Bend over. I'll kick you from here.'

'I know!'

'I used to get roped into fixing up all sorts when I was younger. But now I just say No. I just can't be gassed with the hassle.

I've been bitten too many times. Do you remember that bloody paintball?'

I did.

At Intext Software, where Will and I worked together, every year they had what they called a Summer Jamboree, which was basically an all-day piss-up around some sort of activity.

About eight or nine years ago, Will had been given the job of organising the activity. Which he'd left until the week before, of course. By which time the cocktail-mixing courses and the blend-your-own-whisky experiences were all booked up.

Which is why we ended up with paintball.

Which, on the face of it, sounds like a recipe for fun.

But the absence of alcohol in the activity itself had prompted many in our workforce to engage in some fairly vigorous 'pre-loading' as a compensation. By the time we were pulling on overalls and strapping on coloured tabards and plastic visors, at least half the contingent were about a hundred and three sheets to the wind.

And alcohol, workplace grudges, and simulated firearms do not pleasant bedfellows make.

I'd never seen Hilary, Rose and Trisha (the HRTs) look so vengeful. It's amazing what transformations can be wrought by a mid-morning bucket of Bacardi. The particular focus of their venom was (of course) Dread Ed, our charmless, childlike, ex-military manager. By the time they'd finished with him, he looked like a Jackson Pollock. Jonathan had to pull Trisha's gun off her so she would stop peppering Ed's privates with yellow paint.

I told Will about the vicar and his tenuous connection to someone who'd once been on the telly for three minutes.

'What about that gangster bloke with the trophy wife? Doesn't he have connections in the entertainment world?'

He was talking about Harry Sinclair, East End barrow boy turned highly successful property tycoon and wine connoisseur.

He was one of Artisan Wines' most valuable clients and one whose account Cécile had entrusted me with. It was absolutely true that Harry knew all the right people (and some of the wrong ones) and the glitzy, money-no-object charity ball he'd invited me to was certainly something to aspire to, but his level of entertainment contact seemed about as remote as Mars.

And I was very uncomfortable about asking favours from someone I used to (essentially) work for, particularly now I'd moved on.

I resolved to reach out to the vicar first and see how that conversation panned out.

The reverend Clifford Carmichael had sounded very bushy-tailed on the phone and, judging by the gleaming black Porsche Macan in the driveway of the Old Rectory, was clearly enjoying life.

And had a good-going sideline in drug smuggling.

I balanced Rosemary's lemon drizzle cake in one hand and tugged at the highly polished Victorian brass bell-pull with the other.

The door was opened by a slim man in baggy brown cords and a check shirt, which I assumed was a vicar's off-duty garb. Either that, or it was Dress-Down Tuesday.

I held out the cake.

'I took a gamble on lemon drizzle. I hope you like it.'

His brow furrowed an inch. He held out his hands and took the cake. 'Er, thank you. Makes a welcome change from my usual post.'

I laughed. 'I'm not the postman. I'm Jennifer.'

'Hello, Jennifer.' Brow still furrowed.

'We spoke on the phone.'

'Did we? I don't remember.'

'About the charity gala.'

'Right. And you want me to make an appearance?'

'Well, yes. If you're free. But I wanted to pick your brains about entertainment.'

'Right.'

Aren't you going to invite me in?

'As I said on the phone.'

'Have you cleared this with my agent?'

'You have an agent?'

'Yes. Most writers do.'

'I didn't know you were a writer.'

'Isn't that why you're here?'

'You *are* the Reverend Carmichael?'

A lightbulb. 'Ah. No. I'm not. My name's Nick. Nick Boyd. This is the *Old* Rectory. Clifford lives over there. In the *New* Rectory.'

He pointed to a modest semi across the road, with the Christian fish symbol on the gatepost.

'Oh god. I'm sorry.'

'It's fine. Happens all the time.' He held the cake out to me.

'No. You keep it. Please. I didn't mean to disturb your writing.'

'You're not. I'm watching *Bargain Hunt*.'

'Right. Well, keep the cake anyway. If you like lemon drizzle.'

'I love it, but …'

'No, please. Just keep it. And enjoy it.'

'Right. Well, that's very kind. Thank you.' He smiled.

'Bye then.'

'Bye.'

The New Rectory didn't feel like a rectory at all. It actually felt a lot like my Auntie Brenda and Uncle Bob's place in Bexleyheath, my home during my first few months at Artisan Wines and eminently commutable from its offices in fashionable Shoreditch. Except their semi had been built in the twenties. The Reverend Carmichael's looked no older than eighties.

'The church, like most organisations, is downsizing. There's no longer the money to sustain the grand old rectories of yesteryear. Nor indeed the personnel to fill them. They fetch a pretty penny on the property market. And the church needs every penny, pretty or otherwise, it can get its hands on.' He smiled. 'I don't mind. This place is comfy and easy to clean. Compact and bijou, as the advert used to say.'

'You've got it very nice.' I could say so in all honesty. The wooden floors and the robust and elegant antique furniture gave the place a feel of quality, enhanced by the clean, uncluttered walls.

'Oh, you're very kind. It suits me, anyway.' He nodded towards the street. 'What did you think of our resident celebrity?'

'He seemed very nice. Once we'd got our wires uncrossed. I'm afraid I felt obliged to leave him with the lemon drizzle cake I handed over when I thought he was you.'

Clifford Carmichael laughed. 'I'll make sure he doesn't forget he owes me a cake. Have you read any of his stuff?'

'No. Never heard of him, actually.'

He pulled a paperback off one of his shelves and handed it to me. *The Darkest Grave.* 'They're very good. Psychological thrillers. That one was the first. There've been seven more. They sell very well.'

'That explains the Porsche.' I handed the book back.

'No, keep it. Just the thing for a winter's night. When the Book of Revelation is a bit too scary.'

'Thank you.'

'I can't begrudge him his success. Even if my faith were to allow it. He's very good at putting something back. When funds are running low – and when *aren't* they? – he's perfectly happy to spend a couple of hours at a fete allowing locals to hobnob with him and take selfies, provided I throw a good steak on the barbecue and feed him Rioja.'

'Does the church allow Rioja?'

'We're not Methodists. When God gives you grapes, you make grape-ade.'

'It's a good line. You should work in marketing.'

'I do. Sort of. I've made tea.' He waved towards a pot and two cups.

'Oh, lovely.'

'Are you a MILF?'

'Sorry?'

'MILk in First.'

'Right.' *Are you winding me up?* 'I really don't mind.'

He poured a cup and passed it to me. 'So you're looking for Entertainment with a capital E?'

'Yes. I was foolish enough to agree to take that on.'

'If you want my advice, make this the first and last time you do anything for Anthea Orchard-Lyons. The charities benefit from what she does, of course. But *she* benefits more. She's a dreadful snob. Frankly, I'd rather give her the shirt off my back for charity than spend an hour in her company on a bring-and-buy stall.'

I laughed. His frankness was refreshing. 'You're not a fan.'

'Is anyone, I wonder. And doubtless she's painted me as some sort of latter-day Brian Epstein when, the truth is, my claims to fame are that my granddaughter was in the same class as that girl who came third on *Britain's Got Talent* and I used to know the drummer from The Wurzels. They're still touring. Did you know?'

'Really? My dad used to listen to them when I was tiny. *I Am A Cider Drinker.*'

'Seventy-six. A very hot summer. I wasn't really into folk. Not even their bawdy, silly, pastiche stuff. I was more of a rocker.'

'Really?'

'Oh, yes. I was born a decade too late. It was my mum's musical taste I inherited. Her eyes lit up when she talked about Jerry Lee Lewis and Bill Haley. And, of course, the late great Elvis Presley. And I bought into the whole scene. The drainpipe trousers, the winkle-picker shoes. And I had the sharpest quiff for miles.'

'I can't imagine.'

'I know. Looking at me now. Even in the sixties, there was still a scene, left over from the fifties. The violence. The fistfights and motorbike chains. Newspapers still talked about 'feral youth.'

His face fell under a cloud.

'It seemed like harmless fun. Then somebody laid into a West Indian lad and a few others piled on. He didn't survive. And that was my 'road to Damascus' moment. You can't see that level of violence without wanting to make the world a better place. I try to get the message across. But fewer people are willing to listen.'

I felt like hugging him. He smiled.

'I'm sorry. That turned a bit serious there, didn't it?'

'Serious is fine.'

'The long and the short of it is I'm next to useless to you where entertainment is concerned. But give me a job and I'll roll my sleeves up and muck in. So, when you've got a plan and a date, give me another shout. I'm in.'

12

Wheels

I was glad I'd made the Rev's acquaintance but my entertainment problem was still unresolved.

A slightly more pressing concern was the unsightly damage on the leased Picanto. The lease was up in just over a month – bloody typical that I should have a smash a few weeks before giving it back – and patching it up as good as new was, of course, a requirement.

My insurance excess, it turned out, was five hundred quid – a two-hundred compulsory excess and a three-hundred voluntary I'd opted for (as a cost-cutting measure) to keep the premiums down. Still, Freddie FedEx had reckoned the damage wouldn't stretch to more than two-fifty, which was money I could do without spending but wasn't the end of the world. So the excess was kind of irrelevant.

'Seven hundred and eighty quid?!'

'The bumper alone is three hundred. And we'll have to remove it, knock out the dent, then respray all four rear panels. And fit the new bumper. There's a lot of labour in that job.'

'What do you charge for labour?'

'Forty an hour.'

'God. I should have been a mechanic.'

'If that seems steep, let me tell you there's a Porsche garage in Cowley charges two hundred and ten pounds an hour. I'm not joking. The national average is something like sixty-two. We're cheap.'

I couldn't go on leasing cars that I needed to keep in pristine condition on pain of exorbitant penalties. I needed something more suited to the rough and tumble of country life. And the rough and tumble of my reversing.

What is it about car salesmen that gets everyone's back up? The oily, cocky, patter-merchant car salesman has become a byword for untrustworthiness and, about seventeen seconds into my visit to the glass-fronted dealership just outside Witney, I was reminded that, in every cliché and stereotype, there's a substantial element of truth.

This particular example of the breed – Jordan, the name badge announced – looked like he'd left school that morning. But, if that was true, it'd only taken him a couple of hours to get the salesman persona so off pat it looked like a permanent part of his DNA.

'Are we looking for a vehicle primarily for business or for pleasure?'

'*I* am looking for something robust.'

Jordan slid across the showroom towards a red Audi TT. 'Just the thing. German engineering screams reliability. And the quattro four-wheel drive gives you the go-everywhere performance of an SUV. Plus, she's a looker.' He gave me an oily leer.

I looked at the price tag. Fifty-six thousand two hundred and seventy-five pounds. 'And where would I put my dogs? And a cage of hens when I'm going to the vet?'

Jordan's face fell. 'Okay. So, you need a vehicle with a substantial boot capacity.' He strode past a couple of Hondas and did a sort of gymnastic pirouette in front of a silver Range Rover Sport.

With half my brain, I was giving him a six-point-five for the dismount while, with the other half of my brain, I was clocking the ridiculous figure on the windscreen. Ninety-six thousand nine hundred and ninety-five pounds. Even if I had Victoria Beckham's bank account, I'm pretty sure I couldn't bring myself to spend a hundred grand on a car.

I was beginning to feel irritated.

'Look ... Jordan. You're not going to sell me a flash car. It's not going to happen. And you're actually not going to sell me a brand-new car. What I'm looking for is a secondhand workhorse that is all trousers. No mouth. Just trousers.'

This idiom clearly didn't feature in Jordan's vocabulary. I might as well have been speaking Swahili.

'What I mean is, my car doesn't have to *look* good. I'm not trying to impress anyone. It just has to run well, give me plenty of room for dogs and hens and anything else big and dirty I want to throw in the back. And it needs to still look okay if I reverse it into a concrete bollard. And it needs not to break down very often. Ideally never. Can you help me? At all? Or should I just go somewhere else?'

I must have been raising my voice slightly, because heads were turning my way. At the mention of going elsewhere, an even oilier bald-headed man with a mailbag for a stomach scurried across the shiny floor with his hands clasped in an eager, prayer-like pose. The manager, I presumed.

'We can absolutely help you, madam. If I might escort you outside to the used-car section.'

In a high-fenced compound round the back, far away from the gleaming marble tiles and the ridiculous price tags, I saw her.

My car.

To some, she would have looked ready for the scrapyard, with her faded green paint on her battleship bodywork, but, to me, the little P-reg Land Rover Defender with the full roof rack and the rear ladder looked like me.

She looked like home.

'Good choice. She's a beauty. Only two owners from new in 1996. And it's really rare to find a car at this age with under eighty thousand miles on the clock. Genuine miles. I can show you the service book.'

I contained my excitement behind a frosty, ballsy mask. 'Yes, I'll need to see the service book.'

'Of course. It gives you the full service history. The owners were careful to have the car serviced only at genuine Land Rover dealerships. It really is a remarkable bargain at just under thirteen thousand.'

I gave the man my best Cruella DeVil stare. 'I'll expect some movement on that price, of course.'

'I'm sure we can come to some arrangement.'

I texted David a photo of my new girlfriend. And although it was just after four in the morning in New York, he pinged me a reply immediately.

'Well, that completes the look, doesn't it. You'll need a silk headscarf and a Barbour jacket. That's what the Queen wears when she drives *her* Land Rover.'

'I've already got the jacket.'

'Then I'll send you the scarf. In the morning. When it's no longer dark. And I've had some more sleep.'

'Sorry. I was just excited to tell you.'

'It's fine. I love you.'

'It's a good job.'

'Best job I've ever had.'

***

We were now well over the Spring equinox and the thought that the days were slowly becoming longer than the nights was warming and uplifting me.

Robbie had been working like a Trojan on the grounds and had enlisted the help of his nephew Tom, now 16 and looking for a direction in life. The youngster had a strong back and a faultless work ethic and Robbie was wishing he'd started him earlier, the place was looking so good. I couldn't disagree. The Thornhill estate was starting to look like the kind of place you'd be willing to pay a premium price to spend some time on.

And, after I'd finally plucked up the courage to have the talk with Rosemary that Will had prompted me to have weeks before, Rosemary had moved into the large room round the corner from mine, with a great view of the lake and, in the distance, Over Norton Hill.

She was overjoyed. We were chatting over a mid-morning scone. 'I wish we'd done this years ago. I love my room, and it's really nice you and me being in the big house together.'

I leaned over and kissed her. Then wiped the cream off her cheek.

Thornhill was becoming a busy household once again. And about to get busier.

As Will had reminded me, things can't stay the same for ever.

After George had died, and Camilla had become very frail very quickly, the decision had been taken to move George's very elderly and very frail father, Edmund, into a private nursing home, a circumstance that had brought back all my old feelings of guilt about moving my own mum into Roselands when her immensely capable live-in carer, Leon, could clearly no longer cope.

Now that Edmund had outlived both his son and his daughter-in-law, and the monthly bill for his care at Windrush House was proving a strain on the Thornhill coffers, the time seemed right to review the situation.

If we moved Edmund back into the apartment at the back of the house that had once been his home, and we gave over another of the bedrooms to a live-in carer (whose expenses could be comfortably covered by Edmund's generous army pension), we'd still have twelve guest bedrooms available, for cookery school residents, for overnight corporate clients, and for Hollywood types.

Edmund would come home.

The old campaigner arrived in a minibus, wearing his old blazer and his regimental tie and still brandishing his favourite walking stick.

'For Christ's sake, man, get me out of this bloody van!' he scolded, as the driver lowered the hydraulic ramp.

'I can't go any faster than the ramp.'

'A bad workman always blames his tools,' Edmund countered, as the hapless driver threw me a pained appeal for help.

'Come on, Edmund. Let's get you settled back home. Rosemary's baked you some treats.'

It was immediately clear Edmund had become very much frailer even since I'd last seen him at Camilla's funeral. He smoothed the wisps of white hair over his pate and patted my hand with his skeletal fingers.

In the hall, I saw the empty sadness in his eyes as he gazed up at the portraits of his ancestors, the previous custodians of Thornhill, his own painting showing a vital, handsome man in his thirties, the epitome of square-jawed resolve, staring into the future like he owned it.

If he resented the fact that the estate had been passed to me, he was too much of a gentleman to show it. I'd always seen through his gruff, old-goat exterior and, like Camilla, hadn't stood for any of his curmudgeonly nonsense. I think that's why we'd always got on.

In the kitchen, I pushed a plate of Rosemary's feather-light lemon shortbreads towards him and produced two tumblers of Jura Prophecy, the heavily peated whisky that had been George's favourite and to which I knew Edmund was also partial.

I never normally touch alcohol before lunch – I always fear I might get the habit and turn into one of those woman who pours sherry on her cornflakes – but this was a special occasion and needed to be marked in the appropriate way.

It was clear from Edmund's misty eyes that he appreciated the gesture.

I felt a lump rise in my throat as I raised my glass. 'Welcome home.'

Edmund struggled to lift the tumbler to shoulder height. 'It's very good to be back.'

We clinked, sniffed, and swallowed. Then we sat in companionable silence for a couple of minutes before he piped up.

'I think I'd like to sit in the garden, by the sundial.'

'No problem. I'll find you a couple of blankets and we'll get you bundled up.'

That evening, I settled him in back into his old rooms, helped him to unpack (a couple of suitcases and a box – not much for ninety-three years, but then maybe the Buddhists have got it right: life is about so much more than mere stuff) and installed his most treasured possession, a model of the beloved Mulliner Park Ward Bentley he'd once owned, now on display in the British Motor Museum in Warwick. I remembered the afternoon, a few years earlier, when he'd taken me for a spin, clocking eighty-five on the Little Compton road, his eyes alive with the speed and the power of his cherished machine.

Later, when he'd fallen into a deep sleep, I crept into his room, removed all the shirts and trousers from his chest of drawers, and sat for a couple of hours in the sitting room, unpicking the tiny name tags the staff at Windrush had sewn into everything.

Most of his clothes had seen better days and I made a mental note to replace them the next time I went shopping in Cheltenham.

13

Fairy Godmother

The agency assured me Nutella was one of their top carers.

That wasn't her real name. But it *was* the name Natalia's boyfriend appeared to have etched on her forearm when, armed with a certificate from Witney FE college, a portfolio of skull designs and a hepatitis B jab, Spike had been let loose on his girlfriend's body.

Spike Loves Nutella.

So many questions.

But an excellent carer she proved to be. And Edmund, thankfully, took a real shine to her. I'd imagined the combo of tattoos, facial piercings and multicoloured braids would have sent his regimental blood pressure through the roof. But she seemed to appeal to the maverick in him. Her English was excellent (she was from Moldova) and she took none of Edmund's nonsense, laughing and telling him to 'get back in your cage' whenever he got stroppy.

She was a godsend.

As my old colleague Helen had been years earlier, taking me in after I'd outstayed (in my mind) my welcome with good friends Viv and Roger, my first port of call in the turbulent wake of my breakup with Pete.

Helen was a vegan and a fervent environmental campaigner and I was a bottle blonde in high street fashions and higher heels. But opposites attract and we got on like a house on fire. At least initially. And if Helen despised me for being too 'of this world', she hid it very well. She'd taken me in three weeks before Christmas and had dragged me fully out of the pit of despondency I'd fallen into.

And she'd opened my eyes to the true meaning of kindness. For Helen, all actions had a moral component and she lived her life trying to be the best version of herself in every single interaction with the world: she reused plastic bags until they were shredded, always coaxed wasps and ants and spiders out of the house instead of whacking them with a flipflop (my standard solution), avoided meat on moral, economic and environmental grounds, and persuaded me to buy as much as possible from charity shops instead of funding 'fast-fashion retail, most of which ends up as landfill.'

We'd eventually driven each other if not entirely round the bend then certainly into the corner at quite a speed, prompted mostly by my need to turn her vegan kitchen into a charnel house in preparation for my upcoming role as cook and housekeeper to a saucy old fisherman.

Nevertheless, I had an awful lot to be grateful to her for.

And now she was calling with news. And an opportunity for me to help her out. Helen and tree-hugging husband Paul had brought twins into the world.

'That's wonderful news. Congratulations.'

'Thanks. We're delighted.'

'How was the birth?'

'It strained my principles to the limit, frankly. I came very, very close to taking the drugs.'

'So you didn't have any pain relief at all?'

'No standard medical intervention, no. Breathing, relaxation, an element of hypnobirthing ...'

'Hypnobirthing?'

'It's part relaxation, part hypnosis. A technique based on the theory that our fear of childbirth prevents the release of endorphins that would naturally ease the process.'

'And did it work?'

'Up to a point. But twins are quite a test.'

'I can imagine. What names have you chosen?'

'Willow and Wolf.' I heard her smile. 'And now you're thinking "batty cow".'

'I'm thinking I expected nothing less. I'm also thinking how cool they'll be at school. So how can *I* help?'

'We're having a naming ceremony – a humanist, pagan affair, of course – and each parent chooses a guardian. A godparent, in Judeo-Christian terms. And I'd like you to be mine. If you want to, of course.'

I felt the tears rise. 'Oh, Helen. I'd be absolutely delighted.'

'Then I am mightily happy.'

'What does one bring as a present to a humanist, pagan naming ceremony?'

'Don't worry about a gift. Just do me a favour. I'll tell you on the day.'

***

As I sailed down the M3, I was aware of how good it felt to be back in Hampshire, my home county.

But I was rather daunted by the responsibility of godmotherhood. I was delighted and flattered, of course, but I didn't consider myself to be remotely maternal. I didn't have any siblings, so didn't have little nieces or nephews, and didn't have any close friends with kids. My life had been relatively devoid of children. And my few interactions with them had often been memorable.

I'd once helped out at a children's Christmas party at Intext, and had got roped into assisting the DJ. I thought it might be fun to invite some of the kids up on stage to do little turns and one shy-looking eight-year-old boy came up and asked if he could tell a joke, so I said *Sure* and handed him the mic.

'What's the funniest thing in the kitchen?' he'd asked, his little cheeks aflush.

'We Don't Know!,' the parents chanted.

'The washing machine, silly. Cos it keeps taking the piss out of mummy's knickers.'

When I pulled my little Keswick-green Defender onto the field near the River Itchen, I could see guests had already started to arrive for the naming ceremony. Even from this distance, it was clear I was going to be the least New Age person in the gathering by a mile. A mile of polyester.

Helen looked bewitching in a green velvet robe (green, in Earth Magick, signifies Love and Fertility, she told me, which seemed fitting for the mother of twins). Paul had grown a straggly beard since I'd last seen him, which, coupled with the ponytail, gave him more than a hint of Catweazel.

A flimsy-looking trestle table, covered with a hefty woollen fabric in a deep red (Balance and Harmony), was to serve as a sort of pagan altar and I took my place there beside Helen and Paul and Paul's friend Weaver, at the centre of a 'sun circle' formed around us by the other guests. If it hadn't been for the joyful vibe and the warmth of the smiles, I might have expected someone to set fire to a thirty-foot statue made of straw. With me inside it.

A priestess called upon the elements of Air, Fire, Water and Earth to bless and protect Helen and Paul's little babies ('in a ceremony unbounded by walls') and I felt genuinely moved by the whole ritual. It was a beautiful day spent in the company of good people under a warming April sun.

Four hours later, and with a drive of a couple of hours ahead of me, I sidled over to say goodbye.

'It's been such a lovely day. Thank you.'

'We're so pleased you could be such a central part of it. And so grateful that you've agreed to offer us a solution.'

'Solution?'

'Yes. Remember I asked you to do us a favour? By way of a ceremonial gift.'

I'd completely forgotten. 'Yes, of course.'

'Only they need plenty of space now they're fully grown. More space than we can give them.'

'Now *what* are fully grown?'

'The llamas.'

14

Flash In The Pan

It was almost midnight when I arrived back at Thornhill. And as soon as I opened the door, I knew immediately something was wrong.

The burning smell didn't hit me in the hall. But the frantic barking of Woodbine and Luther, together with the raised voices from the back of the house, were signal enough that bad stuff was happening.

Rosemary was slumped on the floor outside the kitchen door, wiping her tear-stained cheeks.

'I'm so sorry!'

'What's happened?' I reached for the kitchen door.

'Don't go in there! Robbie's told me to stay out. And keep everyone else out.'

I peered through the glass and saw, through a cloud of fog, Robbie covering Rosemary's cooker with foam from a fire extinguisher.

'I fell asleep. I wanted to get a head start on tomorrow's casserole – brown the meat in the pan before throwing it in the slow cooker – and I fell asleep. And when I woke up the flames were three feet high and Robbie was shoving me out the door.'

Through the glass, the fog was clearing and Robbie was laying the extinguisher down and wiping his brow. He turned and saw me.

He shook his head, walked towards the door and came out into the hallway. Rosemary's river of tears burst its banks again.

'I'm so bloody stupid! We're trying to build the place back up and I'm bloody burning it down!'

Robbie sat down on the floor beside her and put his tattooed arm round her heaving shoulder.

'It was an accident. And it's not that bad.'

Rosemary gazed through the glass at the black wall. 'Not that bad? Look at it!'

'Seriously, it looks worse than it is. Agas are indestructible. It'll clean up fine. After that, you're talking about wiping down and painting an eight-foot section of wall and touching up the ceiling. That's it. I'll have it back to normal in a couple of hours.' He smiled. 'But you *will* need a new frying pan.'

'That was my favourite pan!'

I put my arm around her other shoulder. 'I'll buy you a new one. A new old one. A new favourite. It's fine. Nobody died.'

'But what if ...?'

I laid a gentle finger on her lips. 'But it didn't. So it's fine. We're all fine. Come on.'

I helped her to her feet and ushered her up to her room. She lay on the bed in her clothes and stared at the ceiling. Robbie came in with a mug of cocoa.

'Drink that. And relax. I'll fix it up tomorrow.'

I woke early and went down to the kitchen. Robbie had beaten me to it and was up a stepladder wiping down the walls. And he'd already given the Aga a full service, by the gleaming look of it.

'It's come up fine.'

'It looks like a brand new cooker!'

'And this is coming off nicely. Couple of coats of emulsion and you really won't know anything ever happened.'

'Did you hear the alarm?'

'No. It didn't go off. There must be a problem with the wiring. Thankfully, she had the presence of mind to phone me. Think I covered the two hundred yards in about ten seconds. I'm thinking of joining the Jamaican sprint team, now Usain Bolt's hung up his spikes.'

'I'm just glad you were around.'

'Me too. Have you seen her this morning?'

'I popped my head round her door. She was sound.'

'Good. The sleep'll do her good. She'll be alright.'

'I hope so.'

My phone beeped. A text from Anthea. 'Just wondering how plans are coming along for the gala entertainment?' Jesus. That was quite a lot further down my list of priorities than Anthea imagined it was. Nevertheless, I'd given a commitment to sort it out. 'It's in hand. I'll be in touch with news soon.' Nothing like a bit of self-imposed pressure to help you get a job done. And a bit of vagueness to give you a get-out-of-jail-free card.

I girded my loins, bit the bullet, and phoned Harry Sinclair. And got his voicemail. *Bugger.*

A couple of hours later, Rosemary appeared, her whole body dripping with guilt and remorse.

'I've been doing a lot of thinking. I've been thinking most of the night. I didn't get to sleep until five.'

'Oh goodness, Rosemary. I'm sorry. I did look in on you around seven and you seemed sound. And we wanted to let you sleep on.'

'I think it's time.'

'Time for what?'

'James has been on at me for months. To go out there. Meet my grandson.'

Rosemary's family dynamic was unconventional, to say the least. At 17, she'd lost her virginity on a one-night stand with a much older man, in his thirties, a widower. He'd arranged everything relating to the baby's adoption. Then, about three years ago, Rosemary had received a letter with a Boston postmark, from a son she'd never met. Since then, they'd become as thick as thieves. She had a son who loved her. And now there was a grandson.

'How long for?'

She looked me in the eye. 'For good.'

'You're leaving?'

'I think it's best. I think the time's right.'

'Because of … last night?'

'Not really. I've been thinking about it for a long time. And last night was just … the deciding factor. The thing that's made me want to hang up my saucepans for good.' She laughed. 'Before I burn the arse out of them all.'

'You know how I'd feel about losing you? Not just as a housekeeper but as a friend.'

'Housekeepers are ten a penny.'

'Not like you, they're not.'

'And you won't lose me as a friend. I'm a dab hand at Skype these days. And you can come across to Boston from New York when you fly out to see your man.'

'I will definitely take you up on that.'

The old Jennifer would have asked her to reconsider, but the older Jennifer knew it was wrong to try to change a mind already made up.

So, three weeks later, in a kitchen fully recovered from its encounter with the god of fire, I lit the candles on the cake I'd baked for Rosemary and carried it through to the Orangery, to applause from Robbie, Delyth, and special guests Veronica and Kate.

There were tears, hugs, and promises to stay in touch and visit. I handed over the memory book I'd put together over a few evenings in the library, together with a peridot pearl necklace of

Camilla's that Rosemary had always admired, and a leather-bound book of Christina Rossetti poems from George's collection that I often found her reading in the sitting room.

As I walked her down the steps to the taxi, she squeezed my hand.

'George made absolutely the right decision, leaving the place to you. You're just wonderful.'

It was the nicest thing anyone had ever said to me.

15

Two Steps Forward, Seven Back

Y ou never notice how much space someone fills in your life
until the space is empty.

Robbie, Delyth and I were struggling to adjust to life without
Rosemary. I was missing her scones and I know Robbie was missing
her chicken and bacon pie. But those were just the things we talked
about. The things you could put your finger on.

I'd never known Thornhill without her. And without her it
seemed like a different place. A lesser place. It was a feeling I was
struggling to shake off.

The silver lining in the black cloud of her absence was that
I now felt I could drive forward with the plans to revamp
Coachman's Lodge, get it on the rental market, and start bringing
in some money.

I tried to let that positive thought govern my mood.

And I was further uplifted by a call from Harry Sinclair. I'd left
what felt like a couple of dozen sheepish voicemail messages and
had heard nothing back. I assumed I'd dropped off his radar. But
I hadn't.

'So sorry, Jennifer. Work has been hell. And I'm still trying to
get the hang of this new phone and I didn't know that the little tape
sign meant a voice message. Pauline thinks I'm a dinosaur. A stupid
one. Don't worry about your entertainment. I've got your date.

I know it's for charity, so I'll insist on no fee. Leave it with me. I'll fix you up with someone special.'

'I'm so grateful, Harry. Thank you.'

'No problem. I'm just sorry it took me so long to get back to you. Pauline's giving me a lot of grief over that.'

'Please tell her not to. It's fine. And my very best wishes to you both.'

'You're a gem.'

Things were looking up.

But if I was serious about relaunching Thornhill as a thriving commercial enterprise – running a residential cookery school and offering major film productions the use of the house and the estate – I'd need a new Rosemary.

But how do you replace someone irreplaceable?

I emailed a few agencies. They all wanted ridiculous salaries for live-ins. I posted online adverts with *totaljobs* and *indeed* and *jobtoday*. And after three weeks got not one single sniff.

I decided I was being too high-tech. So I placed an old-school ad in the employment section of *The Sentinel* and sat back and waited for the barrage of applications.

I got two.

Gareth was a thick-set man in his early sixties who'd been a pub chef all his life and had learned his trade with Berni Inns in the eighties, churning out its classic fayre of prawn cocktail starter, steak and chips main, and black forest gateau dessert for a staggering three hundred and fifty covers a day.

He was a nice enough guy, and I had no doubt he'd be able to knock up a creditable full English for a cookery school clientele *and* a film crew all at the same time. But I couldn't see him charging round the place changing beds, managing laundry, and being at the beck and call of demanding well-heeled guests, all tasks that Rosemary had taken in her stride.

Annabelle was the exact opposite of Greasy-Spoon Gareth. She looked about nineteen (in point of fact, she was twenty-seven) and dressed like she'd seen a picture in her mum's Sloane Ranger handbook from somewhere around 1984 and had copied the look – white cotton blouse (collar up, natch), knee-length tweed skirt, lilac cashmere tied round the shoulders, all topped off with (and this was England in early May) Jackie-O sunspecs perched on top of her head.

For two years she'd worked as a housekeeper on a super-yacht berthed in Portofino, where some Italian film director I'd never heard of had regularly entertained the world's beautiful people.

Even if she hadn't carried herself like she thought Thornhill was one step down from Fawlty Towers, there were unsettling gaps in her 'career' – and an unexplained termination of employment in Portofino – that made me deeply disinclined to give her the job. I didn't want some millennial Tara Palmer-Tomkinson using Thornhill to pad out her CV.

So back to the drawing-board.

In the meantime, progress was made on two fronts.

Barry from Lexington Locations had emailed with news that the director of a major Second World War blockbuster for Columbia Pictures was very interested in Thornhill and could a team come out in early May?

Yes, they could.

And I'd engaged one of the companies of builders from the business cards given to me by surveyor Peter Potter, and Gerry Starkey and his men were now making very good progress in the Shooting Lodge and had made short work of the roof repairs on the big house that Malcolm Clapp had spent the last several months finding excuses not to do.

Things were looking up.

Then Delyth appeared.

'There's a man with a big van says he's got a delivery for Winstanley.'

When I got to the door, Edmund was already there, directing operations, with an attendant Nutella trying to keep a lid on his impatience.

The van's hydraulic ramp was lowering a huge wooden crate onto the gravel. Robbie appeared carrying a crowbar, much to Edmund's delight.

'Ah. Good man. Let's get this thing cracked open.'

I was wondering whether Edmund had ordered a hippopotamus or a rhino as the driver proferred his little handheld gizmo for me to scribble my signature on and Robbie ripped the front panel off the crate and stood back to let Edmund peer inside.

'What a beauty!'

Nutella put her hand on his shoulder and he patted it with his bony fingers.

The driver and his mate wheeled out the biggest, fanciest-looking mobility scooter I'd ever seen.

I was wondering how much this leviathan had cost, and who'd be paying for it, when Edmund turned to look at me with the eyes of a schoolboy on Christmas morning.

'British racing green!'

'Yes. It's lovely.'

'She'll give me back my freedom. Well …' He patted his stick-like legs. '… to an extent.'

I felt like a complete witch for thinking about money. Nutella had read the earlier look of panic on my face and she walked over to speak to me privately while Edmund continued to eye up his new machine.

'There's a grant scheme. I looked into it. It's all arranged. The government has paid half. The other half is split between a mobility charity and us. Edmund is eligible for support because most of his pension is used to pay for me. And I've arranged a zero-interest credit package. Twenty-four monthly payments of sixty pounds. And if ... something happens, it's returned with nothing more to pay. Is that alright?'

How could it *not* be. 'Of course. It looks so nice. I was worried ...'

'I know. But he understands how hard things are.'

'They won't always be like this. Even so, this is a small price to pay for Edmund being able to move around on his own.'

'He'll be grateful you see it like that.'

Unfortunately, Edmund moving around on his own came at something of a price for the rest of us.

Doubtless harking back to the glory days he spent behind the wheel of his treasured Bentley, he bombed around the house like Stirling Moss on speed, scuffing doors, chipping paintwork on skirting boards, and sending Woodbine into a wiry-haired frenzy.

I tried to turn a blind eye, reminding myself his life at Windrush House had been sterile at best, the highlight of the average week being the Friday afternoon bingo session with confederates who, in most cases, would have struggled to remember their own names. And I'd had personal experience of the sadness of that situation with Mum.

But after one particularly close shave in the kitchen which almost had me decorating his blazer with a pot of steaming minestrone, I had to draw a line in the sand.

'It's not suitable for use inside the house. You're going to do yourself an injury.'

'I know. The throttle is very responsive. I'm finding her hard to control.'

'So we're agreed? Wheelchair in the house. Scooter in the grounds.'

'We're agreed. I'm going to take her for a spin to the main gate. Open her up.'

Ten minutes later, I spied him through the hall window, speeding away up the drive in his roadster, wisps of white hair trailing in the wind, a breathless Nutella sprinting along in his wake.

And, coming up the drive the other way, a four-by-four pulling a horsebox. This particular delivery had completely slipped my mind. I'd need Robbie for this.

A handsome, sandy-haired man stepped out of the car. 'Delivery of llamas for you.'

'Yes.'

'That's not something I say every day.'

'I imagine not. How did you get roped into this?'

'I've got the farm next to Helen and Paul. I've got a horsebox. And I owe them a favour or two.' He held out his hand. 'Dom. We met at the wedding.'

I had no recollection. 'Yes. Hi. Jennifer.'

'Yes. I remember.' He gave me a twinkly smile.

Why is it that when you're desperate, even old duffers with zimmers don't look twice. And when you're settled in a loving, passionate relationship, hunks of all shapes and sizes are falling all over you with their blue eyes and their forearms?

'Strange kind of wedding.'

'I expected nothing less from Helen and Paul.'

He laughed. 'I know what you mean.' He glanced at my left hand. 'Not your kind of ceremony?'

I read him like an open book. 'Not really. And I'm not sure it would suit my fiancé, either.'

'Right.'

Robbie appeared. 'I was thinking the small field by the drive, separate from the sheep.'

'Whatever you think best is fine with me, Robbie.'

I was amused to see the cogs turning in Dom's brain as his eyes went from me to Robbie and back again.

Robbie gestured to the car. 'Shall I show you the way?'

'Yes. Thanks.' Dom stretched his hand out to me a second time. 'Nice to see you again, Jennifer. I hope you don't blame a guy for trying.'

16

Scouting

My two ships of the Andes settled in very well. Robbie had done his homework on how to care for them – plenty of hay, a 'mineral block' to supplement their diet, fresh water – and they seemed to take to him and he to them. I occasionally went into the field with him but I was a bit nervy around them, which they seemed to pick up on, and they made their curious throaty hum whenever I was in the vicinity.

One thing stands out about llamas – they're bloody big. The male, Horatio, was a good foot taller than me and looked like the kind of creature who wouldn't hesitate to trample you to death if you looked at him the wrong way. The female, Lady Hamilton – see what they did there? – was lighter in colour, a little smaller, and a lot less spiky, but an intimidating presence nonetheless.

Every delivery driver that came onto the estate told me how Horatio sprinted along beside them as they motored up the drive to the house, and how uneasy this made them feel. Even with a fence between you and the animal, having a couple of hundred kilos of adult male llama tanking along beside you, screaming and bellowing and spitting at your windscreen, was enough to put Darth Vader off his mid-morning garibaldi.

***

Gerry and his Pacemakers were going great guns on the Shooting Lodge and Miranda came up from London for the weekend to look at how the place was shaping up, take a few measurements, and show me some equipment on the website she'd been living on since we'd first hatched our cookery school plan back in February.

We talked and planned and ordered, and we drank so much gin I tried to persuade her to take on Rosemary's job, then apologised the following morning over coffee and paracetamol. She was sweetness itself.

'I've got a simple brain. I can only do one thing at a time. And if we're going to do this cookery school thing – and I think we'll make a bloody good go of it between us – I'd better focus on that alone.'

'I agree. Ignore me. I'm bonkers on gin.' And I showed her all the marketing I'd done – a draft website knocked up using a set of glossy, idiot-proof templates I'd found online, a Facebook page, a Twitter account, an Instagram page – all peopled with (if I say so myself) quite stylish shots of the estate I'd taken with my Canon, in morning mist, in crisp afternoon sunshine, in the magic hour just before dusk, plus some library shots of classic dishes and cool items of kitchenware. And I'd written some flowing prose about luxury and style and accomplishment. Miranda was impressed.

'My god. That's wonderful. This absolutely cannot fail.'

I was buzzing when I waved her goodbye on the Monday morning.

Then the postman brought me down to earth with a bump – a letter from Her Majesty's Land Registry informing me that Malcolm Clapp had registered a claim for ownership of Woodman's Cottage. I had sixty-five days in which to lodge an objection.

I was so angry my legs started to shake. If Rosemary had still been around, she'd have opened the sherry, or perhaps the brandy, to calm me down.

As it was, I decided to settle for a cup of Earl Grey. After about ten minutes, my legs had stopped shaking and I got on the phone to Patrick Maybole's office and was delighted when his secretary was able to tell me he was now back at work. She put me through.

'Don't worry about it. He must have lied on the submission – you have to have occupied the property in question for ten years continuously.'

'How can I prove he hasn't?'

'When he was hired to do the roofing work, wasn't there anything in writing?'

'No.' This had been the fact I'd taunted him with. Now it looked like this very fact would be working in his favour. *Bollocks!*

'Well, it's going to be a little harder to refute. But we'll compile a dossier of testimonies, from people who were there at the time he spoke to Camilla, which will carry some weight.'

'And what if he compiles a dossier of his own?'

'Do you think that's likely?'

'I don't know.'

I was feeling David's absence like a rock in my stomach – we hadn't seen each other for two and half months – and I could really have done with his arms round me after that talk with Patrick Maybole. I texted him and right away he FaceTimed me.

'It'll be fine. Relax. When you're dealing with – pardon my French – complete arseholes, there's always a way. To get your own way.'

'I can't think of one.'

'You've got sixty-five days. It'll come to you.'

***

I don't know what I expected a film director to look like – maybe cravat, dark glasses, cigar – but Dave Hankin looked more like the warehouse manager from the Winchcombe branch of B&Q than he did a Hollywood mogul.

Barry filled me in while Dave, his Art Director Trudy, and his Location Manager Aidan nosed around in the sitting room and the library.

'He's worked with everyone. Kate Winslet, Brad Pitt, Anthony Hopkins – he's only on the screen for twenty-four minutes in *The Silence of the Lambs*, did you know that?'

I didn't.

'And everyone loves working with Dave because he does his homework, runs a very tight set, never raises his voice. And his films make a lot of money, so producers love him. And he gets substantial budgets to work with. And this one's very substantial.'

I tried not to pop champagne corks in my head. 'Sounds like it'll be fine. If it goes ahead. When will we know?'

'Scheduled to go into production in August. It's a three-week location shoot, at the head of the schedule, interiors and exteriors. They'll switch between both as the weather dictates. They were very keen before the visit. I'm sure nothing they've seen will have changed their mind.'

I was pouring Barry more tea when Dave, Trudy and Aidan came back into the kitchen. Trudy was beaming.

'We'd like to go ahead, if you're sure you're still game.'

'I'm sure.'

Aidan piped up. 'As Barry's said, it's going to be a pretty invasive experience for you. We just want you to be sure you know what you're letting yourself in for.'

'I understand.'

Trudy beamed again. 'Great. It really is the ideal location for what we have in mind.'

Dave laid a document on the table. 'We'd like you to have a lawyer look this over before you sign. We don't want you to feel you've been railroaded into anything.'

I glanced at the day rate they were offering, which was slightly higher than the top figure quoted on the Lexington website.

For that money, you can railroad me as much as you like. I'll even tie myself to the tracks.

I assembled the household – Robbie, Delyth, Edmund and Nutella – and gave them the good news, minus the specific figures. It would be an intrusion, but one so financially advantageous it would cover the full Shooting Lodge refurb, the Coachman's Cottage revamp, *and* the roof repairs. *And* still leave a good amount over with which to develop other plans for the estate.

As an ensemble, we decided a celebration of sorts was in order, off site, with someone else doing the cooking and the clearing-up.

Delyth suggested The Queens near Chipping Norton, a doable journey from Thornhill in a wheelchair taxi. It was under new management, she said, and the place offered 'top-notch posh grub but it's not stuffy – you can still get a pint and a bag of pork scratchings at the bar.'

Edmund, Nutella and Delyth settled themselves at our table while Robbie and I went to the bar to pick up pre-meal drinks.

I was used to people taking me and Robbie for a couple, and this would be useful if some manspreading macho barman felt like dusting off his cheesy chatup lines and digging in for the evening.

But Cameron was a quite different type of inquisitor.

He and his partner James ('the creative cheffy one, sweating in the kitchen while I prance around, front of house') were city boys, from Chingford, and had long harboured the dream of running a country pub. When The Queen's Head had come on the market, the name alone had sold it to them both. And when you threw in the gorgeous location and the proximity to an encampment of men in uniform (at nearby RAF Brize Norton), it had been a no-brainer. A minor name change and here they were.

'And what about you, lady with the cleavage to die for?'

'I'm Jennifer. I'm the new owner of Thornhill.'

What followed was one of those moments you see in films, where all heads turn, time stops, and the darts hang in mid-air.

At the far end of the bar, two old blokes in their seventies who looked like they'd been enjoying the convivial atmosphere since opening time, stood up and sidled over.

The less sozzled one held out his hand. 'Arthur Frickleton. Pleased to meet you, Jennifer. We were very sorry to hear about the old lady of the manor. And we miss having Rosemary and Veronica here at the odd quiz night, don't we, Tom?'

Tom nodded with less co-ordination than he imagined, while Arthur kept the conversation bubbling.

'They were bloody good eggs.' It was the exact phrase Rosemary had used about Camilla at her funeral, and it made me picture them again and realise how much I missed them both. 'And you look like a bloody good egg, as well. It's very good to see you in here. We hope we'll always have a connection to the big house.'

'Thank you.' Cameron delivered our drinks and I asked him to put another one in for Arthur and Tom, at which Arthur insisted on shaking my hand again.

'You're a real lady. And that bastard Clapp – pardon me – had no right to go abusin' the old lady's trust like he did. He's never done an honest day's work in his life, the shameless bugger – pardon me. Done plenty of dishonest days, of course.'

My ears pricked up. 'What do you mean?'

'Been on the sick for years. Claimin' all sorts. Gettin' away with bloody murder – pardon me. Unfit for work? Hah! He's fit enough to shinny up and down a ladder fixin' roofs all over the bleedin' county – pardon me. Been workin' over at the chapel at Shelton for three weeks solid. Someone ought to shop the bugger – pardon me. That's what I think.'

Yes. Maybe someone ought.

17

Clapp Trap

I slept on this thought and, in the morning, felt deeply uneasy about the whole thing. Over an early morning coffee, I called David.

He'd been at the office until midnight and was just climbing into bed. Behind his voice, I could hear the traffic on Riverside Drive, below his apartment window, and, in the distance, the boats on the Hudson. The city that never sleeps was still buzzing at past one in the morning. It made me realise how very far away he was.

'I've never been a snitch. And that's exactly what I'd be.'

'You're looking at it the wrong way. If he were a friend, or even a pleasant acquaintance, and you shopped him, then you'd be a snitch. But he isn't.'

'No.'

'He's an unprincipled, lying, bullying sleazebag.'

'Yes.'

'And, as such, he deserves everything he gets. Everything you're going to give him.'

'Okay.'

'Good.'

I was still pondering it all when I handed my keys to the Romanian guy who'd always done a great job of keeping the little Picanto gleaming inside and out and who I was now expecting to remove the caked-on mud and the dog hairs from my new Defender.

He could see my mind was elsewhere. 'Why are you staring like a cat at a calendar?'

'Sorry?'

'It's phrase from Romanian. It means you look ... confused.'

I wasn't about to discuss my predicament with a stranger. 'Oh, it's nothing.'

He looked at the Defender. 'New car. New job? New life?'

'Sort of, yes. A lot of challenges. I needed a tougher car for a harder life.'

'Life can be hard sometimes.'

'Yes, indeed.'

Something about his demeanour gave me the impression he was speaking from personal experience. But I wasn't sure I was in the mood for a full-on confessional, so I changed tack.

'You do a great job, by the way.'

'I'm not afraid of hard work.'

'No. I can see that.'

'In Romania, I worked very hard. In big hotels. Many hours working in a kitchen, cooking, washing dishes. Also cleaning floors, making rooms nice. And here, picking fruit. Then working in biscuit fucktory.' He pumped the spray that fired out some sort of degreasing pre-wash stuff.

'In a what?'

'Fucktory. Making biscuits. Big ovens.'

'A *factory*. Right.'

He sprayed the liquid over the Defender's bonnet and flanks. 'But zero hours. Then paid off. And now washing cars. It's okay. It's work. I'm Marius, by the way.' He looked at his wet, soapy hand and smiled. 'I won't shake.'

'I'm Jennifer.' I was about to take a gamble. Possibly a big one. 'And do you want to keep on doing this? Washing cars?'

He stopped spraying and looked me in the eye. 'Why? You have better work for me, Jennifer?'

***

I parked the now-sparkling Defender over the road from the Chapel of Our Lady of the Angels in Shelton, about thirty yards from where Malcolm Clapp had stationed his flat-bed truck.

I fixed the 300 mm telephoto lens onto my Canon, pulled my hoodie a little further over my head, took a sip of my takeaway coffee, and waited, feeling like a cross between Sam Spade and Nancy Drew.

Two hours later and I'd seen neither hide nor hair of Malcolm Clapp, who was presumably working somewhere round the back of the chapel. All I'd bagged were some nice close-ups of a goldfinch in a rowan tree and a shot of a young woman in what looked like an old wedding dress and a full-face Margaret Thatcher mask.

Was she walking round like that in broad daylight for a dare? Or was she on her way home from some weird all-night eighties-themed rave?

Feeling like I should have packed some sandwiches for what was turning into a major stakeout, I spotted a bunch of schoolboys in blue blazers tucking into something steaming hot and covered in pastry. I decided to investigate.

I was on my way back to the car with my haul from the Tesco Express round the corner – a steak and mushroom pasty from their hot-food-to-go shelves and a couple of bottles of Vacqueyras for under a tenner each (having, the week before, balked at the sixteen quid they were asking in the Waitrose in Witney) – when I looked across at the chapel and clapped eyes on Clapp, leaning into the cab of his truck. The shock made me drop the bag with the bottles. The sound of the smash filled the little street.

Malcolm Clapp pulled his torso out of the cab and turned to look along the street at where the noise had come from.

Shit! Please God don't let him recognise me!

He stared for three long seconds. Then he smiled his leery, oily smile and shouted along to me. 'That's what you get for drinking in the daytime, love.' And he giggled and walked back towards the chapel and the long ladder now resting against the scaffolding on the chapel's front wall.

I dropped the now-purple bag of broken glass into a bin, made my way back to the Defender, and settled myself into the seat.

And this is what you get for thinking you can frighten me.

I steadied the Canon on my knee and levelled the zoom lens at his fat arse as it ascended the ladder. When he reached the platform at the top, he turned, a half-dozen roof tiles on his shoulder, and presented me with the perfect profile shot.

Bingo.

During the thirty minutes that followed, I assembled a very substantial portfolio of incriminating photographic evidence, all date- and time-coded, ready to present to whomever it concerned.

I reported my day to David.

'Well done. Who are you going to send them to?'

'I'm not going to *send* them at all. I've done a lot of homework. And I've decided this needs the personal touch.'

If anything, the yard was even more cluttered and filthy in June than it had been on my last visit in January. And Clapp's hellhounds, still lashed to the cast-iron clothes poles, seemed even more vicious and unhinged. Envelope in hand, I marched past them to the front door and knocked with the energy of a bailiff.

After a couple of seconds of scuffling behind the door, Malcolm Clapp yanked it open and glared at me. He was, once again, leaning on his faithful friend, the walking stick.

'What the fuck do *you* want?'

'Hello, Mr Clapp. Your usual charming self today, I see.'

'Look, I haven't got all day, sweetheart.'

'Oh, you have, Mr Clapp. In fact, that's *all* you've got. One day.'

'What are you on about?'

'To remove yourself, your brood, your hellhounds and all your crap off my property.'

Malcolm Clapp smiled. An immovable object. 'Or what?'

I, on the other hand, was an unstoppable force. 'Do you know what the penalties are for benefit fraud?'

'You what?' He was smiling. But he was rattled. He glanced at the envelope in my hand.

'Fraud. The penalties. They are many. And they are serious. Very serious.'

'Piss off.'

'How many years have you been claiming income support? Perhaps disability living allowance. Maybe attendance allowance. My sources tell me it's at least five. Five years of, what is it, around four hundred pounds a week?'

Malcolm Clapp smiled.

'Oh, it's a little more than that? Aren't you clever! So you've defrauded the authorities out of, say, one hundred thousand pounds. At a conservative estimate.'

'Your *sources*? Who *are* you? Fucking Perry Mason?'

I held up the envelope. 'I, Mr Clapp, am the person who is in possession of evidence that will ensure you are the subject of criminal prosecution for fraud. When I present this evidence, you will be charged with multiple counts of fraud, resulting in a custodial sentence of at least five years and the forced recovery of all monies fraudulently claimed. Plus a five-thousand-pound administrative fee. So, a hundred and five thousand pounds. At a conservative estimate. Do you have that kind of money lying around, Mr Clapp?'

His face had turned the colour of candle wax. 'You're bluffing.'

'Oh dear. You really think I am, don't you?' I handed him the envelope. He pulled out the half dozen eight-by-ten prints I'd selected to show him to his worst advantage. I noticed there was sweat on his upper lip.

'I have another twenty-five prints in a similar style, all bundled up with copies of these, all ready to go to the National Benefit Fraud Mail Handling site in Wolverhampton. With copies for the Department for Work and Pensions and the Personal Fraud Unit at Thames Valley Police. Oh, and the Oxford Mail, The Sun, the Daily Express and the Daily Mirror. The tabloids love a good human interest story. And the woman at the Daily Mirror was *very* interested when I gave her the broad details of this story. No names, of course. Yet.'

'What do you want?'

'Twenty-four hours. The Land Registry claim dropped. And you lot, and this lot, all gone. If you're not, and it's not …' I pointed to the photos. '… I pull the trigger on this. All of it.'

I leaned in.

'I am deadly serious, Mr Clapp. My advice to you is simple – do not fuck with me.'

18

A Diamond Geezer

Marius had only been at Thornhill for three weeks but I was confident my gamble had paid off.

He never stopped.

He rose at 5 am, went for a run to the main gate and back ('Only three kilometres – I need to find something longer.'), then prepared half a dozen delicious dishes for lunch and dinner. And baked bread. All before he made breakfast. Which was always interesting and delicious. And while the lunch and dinner were bubbling away, he helped Delyth with the housework. He insisted on cleaning all the empty guest ensuites, twice a week.

'But they're not being used.'

'If we keep them sparkling, they'll always be ready. I know bathrooms. The dirtiness creeps up while you're not looking. But we're smarter than it.'

Delyth was impressed. 'He's like lightning. He'll be brilliant when we've got guests. And that soup he makes with the bits of fried pork in – I know it sounds like I'm betraying her, but it makes Rosemary's Scotch broth taste like the water in my bucket.'

So, all in all, a very welcome addition to the household.

Coachman's Lodge – Rosemary's old place – was now fully revamped and listed with letting agents in Stow who'd suggested a monthly rental of £2500, insisting that a fully furnished two-bedroom property of its size and 'pedigree' could easily command that.

But that sounded excessive to me, so I'd insisted on a cap of £2000. Even that seemed a very generous income. At that figure, the agents had told me, it would be snapped up.

Gerry and his Pacemakers had finished work on the Shooting Lodge a whole two weeks ahead of schedule (when does *that* ever happen with builders?) and Miranda had found tenants for her house in Wood Green who were keen to move in as soon as possible.

And, with the Clapps gone (cue a little jig from me), work had already begun on tarting up Woodman's Cottage and making that place also fit to rent out.

Things were looking up indeed.

Then Harry Sinclair phoned me to say the singer he'd had lined up to appear at Anthea's chuffing summer gala (*Do NOT get roped into this again, you stupid cow!*) had come back from Las Vegas with Legionnaires' Disease. She'd done a three-month run as support for Shania Twain and had picked the disease up in the hot tub of a hotel that was currently under investigation by the Southern Nevada Health District.

She was now on oxygen at St George's hospital in Tooting. Which was awful. But which also left me singerless. With two weeks to go.

'Don't worry. I'll find you someone. This is a blue-rinse brigade, you said.'

'Yes. Very twin set and pearls.'

A two-second silence from Harry. Then, 'Do you feel like shaking them up a bit?'

'Sounds like fun. What do you have in mind?'

***

The day of the gala dawned dry and bright. July at its best. A good omen.

The marquee guys arrived early and a battalion of men began erecting the vast white canopy on the lawn on the south side of the house, swiftly followed by Anthea's regiment of volunteers, unloading and setting up dozens of tables and chairs and a very fancy mobile bar.

It was all running like a Swiss watch and I allowed myself to feel relaxed enough to take Luther and Woodbine for a long walk to the lake and back.

I was still basking in a very pleasant daydream (marquee on the sunny lawn, bushels of flowers, string quartet, David and me walking hand in hand to cheers and applause and tears from the wedding guests) when, back in the melée, I was collared by a burly man with a truck and a T-shirt that read *I've Seen The Truth And It Makes No Sense.*

'Excuse me, love. Where d'you want me to drop these chemical toilets?'

The day's events – kids' games like space-hopper racing, welly wanging, and a wet sponge wipeout – all went swimmingly and raised a good few hundred quid. And the charity auction managed, even under Anthea's humourless chairwomanship, to raise close to a thousand pounds, most of it the result of a bidding war between two middle-aged men desperate to get their hands on the prize of delivering a line in the forthcoming Dave Hankin blockbuster, as 'Medical Orderly #3', another coup that boosted my capital with Anthea.

But I knew something she didn't know. And that something would, I was fairly sure, torpedo my standing with Anthea and her salon cronies. I'd be out on my ear. And therefore free of all this nonsense in the years to come.

I'd slipped into my favourite navy dress (which I'd last worn to the very glitzy charity do Harry had invited me to eighteen months earlier) and was just pinning on the exquisite silver brooch George had given me one Christmas when, from my bedroom window, I spotted a familiar orange Austin Allegro trundling up the drive.

My batty old Auntie Brenda hugged me with the force of a champion sumo wrestler while Uncle Bob, my dad's brother, struggled under the bulk of the 18-pack of Andrex Shea Butter three-ply toilet tissue he was carrying.

Normal visitors bring flowers or wine or chocolates. Bob and Brenda bring bulk bathroom supplies.

Brenda scanned the crowd. 'Is this what you do *every* Saturday?'

'No. It's a charity gala. And I offered to host it here.' *Where you've turned up completely unannounced and at absolutely* not *a convenient time.*

'Ooh. A gala. Is that like a church fayre? With stalls?'

Bob and Brenda were the ultimate baby-boomer bargain hunters. Charity shops and car boots and bring-and-buy stalls were to them what crack is to an addict. If you could buy it for a song, it was worth buying. Even if you didn't need it. And if you could buy it in bulk, so much the better.

I asked Robbie to deal with the Andrex, took a deep breath, put a rein on my frustration, and ushered my aunt and uncle over to the bar.

Bob and Brenda had been my saviours when I'd got the job at Artisan Wines in Shoreditch. They'd given me a room in their Bexleyheath semi for a whole month before my boss, Cécile, had shipped me out to Bordeaux to learn the wine trade. So the very least I could do was supply a few drinks and a bed for the night.

Bob soon found his niche – helping the car park stewards direct operations – and I left Brenda at the bar with Delyth, the pair of them sipping strawberry daiquiris, while I went backstage to meet the entertainment.

Lenny Diamond, whippet thin and with close-cropped grey hair, was fixing two giant spidery lashes to his eyelids. I took the perfectly manicured hand he held out to me.

'It's so good of you to step in at the last minute.'

'It's no problem. Harry's been a very supportive friend. So I'm very glad to help out. Are they up for this, d'you think?'

'I think they won't know what's hit them.'

Lenny chuckled and smoothed out a couple of wrinkles in his figure-hugging gold lamé dress. 'It does people good to get a bit of a boot up the jacksie once in a while.' He reached for a giant bouffant wig that Marie Antoinette might have thought a bit much and slotted it expertly into place.

He stood up and struck a pose. 'Voilà!'

I laughed out loud. 'Perfect!'

When I went back to front of house, Anthea was at the mic, holding forth, reporting on the day's successes, and doing her awkward, strait-laced, china-cup-with-the-little-finger-out best to warm the audience up for the entertainment to come. I was glad I hadn't missed it.

The spectacle of Anthea Orchard-Lyons having to announce our star turn.

'Ladies and gentlemen. Please give a warm welcome to …' The old girl lifted her eyes momentarily heavenward, as if praying for a sniper to pick her off before time and fate forced her to utter the words. '… Marilyn Minge!'

The five seconds that followed were a curious blend of polite applause (from the folks who didn't know what the hell was going on), raucous guffaws (from the village lads who'd turned up early to take full advantage of the cheap bar), and apoplectic silence (from every one of Anthea's division of demoiselles).

Lenny Diamond had played enough tough gigs in East End pubs and northern working men's clubs to know how to massage a reluctant audience.

He stalked the stage like a cheetah looking for stragglers in the herd.

'Well … quite a posh do this, isn't it? Big tent on the lawn, plenty of Pimm's behind the bar, Waitrose on speed dial if the buffet runs out of foie gras.'

A few titters from the generality. A smile from Anthea's nice friend, Deirdra. Lenny picked her up on his radar. 'You look like a Waitrose client, madam. Smart dress, slick jewellery, no knickers.' Deidra laughed. Anthea rolled her eyes. 'I bet you're a dab hand at the online shopping. Sorting your inbox. Getting your basket just right. Clicking Submit. I bet you like to submit.'

Guffaws. The audience was warming to Lenny's sauce. Deirdra threw her head back.

'Then the anticipation. Delivery. Where are you going to put that big order? Will it be a tight squeeze in your cupboard?'

The audience was lapping it up. Deirdra had the tissues out now. A few of the other salon dowagers had cracked a smile. And even Anthea, sensing she was in danger of standing out as an arch prude, was beginning to loosen up. Lenny didn't miss a beat.

'I've found, in my HUGE experience of these things, that it's all about the angle of entry. The Greeks knew all about that. Pythagoras, Euclid, Peter Andre. He could measure my hypotenuse any day of the week. The Greek god.'

Gales of laughter.

Then, with the crowd well and truly on his side, Lenny clicked a button on a tiny remote hidden in his palm and the sound system sent the haunting intro to a very famous song out into the brilliant summer evening.

'That's enough of my smut. Time for a bit of class. And they don't come any classier than Dame Shirley Bassey.'

Honestly – if you'd closed your eyes, you'd have believed every word of Lenny's rendition of *Diamonds Are Forever* was belted out by Dame Shirley herself. His voice was astonishing. Powerful, full of emotion, note perfect.

For the next two hours, he blasted through Bassey, Streisand, Cher, Adele, Aretha, Whitney – all with the authenticity of the original artists. It was an absolute *tour de force* that, by the end of the night, had the audience on their feet screaming for more.

I hugged him backstage. 'You were WONDERFUL! Why have I never seen you on TV? You should be on every night. And filling arenas. Five thousand seats.'

He waved away the compliment. 'You're very kind. But nobody wants to see an old queen prancing about on the telly or at the O2. They want youth and beauty. BTS. Little Mix. Justin Bieber. I'm a variety act. And mainstream variety's dead. It died when *The Two Ronnies* were axed in 1987. I did them in 1984. Three minutes.'

He winked. 'Not many old queens can say they did The Two Ronnies.'

19

Wine And The Confessional

It was gone one o'clock when the last van pulled off the Thornhill estate, Bob giving the driver a bit of the unwanted and unneeded 'Right hand down, my friend' instruction that seems to come with the territory when you're a man in his seventies.

When he finally joined us in the kitchen, Brenda and I were on the cheese on toast and the Vacqueyras I'd bought at the full Waitrose price after my Tesco bargain had bitten the dust outside the chapel in Shelton.

An evening spent matching Delyth daiquiri for daiquiri had made Brenda a bit sleepy, but she was getting her second wind on this beefy red from the southern Rhone. And Marius's rye bread was proving a big hit, its complexities of flavour our talking point.

'Is it caraway? They often put that in rye, I think.' She savoured the bread the way Egon Ronay might have. 'Have a bit of this, Bob. And try this wine. It's bloody delicious.'

It was the first time I'd ever heard her swear.

'Wine tastes all the same to me.' Bob was a chestnut mild sort of bloke. Wine was for women. And men who wear dresses. But Brenda wasn't backing down.

'Just try it, you miserable old sod. We're at a party!'

He muttered under his breath. 'If it means you'll drink a bit less I'll give it a go.' He glanced at me, raised his eyebrows in comedy exasperation, and took a big belt. Then he raised his eyebrows again. 'Ooh. Tastes a bit like a glass of port I had once. Can I …?' and he reached for a fresh glass and I poured in a good house measure.

He swilled and savoured. 'That's bloody good.' Another sweary first.

'I know. I *am* a wine expert, after all.'

Brenda radiated pride. 'You are. We keep forgetting that. You've done so well, dear. And this place! I can't believe it!'

'I couldn't believe it either, when it happened, when they told me. Still can't, really. It's been a lot of work, with more work to come, but I'm getting a really good team around me again, and we've got some good ideas for making the place profitable.'

'You're a proper businesswoman.'

'I'm trying to be.'

And then Brenda teared up. 'Your mum would have been so proud.'

I felt a lump rise in my throat. 'I hope so.'

'She was always very proud of you. Of the lovely person you've always been. She always said that. She once said to me, "I couldn't have asked for a better child than Jennifer."'

My eyes filled with tears and I thought about the last few years of Mum's life and how absent I'd been, how I'd left it all – pretty much – to her carer, Leon. I'd played my part during the final months of her life. But it hadn't been enough.

'I could have been a lot better.'

Brenda laid her hand on mine. 'We all think that, dear. Life gets in the way sometimes. We're not perfect. None of us are. But you've come pretty close to it.' Brenda had tears in her eyes, too. And even Bob was looking a bit misty.

They say that, in wine, there is truth. The Romans nailed that fact a couple of thousand years ago. *In vino veritas.* What Brenda had said was very kind. I could only hope it was true.

And while we were all in the mood to open up, perhaps it was time. To broach a subject that had been gnawing away at my brain since a discovery I'd made when clearing my mum's house, and a subsequent conversation I'd had with Mum's lifelong neighbour, Mrs Jennings.

I'd come across a photograph of my dad in his army uniform, taken during his time in Northern Ireland during the Troubles. There was a young boy sitting on his knee. At the time, I'd assumed the boy was some second cousin – Dad had dozens of cousins – but I remembered how uncharacteristically snappish Mum had been when I'd asked her about it once, years before.

When I'd showed the photo to Mrs Jennings, she'd talked about the rocky state of Mum and Dad's relationship in the early years – and how they'd separated for a time – and she started to talk about the little boy, clearly assuming I knew all about him, then backpedalled furiously when she realised I didn't have a clue.

That he was my half brother.

I turned to Bob. 'My mum was such a gentle person. I hardly ever saw her angry, or even irritated. Apart from one time. When I showed her a photograph. Of my dad with a little boy on his knee.'

Bob and Brenda exchanged a glance. Bob looked at the floor. Brenda smiled awkwardly. 'It was a very long time ago.'

'I know. A good few years before I was born.'

'And they were very young. And your dad … well, that time in Northern Ireland was horrible. For both of them.'

'I understand that. I really do.'

Brenda looked across at Bob for help. But Dad's brother was not at all comfortable digging up this old ground. But I wanted answers. He could see that.

'The troubles in Northern Ireland took Ronnie away for months at a time. Too long. Traumatic times. I can't imagine what that was like. Patrolling those hostile streets. Petrol bombs. Nail bombs. Your dad was just a working-class boy. Scared stiff ninety-five per cent of the time. The other five per cent … well, he was a lad. Just wanted a good time. To help forget it all.'

Bob looked up at me.

'And I can't blame him for that. I won't.'

'I'm not blaming anyone. But nobody's ever talked to me about this.'

Bob nodded. 'Well, Ronnie was never home. And Iris never knew when she was going to get a knock on the door with bad news. It was a hellish time for both of them. Enough to put any marriage under strain.'

This was the most I'd ever heard Uncle Bob say in all my forty-three years.

'Then he got home for a week. And Iris was delighted. But Ronnie couldn't get rid of the black cloud that had been hanging over him ever since he'd set foot in Belfast. And he was angry with her for not understanding. And she was angry with *him* for not wanting to make the best of their brief time together. So … they sort of separated. I mean, they were separate most of the time, anyway. But, you know … they decided they were free agents.'

Brenda chipped in. 'Those were just words to your mum. She would never have … strayed. She wasn't like that.'

I smiled. It was very sweet of her, sticking up for my mum.

Bob ploughed on.

'Your dad wasn't like that, either. He was a good bloke. And a very good brother to me.' He was getting misty again. 'But he felt Iris didn't understand what he was going through. And he found someone who did. Because she was going through it, too. She was a Greenfinch. A member of the women's Ulster Defence Regiment. And they just … connected. And the little boy was the result. Born on New Year's Eve.'

A lightbulb moment for me. Mum had always hated the fuss around New Year. Now I knew why.

'Anyway, a couple of years later, his tour was over. And he and your mum patched things up. And they were rock solid after that. And then you came along. That helped. A lot. You were the cement they needed.'

I put my hand on his arm.

'But there was still this other child. There was no getting away from that. They both knew it. Although Iris pretended not to. And Ronnie was good. He kept in touch and sent money. Not much. They didn't have much anyway. Then she got married. Jacqueline. That was her name. Like Onassis.'

'And the boy. What was his name?'

Bob glanced at Brenda again. 'Andrew. His name's Andrew Barker. Your dad used to send him postcards. Then Jacqueline wrote to him and told him to stop. He was cut up about that.'

'I can imagine.'

I let out a deep sigh. We've got no idea, have we? About the challenges and sadnesses and tragedies that fill the lives of ordinary people. People who just get on with it and say nothing.

I put my arms round my Uncle Bob's shoulders as he wiped his eyes. 'Thank you. For being so honest. And for trusting me.'

He smiled. 'Shame on you for getting an old man drunk.' He kissed my hair and reached out and took Brenda's hand. The wine had given him a Cary Grant quality I'd never seen before.

'Come on, old girl. Time for bed.'

20

Feng Shooing

'Trust me. This is the best thing for a hangover.'

Marius dropped a couple of handfuls of spiky flowers into a pot of boiling water, while Bob, Brenda and I grimaced at each other, looking like extras in a zombie movie. It didn't help that this brew made the kitchen smell like last week's hiking socks.

'And food. You need to eat. Sweet things.'

Marius sliced off a few doorstops of sourdough bread, spread them thickly with honey, and slid the plate into the middle of the kitchen table. 'Eat.'

I picked one up, nibbled, and tried hard to keep my stomach below my throat.

Bob sniffed and nibbled. And nodded and took a bigger bite. Brenda eyed the bread with deep suspicion. 'I'm sorry. I can't eat honey. It gives me indigestion. Which I've already got anyway.'

Marius was straining his greeny-brown spiky-flower liquid into a teapot, into which he then dumped about six spoons of sugar. Tablespoons. He stirred the liquid round vigorously then poured out three mugfuls.

'Drink. Milk thistle tea. Sweet.'

It looked like something a squirrel might have done in your birdbath. None of us were keen.

'Seriously. Hold your nose if you have to. But drink. All. You'll feel brilliant in about half an hour.' He smiled. 'Merlin. The magician. You know him?'

We all nodded.

'He was from Romania.'

Brenda piped up. 'I thought he was English.'

Bob rolled his eyes. 'He was neither. He was a character in a story.'

Marius shook his head. 'Not true. It's a legend, yes. But based on real people. Real events.'

'So King Arthur is Romanian? That's what you're telling us?'

'The king was Welsh or maybe Scottish. But Merlin came from the part of Europe we now call Romania. My country.'

Bob looked like his face was trying to spell the word 'sceptical.'

But Brenda was happy to play the game. 'Imagine that. Did you know that, Jennifer?' I was sniffing the milk thistle tea and trying to pluck up the courage. 'No. I didn't.' Marius was stirring something in one of Rosemary's big jam pans. 'A lot of Western plant knowledge comes from Central Europe. And we got it from the Chinese.'

Bob sniffed his brew. 'Is that where this tea comes from? China?'

Marius smiled. 'Don't ask questions. Just drink.'

We three looked at each other. Bob picked up his mug. 'Come on, then.'

And we knocked it back.

Brenda's goodbye hug was softer. More meaningful. I felt I'd learned more about them – seen them as people, not just as my batty old relatives – than I'd ever known before. And I felt closer to them. And I knew they felt the same.

And now I knew his name.

Andrew Barker.

***

Trudy and Aidan – Dave Hankin's Art Director and Location Manager – were now on site, together with Production Designer, Justin.

The schedule allowed them just one week to prepare Thornhill – inside and out – for its first outing as a bona fide film location.

Their team – about twenty very young men and women, most of them in T-shirts and shorts and with walkie-talkies – moved with a focus and an energy that I found hugely impressive. They knew exactly what they were doing and they worked together to achieve it with maximum efficiency.

I can earn from this. And I can learn *from it.*

The sitting room and the library were repainted in a matter of hours. All the furniture and soft furnishings were removed and stored in steel containers jacked up on the lawns. Sets of steel gantries were erected ('For lights, mostly,' a twenty-something girl with fiery hair told me) and the production's furniture and furnishings carried in and set up, with Trudy directing operations, a tablet in one hand and a sheaf of notes in the other. Then dozens of period props – phones, a bath chair, a gramophone, cigar boxes, decanters and glasses – were hauled in and laid down for positioning later.

And the Orangery was stripped of its contents and refitted as a hospital ward.

Justin, forties, hipster beard, came over to me with a clipboard. 'Do you mind if we remove a couple of your windows? The whole lot can be reglazed after, if you want, with whatever glass you want. It's just that we need bullet holes.'

'You're going to shoot the windows?'

He smiled. 'No. We'll replace the panes with polycarbonate panels that have the bullet holes pre-made.'

'Right. No, I don't mind. Go ahead.'

Outside, the grounds were being licked into period shape. Which, for the most part, meant doing up what was already there.

Gravel paths were spruced up – with whole sections actually relaid – and their borders clipped, sections of the walled garden were replanted, the wisteria on the south wall was trimmed, the sundial was buffed to a high brass gloss.

And, much to Edmund's delight, a whole battalion of period vehicles were delivered on two transporters. Edmund wheeled over in his scooter and namechecked them all for me as they came off the trucks – two Ford Anglias, two Austin 8s, a couple of 'bullnose' Wolseley 10s, an Austin K2 army ambulance and, to his great delight, an Alvis Silver Crest.

'Only four point two litres, but that's a lot of power in what is essentially a two seater.' His eyes took on a faraway look. 'By God. I wish I still had the legs to drive that beauty. She's a belter. Must be for someone playing a senior officer.'

We'd now been given details of the cast.

Most were British names very familiar to us all from the top TV series that had gone round the world – *The Crown*, *Sherlock*, *Peaky Blinders*, *Line of Duty* – plus a few American names from the middle echelons of Hollywood. It was all very exciting.

But Dave Hankin's biggest coup was bagging the services, for a full two weeks, of a genuine Hollywood legend.

In the 1990s, there had been nobody bigger than Lola Montgomery. She was young, pretty, had an enviable cleavage, and was a powerful performer. As a young teenager, I saw her opposite Dennis Quaid (my major teenage crush) and kind of fell in love with her.

She was still getting sexy roles in the noughties, playing a hot forty-something waitress opposite Al Pacino, and later lighting up the screen as Harrison Ford's ballsy but sexy boss in a saucy romcom.

Fifteen years on, here she was in her sixties. And doing nothing. It seemed she was too old for sexy roles but too sexy to play grandmas. She was in Hollywood's No Woman's Land.

So she was looking for work.

And, market forces being what they are, she was willing to work for a fraction of her usual fee.

'Three to five,' said Aidan, when I told him how excited I was at the prospect of meeting her.

'Three to five thousand pounds per day?'

Aidan smiled. 'Between three and five million dollars per picture.'

I had to hold onto the wall. 'Five MILLION?'

'That's right. And, if the schedule is tight, that could be for one week's work.'

'You're kidding!'

'I'm not. Big stars, and their agents, understand their value at the box office. A major Hollywood picture can cost upwards of two hundred million to make. Sixty or seventy percent of that will be talent. In other words, the actors' fees. But if the picture makes four hundred million at the box office, it's money well spent. We all get paid and the financiers get a good return on their investment.'

'My god.'

'I know. Sounds crazy. But it's very big business.'

'So what is she getting on this film?'

'I have no idea. Honestly. Nothing close to that, I'd imagine. But still a very good wage to you and me.'

'Yes. I'm sure.'

'Have they told you about Baba G?'

'What's that? Her favourite skincare product?'

'It's a *who*, not a what. He's kind of her guru. He controls her diet, her fitness, her sleep patterns, the lot. And he's the guy we'll all have on our backs if her personal spaces are not sound. Spiritually.'

'What does that mean?'

'I don't really get it. It's bits of feng shui with some shamanistic stuff mixed in. So you get a sort of New Age philosophical soup.'

'Sounds interesting.'

He leaned in. 'It's bollocks, actually. But I didn't say that. And it keeps her happy.'

I guess, much like film directors, spiritual gurus come in all shapes and sizes. And some are very different from the stereotype we all carry around in our heads. In *my* head, a spiritual guru is an old man in a white robe with a long grey beard and hair to match.

Baba G was a skinny mid-thirties with an afro-style 70s perm and a horseshoe moustache. The purple crushed velvet trousers and mustard silk shirt completed the cheesy pornstar look.

For Lola Montgomery, I'd earmarked (of course) the biggest suite on the first floor, with the killer evening view of sunset over the lake. The bedroom-cum-sitting-room had a Sheraton couch, two Chesterfield armchairs, and several pieces of Georgian furniture in burr walnut. The spacious ensuite had a double walk-in shower, twin basins, enough storage for Gwyneth Paltrow's whole range.

Baba G (was his real name Gary, or perhaps Graham? I thought I detected a hint of Lancashire) wasn't impressed. 'It's very brown. What can we to do lighten it, spiritually?'

Well, we could heave you out of a window, for starters.

'I don't know. Brighter bed linen? More table lamps? Flowers?'

'Hm. That table's interrupting the flow.' He pointed to an antique table by one of the windows that I'd been considering selling to a dealer in Bourton who'd offered two and a half grand. 'Can it go?'

'Go?'

'Out of the room.'

'Sure.'

'And the bed.'

'You want the bed out?'

'Moved.'

'Okay. Where to?'

He walked round and round a tiny spot in the centre of the room. 'Here would be good.'

'In the middle of the room?'

'The Western tendency to have beds pushed up against a wall militates against a room's chi.'

I wondered how on earth this young guy had landed this fabulous (presumably immensely lucrative) gig of spiritual guru to a major star. Had he simply done a City and Guilds in Feng Shui and an HNC in Bullshitting at Scunthorpe Community College and put together some artsy website, written regular blogs with a million followers, and carried out a killer networking campaign on Twitter and LinkedIn?

It all looked, felt and sounded like a total con.

'The room's chi. Right. Sure. Let's move the bed to the middle of the room. I moved over to the headboard and prepared to lift. Baba G (I'm going with Grant. Grant Babcock.) smiled. 'Oh, I don't do lifting.'

'Okay. You want me to move this oak-framed superking bed on my own?'

'I'll get Aidan to send up some muscle. And I'll deal with the changes we've agreed on. Now, I need to speak to your chef.'

'You'll find him in the kitchen.'

And I think you'll find you've met your match.

21

Lights, Camera, Friction

Baba G looked a little paler after his run-in with Marius – a stern lecture on the health-giving properties of Central European cuisine seemed to have given his chakras a bit of a boot in the goolies. Nevertheless, the two men had reached a workable compromise on Lola Montgomery's regimen, and Baba G had now certified the house as spiritually acceptable, to the immense relief of everyone involved.

I haven't met many real stars. I once sat down at a table in a Soho wine bar – some time in the early noughties – and I turned round to speak to the waiter and noticed that the singer Debbie Harry was at the next table. She was so beautiful and radiant and electrifyingly sexy that I lost the power of speech for about thirty seconds and the waiter moved on to another table where the people weren't comatose buffoons.

But I was prepared for this meeting with Lola Montgomery, and I made sure to hold onto what little cool I possessed.

Dave escorted her across the hall towards me and she smiled her trademark smile and held out her hand.

'It's so very good of you to make your beautiful home available to me.' She sounded less American than she always did on screen and I resolved to google her background later.

'You're very welcome. I'm delighted to meet you and it's a real pleasure to have you as our guest.' The air seemed a little more fragrant around her and I inhaled it discreetly.

'You're very kind. It really makes a difference to be living virtually on set, and in such elegant surroundings.'

'I'm very glad you're pleased, Ms Montgomery. You and your ... consultant.'

She laughed. 'Don't mind him. He likes to think I'm a porcelain doll. And, please, call me Lola.'

Over her shoulder, Dave Hankin lifted his eyebrows an inch, as if a precedent had been broken and I was entering a very exclusive club.

'Thank you ... Lola. Is there anything you need for the room that you don't have?'

'The room is perfect.' A middle-aged woman with glasses on a chain who looked like she'd been dressed by Oxfam was now hovering next to Dave. Without looking, Lola seemed to know she was there. 'They need me for hair and makeup. Very nice to meet you, Jennifer. And thank you, again.'

And off she glided.

A film set runs on a rollercoaster of extremes: there's about an hour of noise and frenzied activity while the lights are set up and moved around – which involves engineers threading huge cables all over the place like giant liquorice – then the camera (smaller than I imagined) is set up – either on a little truck on a sort of short railway track, or on a harness strapped to the camerawoman's body and reaching up and over her head. Then an assortment of extras are marshalled into position by a number of people (assistant directors, it seems), and their movements co-ordinated, while the sound guys make sure nothing's rustling or clicking or creaking when people move, adjusting microphones, laying down mats. Then, when everything's organised, the actors are brought in, there's a couple of minutes of discussion, then, as if under a spell, everyone falls silent.

Then the magic happens.

The action you see before your eyes is transformed, by the considerable skill and hard work of everyone involved, into the beautiful images we see on our screens.

For about ten seconds.

Then frenzy and noise again for another hour.

Then silence.

And so it goes on.

It's absolutely fascinating. By lunchtime on the first day, I'd become totally bewitched.

Edmund, Nutella and I stood on the fringes of the crowd gathered at the kitchen truck. They seemed as dazzled as me. Then Woodbine trotted past with a chunk of pulled pork sandwich in his mouth and the camerawoman shouted across to me.

'Sorry! Is that okay? He just lifted a paw and gave me his cute face and I couldn't resist.'

'It's fine. Just make sure *you* get enough to eat. I've seen how hard you work.'

'Oh, don't worry about me. We mostly run on caffeine and nerves.' She waved the remains of her sandwich. 'This is just a bit of added interest. I don't really need it.'

It was all utterly charming.

But the mood changed in the afternoon.

What had been good-humoured bustle in the morning seemed wrapped in a blanket of tension for the first scene after lunch.

A young man in a black T-shirt with the word *Arriflex* on it marched past me on his way to one of the trucks on the lawn, looking cheesed off.

'Is everything okay?'

'Oh, it's fine. It's just … well, sometimes, the bigger the star, the bigger the pain in the arse.'

In the Orangery, Dave Hankin looked like a man at the end of his tether. A very short tether. A silver-haired man I'd never seen before was smiling at a disgruntled-looking Lola in an outfit straight off the cover of a 1939 edition of *Vogue*. I thought of the Joan Crawford films my mum used to devour on a Sunday afternoon.

A twenty-something girl handed Lola a bottle of water and Lola took one look at the label and handed it back to her and the girl trotted off to get another, while, all the time, the silver-haired man smiled and soothed and Lola scowled and seethed.

After about two hours of exchanges of pissed-off glances between just about everyone on the set, the now-familiar silence fell and work began again.

At the end of a long day in which I'd done nothing but hang around and ogle, and equipment was being switched off and unplugged, I collared the young man in the Arriflex T-shirt.

'How did that go?'

'Not bad. But two pages is pretty shit.'

'Two pages?'

'Of script. If we only shoot two pages a day, we'll be a week behind after two days. We're supposed to get through six pages a day. But it never goes according to schedule when she's around.'

'Lola?'

'Yeah. We all run around like blue-arsed flies trying to keep her happy. Which makes everyone else unhappy. But it goes with the territory.'

'She seemed really nice when I spoke to her this morning.'

'She is. Until you put her in front of a camera. Then she morphs into the Wicked Witch of the West.'

'Why do people work with her, then?'

'She sells seats. As soon as you put her name on a poster, millions of people turn up and pay their twelve quid or whatever. And that keeps the money guys happy. Which keeps us all in a job.'

'I'm sorry.'

'It's fine. We just have to get on with it.'

When the set had shut down for the day, I went to catch up with Edmund. I suspected he'd be grumbling about having his movements restricted by the demands and requirements of the crew and I wondered if Nutella had had to sedate him with industrial-strength puffs from her vaping 'mod' and he'd be lying on his couch in a cloud of Black Mamba or Blue Voodoo.

But he was sitting in an armchair with a photo album on his knee, a whisky at his elbow, and a faraway look in his eyes.

I sat on the carpet beside him.

'I remember it all, you know.' He turned misty eyes towards me. 'Old fools like me are often guilty of romanticising those times. And there *was* a lot to be romantic about: there were incredible acts of bravery, committed by ordinary people just getting on with what needed to be done. But death was everywhere. And it has a horrible smell.'

I put my hand on his arm and he patted it, then took a sip of his whisky.

'Hurricanes used to fly over here. Right over the house. There was a squadron based in Gloucester. One night, in the early days of the Battle of Britain, a Hurricane got into trouble not long after take-off and had to ditch near here. But it had to try to unload its bombs first, safely. Not all Hurricanes carried bombs, but these did. Two five-hundred-pound bombs.'

'Were you scared?'

'I was excited. A bomb to a young boy was an exciting thing. I wanted to see the big explosion.'

'And did you?'

'No. We ran towards where we thought it would go down – I was with a boy from the village whose face I can see but whose name escapes me now – but it passed over a bank of trees and we lost sight of it. Then a few seconds later, the ground shook and we knew the bombs must have landed.'

'What did you do then?'

'We kept running. Like idiots. Towards where the noise had come from, to see if we could see the crater.'

'Did you find it?'

Edmund stared into his glass. 'The bombs had landed in a field, about a mile away. I think that's the fastest I've ever covered the distance of one mile on foot. And it was … horrible. The mangled bodies of cattle, strewn everywhere. Dozens of them. Limbs blown off. Bloody intestines cast around like some sort of ghoulish tinsel. I saw the dismembered head of a cow, its big soft brown eyes still open. And I realised. War wasn't about uniforms and medals and shiny planes. It was about death. But not clean, peaceful death. Violent, blood-spattered carnage.'

'What an awful experience.'

Edmund nodded and fell silent for a few seconds. 'My father never returned from the war. And I can't really remember him. What he was like. And when I do think of him, all I see is an image of dead eyes. Dead, open eyes.'

This talk about the fragility of life had spooked me and I texted David – midnight our time was clocking-off time in New York and I hoped he wouldn't be working late. He called me back immediately.

'How's the filming going? Are you fed up yet?'

'It's only been one day.'

'I know. But they kind of take over, don't they?'

'Well, yes. But it's quite exciting. And everyone's very polite. To me, anyway. And grateful.'

'What about *la grande dame*?'

'She's been perfectly charming to me. All smiles and graciousness and *Call me Lola.*'

'Wow. First names terms with Hollywood royalty. You're too good for me now.'

'I know. You'll have to up your game, mister.'

'How will I do that, I wonder?'

'You will do what you always do. Look into my soul and make it complete.'

'I have that power? I'm beginning to think I'm underpaid.'

'I can only pay you in kind. I'm rich in assets but very poor in cash.'

'I am perfectly happy for you to pay me with your assets.'

'For a very posh, very well educated man, you are surprisingly filthy.'

'Only because I know you like surprises. I love you, Jennifer Brown.'

'It's a good job.'

'Best job I've ever had.'

Filming continued over the next couple of weeks, and I dropped in on the set only when needed, to okay decisions on moving furniture, replacing lights, and unhinging the odd door. Arriflex T-shirt guy – Toby – became someone I shared the occasional sandwich with at the kitchen truck and he gave me updates on progress and on Lola's moods.

'Five pages yesterday. That's not bad. And she only had one major strop. We count that as a result.'

'Well done. By the way, who's the grey-haired guy?'

'Nigel Evans. The Producer. The head honcho. We only see him when Lola's on the call sheet. He knows he'll need to be around to talk her down.'

'Right.'

'And he always manages to.'

'It's a good job.'

'Yeah. Anyway, if we can pick up the pace a little, only one more week and we're out of your hair. Has Dave spoken to you about the schedule?'

'Yes. It's fine.'

It was very fine, in fact. The contract we'd signed stated that any extra days would be paid at double a day rate that was already very generous indeed.

Double.

Given that the estate's business wouldn't be properly off the ground for several weeks at the earliest, a few extra days wouldn't hurt. Quite the opposite. If Lola's 'strops' were causing delays to their schedule, that was clearly a pain for all concerned. Except me.

As I sat on the bench by the lake one warm evening, giving the dogs the rare treat of a dip in the water, I was just wondering if anyone on the team thought I was bribing Lola to act up on set as a way of bumping up my location fees when I was startled by a voice.

'It's so peaceful here.'

I turned to see the face I'd seen a thousand times on screen and on the cover of magazines. Lola Montgomery gestured to the bench.

'Mind if I join you?'

'No. Please do.'

She was wearing joggers and a loose T-shirt and had her hair scraped back into a ponytail. She looked younger. More vulnerable.

We sat in silence for a few seconds, watching a pair of mallards swoop down towards the water then, harassed by a vociferous Woodbine, pull up their landing gear again and arc back up into the clear August evening sky.

The silence was starting to feel awkward, so I broke it.

'It's good fun watching you all make a film. I feel very privileged.'

Her smile was tinged with something – a hint of sadness. 'It used to be. Good fun. I don't think I enjoy it the way I used to.'

'That's true of a lot of things, isn't it? As we get older.'

She smiled. 'Well, I *am* older, that's for sure.'

'No, I didn't mean that.'

Lola Montgomery put her hand on my arm. 'I know.'

'But everything that was once exciting becomes, through familiarity, less so. Gradually.'

'I guess.' She looked cast down. I felt the need to pick her up.

'People love it, though. What you do. What you give them. I do. Your characters are … strong. And beautiful, of course. I've always admired them. Admired *you*.'

The eyes she turned on me were moist. 'You're very kind.'

'I'm not being kind. I'm just being honest.' I couldn't believe I was having what felt like an intimate conversation with a Hollywood legend.

'Clark Gable had false teeth. Did you know that?'

'No.' He'd always been one of my mum's favourites. She'd have been shocked to learn that. She wouldn't have wanted to know.

'And he loved England. He'd been stationed here during the war. He flew combat missions from an air force base somewhere. And after the war, he often came back and visited with the friends he'd made during that time. At the very height of his fame, just a few years after *Gone With The Wind* had made him the biggest male star in the world, he'd walk about villages here with his friends and go to the post office and the pub and nobody bothered him. And at night, he'd take off his corset and take out his false teeth and look in the mirror and laugh at the notion he was America's sweetheart. I read that somewhere. I don't remember where.'

'That's sad.'

Lola turned to me. 'I don't think it is. I think it's positive. Empowering. You see, he didn't buy it. The whole fame thing. He played the part he was required to play – giving interviews, getting his picture taken, cutting ribbons for stuff – but he never believed it. Was never fooled by it. He knew what was real.'

'Good for him.'

'Yes. Good for him.'

'But not for you?'

The sad smile again. 'I haven't been able to pull it off. Now, maybe a little. Maybe that's why this business makes me sad. Because I know it's beaten me. It's won.'

'But you're rich and beautiful and admired by millions. *You've* won, surely.'

'Don't get me wrong. I've had a very comfortable life.'

'It's not over.'

'No. But I've played the game. And now I wish I hadn't.'

'In what way?'

'I've made the mistake of believing the people around me. My manager. My agent. My goddamn spiritual guru.'

'They're there to help you, aren't they? To serve you?'

'That's the theory. But you end up buying their bullshit. About the value of your image – the importance of playing the bitch, the diva. And your 'bankability'. God! I *hate* that word.' She looked at me and shook her head. 'I'm sorry. I shouldn't be dumping all this shit on you.'

'It's fine.'

'No, it's not. You've been very generous and gracious.'

I smiled. 'That's funny. That's the exact word I used about *you* when I was talking about you to my partner.'

She beamed her Hollywood smile. 'That's so nice.' She put her hand on mine. 'You're a real person, Jennifer. That may not sound like much of a compliment but, in my world, there is no higher praise. Believe me.'

'Thank you.'

'So, your ... partner?'

'It's an odd word, isn't it. I just can't bring myself to say 'boyfriend'. I'm about thirty years too old for that.'

'And 'lover' makes it sound like we're Mata Hari, doesn't it. So, what's he like? Someone as genuine as you must have a pretty good guy.'

'We haven't been together that long – less than a year – so it's fairly early days. But we've known each other much longer. Our paths kept crossing, in a way that felt like it was meant to be. I was attracted to him from the very start, but didn't dare hope he felt the same. Then he got married and that seemed to be the end of that daydream.'

'Wow. Sounds very Hollywood. What happened?'

'Their marriage, which seemed perfect – she seemed exactly the type of woman someone like David should be with – well, it only lasted a few months.'

'Because of his feelings for you?'

'No. Although he says he had them. No, they just both realised, separately, that there really wasn't very much there. That they'd gone into it because it was what everyone else wanted and expected. Because it was good on paper. Then our paths crossed again. And my daydream came true.'

'That's so lovely.'

'And then he moved to New York.'

'WHAT?!'

'Exactly. A two-year placement. Well, only eighteen months left now. But still …'

'Long-distance relationships are tricky. I know all about that. How's it going?'

A family of coots had the cheek to venture out from a bank fifty yards away and Woodbine launched himself back into the water to terrorise them.

'As well as it can go when you're thousands of miles away from each other in different time zones. He's been back for just one visit in the last four months. We Skype and FaceTime a lot. But it's not the same.'

'It certainly isn't. But it sounds good. Solid. Real.'

'I hope so.'

'I'm sure it is. He left the fake relationship behind and chose the real one. I don't think I've ever had that.'

'I'm sure that's not true.'

'The problem is, I can never know. Someone like me can never know. If a guy really wants me. Or if he just wants the woman on the screen. Every time you go into something, you think, Maybe this one's for real. But it never is.'

'Well, if not so far, maybe a good relationship is around the corner.'

'I hope so.' She took a deep breath. 'I'm enjoying this. Just talking.'

'And we're women. So we're good at multi-tasking.'

Her beautiful brow crinkled half an inch. 'What do you have in mind?'

'Well, I don't know if it's allowed – on your regime – but I'm quite good at talking *and* drinking wine.'

'I think I can pull that off.'

***

I was genuinely sad to see the production wind up at Thornhill.

The estate bank balance was a few tens of thousands healthier as a result, and they weren't kidding when they said they'd leave the place in better shape than before – the sitting room, the library, the Orangery, four of the bedrooms, and a good chunk of the grounds now looked fit for the glossy pages of *Country Living* – and I'd enjoyed the buzz that came with having them around.

And my intimate conversation with Lola had led to three or four kitchen get-togethers in the evenings over bottles of my finest stuff. We'd exchanged numbers and emails and sincere promises to stay in touch.

'I mean it. I only have time for what's real now. You've helped me to see that. Promise me you'll stay in touch.'

'I promise.'

Will was seething with envy.

'You've *got* to give me her number. Kavi's a massive fan. He loves her even more than I do.'

'Absolutely not. I'm not a fan – I'm a friend.'

'You're a stuck-up cow.'

'She's a lovely person whose privacy is very precious to her. I'm not going to betray that trust.'

'You're a snotty bitch.'

'You can call me all the names you want, but you're not getting her number. I can send you a photograph. That's about it. She's given me half a dozen for close friends.'

'Can you get her to sign it? To my best friends Will and Kavi. Love Lola.'

'They've all gone now. *She's* gone.'

'Just you sign it then.'

'What?'

'Sign it as if it was from her. So I can put it on my desk and make everyone in the office jealous.'

'It'll be my writing, though.'

'They won't know it's not hers.'

'I'm hanging up now.'

22

Not Yet Mellow But Very Fruitful

I strolled past the flagpole cherry trees that lined the walled garden and looked forward to the dazzling autumn show they'd be putting on in five or six weeks. I headed over to catch up with Robbie and his nephew Tom, to help out with a spot of hand weeding.

The kitchen garden had fully returned to its former glory – the raised beds were bursting with green beans and mangetout peas and courgettes and butternut squash, all ripe for the picking. The onions and garlic were bursting with goodness. And the winter veg – carrots, beetroot, leeks, kale – were all shaping up nicely.

Miranda would be able to claim that all the vegetables used in her classes were grown on site. It was a claim of which we would both be extraordinarily proud.

And Marius would make excellent use of all this gorgeous produce for the delicious lunches and dinners that we were confident would help us to rack up five-star reviews on Trustpilot, both from the guests on our cookery courses and from the hospitality guests we'd soon be welcoming in a few weeks' time.

David called me as I was making my way to the kitchen for a mid-morning cuppa. I told him how the estate was shaping up and he was impressed.

'It sounds like the place is thriving.'

'Yes, it really is.' I looked at my watch. 'But it must be the middle of the night there. How come you're calling so early?' I dropped my gardening gloves at the kitchen door and saw that Marius was laying out tea and a plate of the scones he'd been practising for weeks.

'I wanted to let you know I'm taking a week off and I'd like to come over.'

'One whole week?'

'Yes. An entire week. With you. At Thornhill.'

'How did you wangle that?'

'I just told them they needed to manage without me. Which they will. Because I've foreseen everything that could go wrong and dealt with it before it happens.'

I took a bite from one of Marius's scones. 'So that's your new superpower? You can see into my soul and now you can see into the future?'

'Yes. And I foresee a long and happy future. For me. With you. I've been assuming you're flexible about dates. Is that right?'

'To fit in a visit from you, my darling, I can be as flexible as you like.' The scone was pretty good. Not quite up to Rosemary's standard of fluffiness, but not bad at all. I swept crumbs from the kitchen table into my hand.

'Good. Because ...' He sounded sheepish.

'Because what?'

The front doorbell clanged and echoed through the hall and along the corridor to the kitchen.

'Because that doorbell noise is me.'

A glorious week of lazy days followed. As if to order, the weather treated us to clear blue late-summer skies for morning walks round the estate, Luther trotting along beside us and Woodbine nosing noisily round the llamas (and sending Horatio into a macho tailspin) and shooing any jackdaws and magpies that had the temerity to use our lawns for a playground.

'The place is an absolute credit to you.'

'Oh, I don't do much of the actual spade work. Robbie and Tom have worked wonders round the grounds and Delyth and Marius are keeping everything tight indoors, and Miranda will be an absolute natural in the cookery school – she'll really make it work.'

'As always, you are very quick to recognise the efforts of others and prone to overlook the tremendous value of your own input. You are the one with the vision. You are the one who steers things. Provides the focus. The drive.'

'It's a team effort.'

'Yes. And you are leading that team. And, in less than a year, you have – once again – turned the place into a thriving commercial enterprise.'

'We've had some good luck.'

'Every business success needs a bit of luck – it's only a hubristic fool who fails to acknowledge that – but most of what you're seeing now is down to hard work. Marshalled and guided and shepherded by you. So take some credit.'

'I'll try.'

We reached the sundial and George's bench and we sat down with the dogs at our feet. David pointed to my favourite flower in the whole garden.

'What a gorgeous rose!'

'That's uncanny.'

'What?'

'That, with the whole garden to look at, your eyes would settle on the flower that is my absolute favourite.'

'It's beautiful. That creamy yellow colour with just a hint of pink at the edges. It's stunning.'

'I love it for its beauty. But I also love it for its backstory.'

David settled back on the bench, the August sun on his handsome face.

'I'm all ears.'

'It's a hybrid tea variety, called Rosa Madame Meilland. It was grown by a Frenchman and he named it after his mother. In the late thirties. Then, when it looked like France was going to be invaded, he sent cuttings to friends around Europe and asked them to grow and propagate them, to protect the variety. Friends in Italy and Turkey and a few other countries.

'And after the war, when France was liberated, and the variety had survived, he wanted to change the name to Alanbrooke, after the British Field Marshal who'd masterminded the liberation. But Alanbrooke, who didn't always get on with Churchill – Edmund will give you chapter and verse if you're interested – felt a bit awkward about the rose being given his name, and he suggested calling the variety 'Peace'.

'And that appealed to Meilland. And one of these roses was given as a gift to each delegate at the first ever meeting of the United Nations. 1946. And now it's known as the Peace Rose.'

David had listened to the whole story with a smile on his face.

I was suddenly overwhelmed by happiness.

'I don't think there's anywhere else I'd rather be, right now, in the whole world, than sitting here with you.'

'And that's *your* superpower.'

'What?'

'Saying exactly the thing I'm thinking before I get the chance to say it myself.'

David's warm, soft, hazel eyes washed all over me and he stroked my cheek with his hand and gave me a long, lingering, searching kiss that saw all thoughts of roses and of spreadsheets and business plans replaced by impulses generally reserved for the evenings.

'Is it too early for a "nap"?'

***

When David's taxi pulled away, although I was very sorry to see him go – we'd had a fabulously relaxing, warm, intimate week together and I was going to miss him enormously – the edge had gone from my usual desperation. And when I looked at my feelings, I was fairly sure I knew what had happened.

I'd gone from simply being 'in love' with David to loving him. Deeply. Wholly. We'd become creatures who know their way back to each other. A hand goes out and another one takes it. Automatically. It was, for the most part, unspoken but all the stronger for not being talked about all the time. It just … was.

And that familiarity, that certainty, put me at ease with everything. With the separations of the months ahead. Because, after those months – just another twelve months or so – there would be no separation. Only togetherness.

Forever.

23

Get Natted

Miranda had now welcomed her first cohort of paying students into what we'd decided to call the Montpellier Cookery School, sited in the fully refurbished Shooting Lodge.

'They love the place. They're very impressed by the estate, the house, and the kitchens. And the very positive and detailed feedback on course content is suggesting we need make very few adjustments, if any.'

'Sounds good.'

She took both my hands in hers and looked me in the eye. 'It's so good to be teaching people who actually *want* to learn. They're so engaged and appreciative. I'm loving it all. And being in business with you is the best idea I've ever had. Well, you had the idea, but you know what I mean. Thank you.'

'We're a good team. It's a terrific venture. And it's working. As we knew it would.'

'And thank you for that lovely room.'

Miranda had now moved into the suite that had been Lola's. Four of the school's six guests occupied the bedrooms newly refurbished by the film crew and the other two were in rooms that had been quickly and easily brought up to scratch by Robbie and me over the course of a single weekend.

Coachman's Cottage, Rosemary's old place, was now occupied by a lovely young couple with a three-year-old boy and another baby on the way. How on earth a couple in their late twenties could afford a rent of two grand a month was a complete mystery to me. Jo didn't work at all and Sam worked in marketing, for a publisher in Cheltenham, which I didn't imagine paid that wonderfully well.

Maybe he had a sideline as a bank robber.

Woodman's Cottage, the place I'd managed to de-Clapp with a shedload of research and a sprinkling of De Niro, was also now occupied, on a twelve-month lease, by a German man called Werner Klampfleitner who was a visiting lecturer in Business at the University of Hertfordshire (didn't know there *was* one) and was happy to make the hour-and-a-half drive from Thornhill to St Albans and back every day.

I was making my way up to the house from a long walk with the dogs, and feeling good about life, when I heard raised voices coming from the drive.

A taxi was parked by the steps and the driver was having very strong words with a person leaning in at his window.

'Look. If you don't settle the bill, I'm calling the police.'

'Stop shouting. Just let me call my friend.'

The figure straightened herself.

Nat!

My best friend from school had been making a habit of turning up unannounced for the last few years, notably in Bordeaux during my training at Château Paulus. Nat had been (I'd later learned) going through a very messy breakup with the older man she'd hooked up with twenty years earlier, about ten minutes after the pair of us had left Brookhill High.

At school, Natalie Nicholson, a Kylie Minogue lookalike, had been the girl we'd all wanted to be. Cool, sexy, from a well-heeled family with a very comfortable house on the very posh side of town, she'd had the knack of being able to wrap pupils and teachers alike round her little finger.

The emotionally fragile, drink-addled woman who, twenty years later, had shown me her scars and reached out to me for help, had been very hard to connect to the golden girl of our school years. She'd used every emotional blackmail trick in the book to shoehorn herself into the household of Philippe and Madeleine, close friends of my boss Cécile and my hosts for the practical element of my training at Artisan Wines, and our time together in France had been fraught with tensions created largely by Nat's outlandishly bad behaviour.

But we'd eventually parted on good terms when I'd come round to seeing her flaws as the results of an adult life laced with sadness and tragedy.

The last time I'd seen her, at a Brookhill High reunion, she'd been humiliated by a very polite rebuff from the man who'd been her golden-boy counterpart at school, Scott Chandler. The Brookhill heartthrob had, unlike Nat, aged wonderfully well and had blossomed into a very likeable man.

And, also unlike Nat, he was gay.

So, likeable though she was, and strongly though I felt my duty towards her to be as her closest childhood friend, there was no denying the fact that, whenever Natalie was around, the forecast was for awkwardness and embarrassment, with a distinct chance of mayhem.

My phone rang in my pocket as I was ten yards from the taxi and I took the call and heard Nat's voice both over the phone and across the drive.

'Jen. Sorry. I'm here. Outside your house. Can you help me?'

'Turn round.'

She clocked me and I waved and she half-smiled in a panicky, slightly unhinged way and tottered over the gravel towards me in heels that would only work if you were on a dance floor.

And if you were twenty-two.

'My card's been declined and this arsehole's talking about calling the police.'

'Hi, Nat.'

'Can you …? Sorry. I don't have any cash on me.'

I pulled my purse out of my pocket and walked over to the driver. 'What does she owe you?'

'Forty-seven fifty.'

'What? Where has she come from? Vladivostok?'

'Birmingham Airport.'

'Bloody hell. Right. There you go.' He slotted my card into his gizmo while Nat started unloading bags from the boot. She shouted over the taxi roof.

'Don't give him a tip. Miserable bastard.'

The driver shook his head. 'Friend of yours, is she?'

'Yeah. She means well.'

'She's a bloody bombscare. Good luck.'

I smiled. 'I know. Thanks. I'll need it.'

24

Man(-Eater) Trouble

We dumped Nat's bags in the hall and I took her through to the kitchen and sat her down at the big refectory table.

I'd learned, in recent years, that subtlety didn't work with Nat.

'So. Where have you been and what are you doing here?'

She looked gaunt. 'I'm sorry. I just … needed you. I got off the plane in Birmingham and had a bit of a panic. I sat in the toilets in Arrivals and … ' Nat's eyes filled with tears. '… kind of fell to pieces. Again. A teenage girl – who really shouldn't have been treated to the sight of a middle-aged woman spilling her marbles all over the bathroom floor – went to fetch someone. Two very nice women in high-vis tabards took me into an office and poured coffee into me – I'd hit the prosecco a bit on the plane – and asked me if I had anyone.' She teared up again. 'And the only person I could think of was you.'

I put my arm round her. 'Come on. Let's go into the garden for some fresh air. And you can tell me all about it.'

We sat on the bench by the sundial with a pot of tea and some German-style biscuits of Marius's that I'd been trying to get a taste for.

The last time I'd seen Nat, I'd sensed she'd turned a bit of a corner and left behind the very troubled existence that had been most of her adult life.

Way back when we were best friends, Nat had run off with an older man – Rodney, an 'artist'. It had been a genuine love affair, even though she was only just eighteen and he was well past his thirtieth birthday. And they'd run off to southern France together with dreamy plans to live the bohemian life – him painting and selling his art, and supplementing sales of his work with teaching, and Natalie hanging around in floaty silk dresses decorating their lives with her beauty. And Nat in her late teens was eye-poppingly lovely – gorgeously tumbling blonde locks, flawless skin, tiny waist, fabulous breasts. The kind of woman young men gazed at on Athena posters on their bedroom walls. Only better.

That life worked pretty well for a while. Then Rodney's art stopped being the kind of thing anyone wanted to buy, he lost confidence in himself, started to drink more than just a casual Muscadet over lunch on the sunny terrace, and turned into a cliché – the older man in search of increasingly younger women to bolster his ego. And, although he and Nat stayed together for another couple of decades, he'd effectively kicked her into touch where trouser-related activity was concerned and, although he made no secret of his dalliances, she pretended not to know. Because it suited her. Until it didn't.

And it all came to a head when, after twenty-odd years of barely being in touch, she sought me out during my time in Bordeaux and I saw the physical toll those miserable years had taken on her. She was still a desirable woman – the fabulous figure was still there – but there was a look of worn-out desperation etched into her features that I imagined a lot of men might find hard to ignore.

We'd said our goodbyes after a boozy catch-up in a restaurant on Bordeaux's Place de la Bourse and I'd thought it'd be another couple of decades before our paths crossed again.

Then, a couple of weeks later, she turned up out of the blue, in a state, in Saint Emilion, where I was living and working, and promptly announced she'd finally left her womanising drunk of a failed artist husband.

And here she was again. Unannounced and in a state.

And, once again, Rodney was the cause.

'I thought you were divorced.'

'We are.'

'So what the bloody hell were you doing going back over there?'

'Well … he's basically dying. Or at least he says he is.'

'I'm sorry, Nat. I know it sounds heartless. But that's not your problem.'

'I know. But we did have some good years together.'

'I'm not saying you didn't. But he behaved abominably. Unforgivably so, in my book.'

'I know. But he reached out. And it's hard to say no.'

'It *is* hard. But you have to try. For *you*. For your own self-esteem.'

'I'm weak.'

'You're kind. But a bit soft. What happened?'

'Well, I get a phone message. He sounds dreadful. Can hardly speak. Says he's only got months. Maybe only a few weeks. Starts talking about the past. The good times we had together.'

'That's laying the emotional blackmail on a bit thick.'

'I know. I'm a sucker for all that.'

'He knows it, too.'

'I know. You're right. Anyway, I drop everything.'

'Drop what? Where are you working?'

'I do three days a week in – irony of ironies – an art gallery in Oxford. On the desk. Admin. Basic stuff. Not much more than minimum wage. But it pays the rent for a small flat in Cowley, above a Timpson's. I can't afford Iffley.'

'Right. So you sack off the gallery for a few days and fly out to Provence. What then?'

'Well, it's all really lovely for a couple of days. He's sixty-two now but he looks a lot better – healthier – than when I saw him last. And it sounds like he's doing okay. Not drinking. Sold the house in Aix and is in a lovely flat in Les Baux. Balconies. Good light. And he's painting again. But he's got MS.'

'That's quite a trump card.'

She smiled a wry smile. 'I wish I was more like you.'

'Sorry. I don't mean to be … mean.'

'No. You're quite right to be. Anyway, he's charming. Of course. And he talks about the past. *Our* past. And good times. All of which is true.'

'Selectively, yes.'

'Yes. And at first I think I'm just there to say goodbye. He's dying. It's a rapidly progressing form of the condition, he says. So I think, He's putting his house in order. He's making up for the shitty way he behaved. Making it all right before he, you know, shuffles off this mortal coil.'

'But that's not it?'

'No. That's not it.'

'So …?'

'So. It gradually emerges that there *is* no MS – at least, not definitely.'

'He's made it up?'

'Not entirely. He's got symptoms – muscle stiffness and weakness in his arms, his vision's going, he's got problems with his bladder.'

'He's sixty-two. Ropy eyesight and a dodgy bladder are in the job description. And it's hardly surprising he's got stiff arms – he's been holding a paintbrush all his life. And lifting twenty-five glasses of wine a day. What are the doctors saying?'

'He hasn't see one.'

I blinked in disbelief. 'What?'

'He's terrified of them. But Camille's googled the symptoms and put two and two together.'

'Hang on. Who's Camille?'

'She's his girlfriend. And she's very much at the heart of this story.'

'Shocker. Age?'

'She's twenty-seven.'

'Right. I don't like where this is going. And she's been there during this stroll down memory lane?'

'No. She's stayed out of the way. Then he brings her over, on the third evening.'

'Right. I *really* don't like where this is going.'

'I don't blame you.'

'Where *is* it going?'

'Well ... between them, they've decided he's dying. Of a ragingly degenerative form of multiple sclerosis. The kind that finishes you off in weeks, Google says. So he's looked at his life insurance. And it turns out he hasn't got any. He *did* have, but it was some weird, cheap policy that ended on his sixtieth birthday. So there'll be nothing. And he owes money on the flat. Twenty-two thousand euros.'

'I thought he'd sold the house in Aix.'

'He did. But the proceeds from that got frittered away.'

'Shocker Number Two.'

'So he had to take out a loan – a mortgage of sorts – to part-fund the purchase of the flat. And he's fallen behind on the payments. Hasn't paid them for the past twelve months, in fact. So now the bank is threatening to call in the loan. So when he dies, Camille will have nowhere to live. And he doesn't want her to have that worry.'

'So he asked *you* for the money?'

Nat could only nod.

'To fund the lifestyle that his young girlfriend has become accustomed to. In her very nice flat in Provence. With the balconies and the lovely light.'

Nat's eyes filled with tears and she nodded again.

'Even though there's a strong possibility he won't die. At all. But he wants his debts cleared anyway. Just in case. By you.'

Nat buried her head in her hands and sobbed quietly for a minute or two, then laid her head on my shoulder. And I stroked her hair while I wrestled with visions of me planting a dagger I don't own into the heart of a man I've never met.

Nat finally pulled herself upright.

'It's my stupidity that upsets me most.'

'It's not what upsets *me* most. It's him. I want to rip his bloody head off.'

She managed a faint smile. 'I practically did.'

'Good. What did you do?'

'I called him a Wanker. And I called her a Stupid Tart. And told him he could go fuck himself if he thought I was bailing him out – him and his new bit of stuff. With money I don't fucking have anyway. Then I smashed a few glasses and plates for good measure – one plate over his back. Then I called a taxi and headed out to the airport.

'And in the taxi and on the plane I felt pretty good about the glasses and the plates. Then when we hit the ground in Birmingham, I felt stupid. Like some gullible old tart who never learns. And I hated myself. And that feeling sort of closed in around me like a black fog. And I went to pieces. And here I am. Leaning on you. Again. In pieces.'

Tears rolled down her cheeks and I wiped them away with my fingers.

'It's fine. Have you phoned the gallery?'

'Not yet.'

'Take a deep breath. Give them a ring. Tell them you need a leave of absence. A couple of weeks. Make something up if you have to. And I'll take your bags up to one of our rooms.'

'You're a bloody good friend, Jennifer Brown.'

'Like you, I'm a total softie.'

In the days that followed, Nat settled down and made herself useful. She helped Delyth with general housework, rolled her sleeves up in the kitchen to help Marius prepare breakfasts and evening meals for the Montpellier guests and, once they'd left, rolled her sleeves up again and helped with cleaning down the

Shooting Lodge kitchen and making the place ready for a new intake of guests, arriving the following week.

And she was discreet enough to stay out of the way when Miranda and I were talking business. Her way of staying out of the way was to wander round the grounds in search of opportunities to spend time 'helping' Robbie, a not-entirely-selfless gesture, it emerged.

One evening in the library, I poured us each a glass of wine while I went over the revenue projections for the cookery school. Nat folded her slender legs up onto the big brown Chesterfield armchair that had been George's favourite before he'd lost the use of his legs.

'Your gardener's rather dishy, isn't he?'

I peered at Nat over the top of my reading glasses. 'He's a very nice man. He's also very shy. And he lives with his ageing and infirm mother. He's a total gentleman.'

The old man-eating Nat of our high school days was never very far beneath the surface.

'Now you're just deliberately trying to make him more attractive.'

'I'm trying to tell you to back off. He's a nice guy. I don't want you corrupting him, you with your blondeness and your killer boobs. Put your boobs back in their box.'

'I'm just saying he's a bit of a dish. I like a man with tattoos. And under different circumstances …'

I glared at Nat over the top of my laptop. 'Under these circumstances, he is to be regarded as out of bounds. Kapeesh?'

'Understood, Don Corleone. I'll be on my best behaviour.'

'Hm.'

'If I chat him up, what happens? Do I get a severed llama head in my bed?'

'Yes. And that's all you'll be getting in your bed. No chatting up. Or chatting down. Anyway, why Robbie and not Marius? I reckon most women would go for him first. That statement is not an invitation, you understand.'

Nat pulled a face. 'Oh no. He reminds me of that woman from the Bond film.'

'Pussy Galore?'

'No. The one with the knives in her shoes.'

I laughed out loud. 'Rosa Klebb.'

'That's her.'

'I know what you mean.'

'With everything he says, you feel like you're being told off. Or kind of lectured about something.'

'He certainly has very firm opinions. But he's an absolute wizard around this place. He's been a godsend.'

'I can see that. It'd just be nice if he … loosened up a bit.'

'I don't think he does loose. You, on the other hand …'

'Stop it. I'm a reformed woman.'

'Except where Robbie's concerned.'

'Well, he could, so to speak, tempt me to fall off the wagon. And into his lovely arms.'

Well, don't fall anywhere. This place needs his arms. I can't be having them cluttered up with sex-starved man-eater.'

'You're a very good friend, Jennifer Brown. But you're also a bit of a cow.'

'One tries one's best.'

Superficially, I was enjoying having Nat around, now that she'd recovered from the ill-advised trip to France to see her exceptionable ex.

But something I couldn't put my finger on was unsettling me. Perhaps it was memories of our recent times together – her awkwardly drunken behaviour over lunch in Bordeaux, her insinuating herself into my life in Saint Emilion and the awful way that episode had ended (with Nat being vilely groped by a thoroughly objectionable arsehole of a client on some wine-tasting holiday), her cringeworthy attempt to chat up, at a high-school reunion about a year previously, the golden boy of our cohort, a man who everyone in the room seemed to know was gay. Everyone except Nat.

Trouble of some sort seemed to follow her around like a bad smell. And that feeling – that bad stuff was about to happen – was, I think, what was unsettling me.

I hadn't been sleeping great since she'd pitched up on the Thornhill gravel. Luckily for me, 3.36 am in the heart of the Oxfordshire countryside is late evening in New York City.

David was in a taxi, on his way home from a Broadway show with clients.

'What show?'

'A thing called *Girl From The North Country*.'

'Never heard of it.'

'Me neither.'

'Any good?'

'It's pretty grim stuff, for a musical. They sing a lot of Bob Dylan songs and tell a story about teenage pregnancy and poor mental health and tragedy.'

'It's not *Mary Poppins*, is it?'

'No. Although I don't really get musicals. Any of them. All that breaking off from doing the dishes to sing a big number and dance about the place. It's really not my thing. And this one really, *really* wasn't my thing. But a couple of our clients liked the idea – one of them grew up listening to her dad's Dylan albums – so we did our duty. How are things at Thornhill?'

'Business is great. A steady flow of guests in the cookery school. Feedback from the guests so far has been almost unanimously excellent and we now have armfuls of terrific reviews on Trustpilot. And the rental income from the two cottages is great to have. So the estate coffers are filling up nicely. But ...'

And I went on to explain about Nat pitching up and about her tendency to carry around a big spanner ready to throw in the works.

'It sounds like she's had a rough time, but also that she's settled down a bit.'

'You think I'm being a cow?'

'No. But maybe you're worrying about nothing.'

'I hope so. Anyway, let's rewind a bit. You're taking young women out to Broadway shows?'

'Yes. Strictly in the line of duty.'

'You know I would be devastated if you parked me at the kerb and drove off with a younger model? That's basically the story of Natalie's married life. And I'd be devastated. For about a week. Then I'd hunt you down and plunge a dagger right into your heart of darkness.'

'I don't want a younger model. Even without the threat of the Van Helsing treatment.'

'Good.'

'Because I love *you*, Jennifer Brown. And have for some time now. A long time. Even when you didn't know it.'

Those few words made my eyes glisten. 'It's a good job.'

'Best job I've ever had.'

25

An Ill Wind Blows East

A bright morning in early September saw me at the long kitchen table on my laptop applying for an e-visa.

For India.

My medium-term travel plans, such as they'd been vaguely formed by a brain wrapped up in business plans and revenue streams, had been confined to a possible trip to New York – lunches with David at a café terrace in Bryant Park, near his office; afternoon strolls round the Museum of Modern Art while he worked; perhaps an early evening cocktail with Lola in some exclusive joint crammed with film stars (De Niro lives in New York too, doesn't he?); cosy evenings in David's apartment, sipping cosmopolitans on his balcony overlooking the Hudson.

That daydream had been exploded by a call from Will.

'Kavi's left me!'

'What?'

'He's gone back to India.'

'What did you do?'

'I didn't fucking well *do* anything!'

'Well, what happened?'

'He got a phone call. Yesterday. His mother's very ill.'

'Bloody hell, Will! He hasn't *left* you, you daft sod. He's just gone away for a bit to attend to very serious family business. He'll be back.'

'That's the thing. I don't think he *will* be back.'

'Why the hell would you think that? He loves you.'

'He's left his phone here. I can't reach him. I don't think he wants me to.'

I scratched around for something comforting to say. 'He's probably got a second phone he uses just for India. They'll have different networks over there. When did he leave?'

'This morning. When I woke up, he wasn't there. Just a note. *Sorry. I have to go.*'

'Go to see his very ill mother. Not leave you.'

'I need to go. I need to speak to him.'

'You're being ridiculous. He'll probably phone you tonight, once he lands.'

'He won't. They're in the middle of nowhere. Some tiny fucking village hundreds of miles from Kochi.'

'Where?'

'Exactly! They probably don't even *have* fucking phones!'

'Will. Calm down. He's gone because he's worried about his mum. Of course he is. You'd do exactly the same in his shoes. And you'd call him just to hear his voice and let him know you were safe. And that's what *he'll* do. Everywhere's got phones these days. There's a bloody Carphone Warehouse at the South Pole.'

'Is there?'

'No, you plonker! I'm making a point! And the point is, you're a daft old queen who's got his knickers in a twist about nothing.'

'I can't sit here and wait for a phone call that might never come. I just can't. I need to go.'

'You know that's mad, right?'

'Come with me.'

'To India?!'

'PLEEEASE!'

***

London Heathrow on a Saturday evening has all the relaxed tranquility of a street market in Southsea on Christmas Eve.

Our progress through security felt like what I imagine it's like going a few rounds with Nicola Adams. But, after a couple of hours of boredom enlivened by brief bouts of physical assault, Will and I were settled into our seats on an Air India Boeing 777.

I adjusted my seatbelt while Will pulled his phone out of his pocket. For perhaps the five hundredth time in the last twenty-four hours. My poor friend looked like he'd never relax again and turned red eyes towards me and held out his phone. It showed a photo of him and Kavi, each of them looking relaxed, handsome and in love.

'Our first weekend break. We'd been together six weeks. Brighton. We did the Pier. Then the Pavilion. Then the bookshops and antique shops near the front. And in the William Morris antiques place I told him I loved him.' Tears rolled down his cheeks and I put my arm round him. An eight-year-old girl across the aisle pulled a sympathetic face.

'Doesn't your husband like flying?'

I smiled. 'No. Not much. But he'll be alright.'

Will slept for most of the flight – sleep was something I suspected he hadn't properly done since he'd found Kavi's note – and I had to wake him when the plane touched down in Kochi nine hours later.

In the air-conditioned taxi to the hotel, it hit me how ridiculously tenuous this whole enterprise was. Will had no actual address for Kavi, and wasn't even sure of the name of the village – just that it began with a K and was near the Cardamom Hills. All he knew for certain was that Kavi's sister, Asha, worked in that village in a tiny hotel called the Methi. The name had stuck because Will had always thought *methi* on an Indian menu meant spinach. Kavi told him no – it means fenugreek.

So … for our mission to find Kavi, the intel was: the name of a hotel, in a village beginning with K, somewhere near the Cardamom

Hills. A mountain range extending over some two thousand eight hundred square kilometres.

Piece of cake.

The Jasmine Hotel was in a district of Kochi that seemed to consist largely of dwellings made of plastic and cardboard, with the odd breeze-block chai shop dotted around for good measure. I didn't imagine it was a district they trumpeted much on the Kochi Tourist Board website.

And the Jasmine Hotel wouldn't be in anybody's top ten (unless it was Top Ten Hotels You'd Really Rather Not Spend The Night In). But Will had made all the arrangements in a panic-fuelled, tear-flooded couple of hours, so it would have been churlish of me to pull my face.

The man on the desk looked friendly enough. He smiled at us from behind a vase full of plastic jasmine flowers, his broad beam revealing a gap in his front teeth you could have driven a car through (a car full of dentists).

'We're very pleased you're staying with us,' he said, and seemed to mean it. Then he hopped out from behind the desk to pick up our bags – my case and backpack and Will's holdall. His slight frame looked ill-equipped to handle the burden and I stepped forward to give him a hand.

'No, mam. Please. You are the guest. And for you we have a special room. Please.' And he skipped off down a dark hallway that smelled of incense and Jeyes cleaning fluid, with Will and me trailing behind.

The corridor was airless and I was aware of never having felt so oppressed by heat in all my life. The sensation of stuffiness was so intense I thought I might actually throw up all over this nice man's 1970s orange floral lino.

He pushed open a door, stood back, and ushered me into the room with a grand sweep of his arm.

I have to say the room looked very clean. A reassuring smell of bleach hung heavy in the air as I staggered over to the window, which overlooked the main street with its row of makeshift dwellings. I pushed the window open and a wall of intensely hot and less-than-fragrant air hit me squarely in the face. A skinny brown cow with frighteningly long horns looked over at me from its station on the other side of the road.

I turned to the smiling hotel man.

'Is there air conditioning?'

He greeted the question with a curious gesture that was half nod, half shake of the head, and skipped across to flick a switch on the wall. He pointed to the ceiling.

A giant fan only slightly smaller than the propeller on the Titanic lurched into action and the three of us watched for perhaps ten seconds as it settled into a stately rhythm. I turned my face upwards and felt a faint breeze – the kind you'd feel if a small child was waving a paper hankie from the other end of a very long street.

'Great. Thanks.'

He did the nod-shake thing again. 'If you need anything, mam, find me in reception area.'

And off he skipped to give a dejected-looking Will the tour of the room next door.

I flopped down on the bed and consoled myself with the thought that this was only for one night.

The following day, we were heading inland.

On a wild goose chase.

Will had narrowed the villages down to two: Kankudy and Kanchithal.

'It's definitely *Kan*-something.'

The spirit of the quest seemed to have lifted his mood quite a bit from the previous day's tearful doldrums.

'I feel good about this. We're going to find him. I know it.'

Kavi clearly hadn't called Will. I was working hard to convince myself there'd be practical reasons for this, but his doom and gloom had infected me a bit and I was starting to think maybe Kavi really had left him. If he *had*, it was a pretty shitty way of breaking things off. After the three years they'd had together.

'I'm sure you're right.'

Both these villages were a good few hours inland. As the crow flies, we were only talking forty miles or so (not the hundreds Will had imagined). But the inland roads in this part of Kerala were not, I was to learn, always worthy of the name.

Plus, only part of our journey was to be made by road. The rest was to be made by water. On something called a rice barge.

But the first leg we would make in a tuk-tuk.

If you've never ridden in one, imagine a cross between a motorised tricycle and a lawnmower. Then stick a very small couch on the back. Then build some bodywork round it using old bits of tea tray.

Then hire a driver with a death wish.

I don't know whether traffic in all cities in India is as mental as the traffic in Kochi. It's not that there aren't rules. Or signs. It's just that absolutely nobody follows them. Our lives were very nearly snuffed out, violently, about five times in the first three minutes.

The monologue in my head ran like this: *He's not seriously going to try to get through that tiny gap between the bus and the gravel truck, is he? Oh my fucking god, he bloody well IS!*

Then I'd close my eyes, cling onto Will, and wait for a death I hoped would be instant.

Then open my eyes, resolve to enjoy the next seven seconds of life, then go through the whole performance again, as our driver hurtled headlong towards a motorbike carrying a man, his wife, their baby, a four-year-old girl with a sack of rice on her knee, and a teenage boy on the back. Carrying a ladder.

Alton Towers should really invent a ride called *Indian City Death Race*. Except all the hardcore thrillseekers who pretend they enjoy the likes of *Nemesis* and *Oblivion* would take one look and go, *No bloody chance!*

Will paid the driver the four hundred rupees he asked for and I tipped him another two hundred simply because I was glad to be alive.

The hire car came with a driver, Aji.

'I take you as far as the river. Twenty miles. Two thousand rupees. Okay?'

Twenty pounds. A pound a mile. 'That's fine. Just keep us alive.'

Will dug me in the ribs. 'Relax.'

Aji smiled. 'Indian roads very bad. In the city. Outside the city, not so bad. Don't worry. Traffic will not kill you.'

'Great. Thank you.'

'Snakes. They kill you. And tigers.'

'What?'

Will dug me in the ribs again. 'Bloody hell, Jen. He's joking.'

I looked at Aji's face in the rearview mirror. 'Are you? Joking?' And he did the same nod-shake thing the bloke in the hotel had done.

So I was none the wiser.

After a final few minutes of urban sprawl, we hit open country. And it was spectacular.

Wherever you looked, there was vegetation. Coconut palms, rubber trees, grasses that towered over the road. A hundred and fifty shades of green.

And the tropical air was no less sticky but, with the windows down on Aji's little red Toyota, at least it was moving. I closed my eyes and turned my face upwards to the sun.

'You're loving this, aren't you?'

I turned to see Will smiling at me. 'I'm sorry. I know this isn't a holiday.'

'It's fine. I blackmailed you into coming out here. The least I can do is hope you enjoy the trip.'

'You didn't blackmail me. I'm happy to be here. To support you. God knows you've supported me often enough over the years.'

He squeezed my hand and teared up. 'What am I going to do, Jen? If it's all over between us?'

'If it is, you will hurt. For quite a while. Then you'll recover. Gradually.'

'I thought this was it. The one.'

'I don't think there is. Only one.'

'What would you do if you lost David?'

I looked out of the window. A woman knee-deep in the water of what I took to be a rice field straightened up and stretched her back, her red cotton skirt soaked all the way up to the waistband. 'Fall to pieces. Be a wreck. Then eventually get over it. And live.'

'And find someone else?'

'I don't know. I don't think I'd look for anyone else for quite some time.'

'I'm not sure I can live without him.'

'You can. You could. But maybe you won't have to.'

Will looked out of the window. 'Maybe.'

26

A Watery End

A ji dropped us at a place that felt like the Norfolk Broads on Easter weekend.

Although we'd hardly seen a settlement since we'd left the outskirts of Kochi, this random collection of mud-and-straw huts was clearly Boat Central in this part of Kerala.

Hundreds of small craft buzzed about, their skippers shouting to (or at) each other, announcing destinations to the crowds gathered on the bank, or barking what sounded like orders at nobody in particular.

I had no idea what the script was, and neither did Will. We wandered around aimlessly for ten minutes or so, assaulted by moist heat and noise, and I spotted a group of people who looked European being herded towards the water – presumably on one of those holidays they charge eight grand for and advertise during reruns of *Inspector Morse* – and I went over to see if someone could help.

I buttonholed a silver-haired man in a linen jacket with the demeanour of the chairman of your local Conservative Association.

'Excuse me. Do you speak English?'

'I'm afraid it's the only language I speak.'

'My friend and I are, I think, booked on a rice barge to take us up the river to a village beginning with K – don't ask – and I have no idea what a rice barge looks like.'

'Ah. That I *can* help you with.' He pointed. 'See that long vessel – one, two, three, four, five boats away, with a canopy that looks like it's woven out of raffia or somesuch?'

'With the red stripe on its side?'

'That's the one. That's a rice barge. I don't know if it's *your* rice barge, of course …'

'That's helpful. Thank you.' I looked at the guide book he was clutching. 'Are you on holiday?'

He pulled a face. 'Yes. They don't talk about this place in the *brochure.*' He pronounced that word like it was French. 'We're meant to be cruising – in some style, I'm told – down to a place called Coconut Lagoon, where we will live like kings for three days.'

'Sounds wonderful.'

'Yes, it does rather, doesn't it? However, whether we actually make it there is uncertain. You see, our boat is not here. And the guide is in quite a flap about that, poor man. Some of the other travellers have rather made his life a misery. There *have* been one or two hiccups along the way and they've wasted no time in pointing them out.'

'Oh dear.'

'I see their point in a way – we've paid a lot of money – but I don't think that gives one the right to be unpleasant.'

'Well, I hope the trip gets smoother from here.'

'Oh, I'm quite relaxed about it. It's lovely just being in this dazzling country, isn't it?'

'Well, it's certainly an assault on the senses.'

Will turned up at my side and the man smiled at him. 'Well, I hope you find your barge. Good luck.'

I thanked him and pulled Will through the crowds and towards the boat with the raffia roof.

It really wasn't clear from my conversation with the boatman that this was actually the one Will had booked, given that the concept of booking something in advance appeared to be alien to this gentleman.

Nevertheless, he looked at the map we showed him, suggested a price that worked out at around a tenner, we bit his hand off, and he ushered us on board.

Rice barges may come in different sizes and different levels of comfort – I wouldn't know – but I have to tell you this one was very comfortable indeed. Will and I were the only passengers, but there were chairs and couches enough for a dozen or more. There was a polished wooden floor and a gorgeous little campaign table with a bowl of fragrantly ripe mangoes on it. And you might think the open, windowless sides would have waved in the heat and the river smells but, on board, an airy freshness reigned.

I was beginning to think we'd bagged the thing my silver-haired guide and his party were expecting to cruise down the river on to Coconut Lagoon.

I turned to Will, who was looking lost in his own thoughts. 'This is the life, isn't it? All that's missing is champagne.'

Will turned a watery smile on me. Clearly, all the doubts and fears of yesterday were crowding in again.

The boat's skipper tied a rope round the wheel and hopped past me to a little cupboard beside one of the armchairs. He pulled open the door to reveal a small fridge with three or fours bottles and half a dozen glasses. He pulled out one of the bottles and held it up to me with a questioning gesture.

'Wine. From India. Not champagne. Sorry.'

I was taken aback. 'Oh. Great. Thank you.' I started to dig into my handbag for my purse but he waved his hand. 'No. Madam. Please. My pleasure.' And he took two glasses, opened the bottle, and poured a golden white wine into each of them and handed them to me and Will.

'Aren't you going to join us?'

He smiled. 'For me, it's not allowed. Muslim.'

'Oh. Sorry. Of course. Well, thank you.' I held out my hand. 'I'm Jennifer. And this is Will.'

The boatman put his hand on his chest. 'Latif.' He reached out and shook Will's hand. Then he placed his hand back on his chest, looked at me, and executed a short bow. Then he did the nod-shake thing, hopped past me, unroped the wheel, and went back to his job.

His kindness had made me a bit tearful and Will had tears in his eyes, too, although his were the product of a whole whirlpool of emotions. I held up my glass.

'To the future, whatever it holds,' I said, my voice wobbling over the words.

Will couldn't speak. He held up his glass and we clinked.

An hour and a half later, the driver cut the engine and brought the boat to a halt alongside a wooden jetty.

'Kankudy, madam.'

'Oh. Thank you.' I looked across at the shore and saw only thick vegetation and a pyramid-shaped building, bright orange – some sort of temple, presumably.

'This is the village?'

'Inside. Maybe, one half mile.'

'Okay. Will you wait here?'

The nod-shake gesture again.

'Right. Thank you.'

Will and I stood. My best friend suddenly looked terrified and turned to the boatman. 'Is there a hotel in the village?'

'I don't know. Sorry.'

I reassured him. 'It's fine. Don't worry. We're happy to explore. But you *will* wait for us?'

'Of course.'

Will and I climbed ashore and set off into the unknown.

The road into the village was lined with thick ranks of towering palm trees. Through the odd gap in the trees, watery fields seemed to extend for miles, to the Cardamom Hills in the hazy distance. I half expected Mowgli to come bouncing through the undergrowth, with a watchful Bagheera at his side.

Then something spookily wonderful happened.

A second after I'd had that thought, a man appeared from around the corner, wearing orange trousers and a lilac shirt. He was followed by a majestic elephant, more than twice his height, carrying a huge bunch of palm branches, ten or fifteen feet long, in its trunk.

Will and I exchanged a dumbfounded glance as man and elephant sauntered towards us, each at ease with themselves and each other, simply playing out a scene from everyday life in Kerala.

We stood aside as they passed, the leaves from the elephant's branches sweeping the dusty ground inches from my sandals, its huge grey-brown bulk blocking the sunlight for a couple of seconds, then gone.

I realised I had a ridiculous, childish grin on my face. Will's eyes were wide open.

'Wow!'

'We will never have an experience like that again.'

'No. We don't get many elephants on the streets of Portsmouth.'

'I guess not. And that makes my llamas at Thornhill seem like a third-rate sideshow. Just wonderful!'

We smiled and breathed.

Then we turned the corner and there it was – the Methi Hotel.

Will stopped dead in his tracks and grabbed my wrist. 'I can't do this.'

I looked him in the eye. 'You have to.'

'Come with me.'

'Come on. We both know you've got to do this on your own. You go on ahead.' There was a low stone wall ten yards away. 'I'll sit on that wall and wait for you. Take your time.'

Will nodded, took a deep breath, and set off towards the truth.

I watched him stride off up the road, gathering all the confidence and determination he could muster. When he reached the hotel, a hundred yards away, he stopped, took another deep breath, and marched inside.

I took a sip from a water bottle – the wine, delicious though it had been, was starting to feel like a bad idea in this heat – then pulled from my bag the compact Canon Power Shot that goes with me on any trip I suspect will offer good subjects.

Within ten minutes, I'd bagged a couple of dozen shots of amazing stuff – a big monkey with a white mane, eating a mango; a grey bird with a huge, curved, orange beak and a call that sounded like the horn of a container truck; a gorgeous young woman working in a rice field who saw me shooting and struck a pose of flamboyant stylishness then fell about laughing (a couple of shots of her smile looked like something straight out of a copy of *National Geographic*).

Then I looked back up the road and saw Will emerge from the hotel. He looked downtrodden. He waved at me down the road then pointed behind him, turned, and headed off further into the village. I guessed the conversation with Asha had furnished Kavi's family's home address.

My heart started to beat faster and I wondered what the next half hour would hold for my friend.

I thought about the conversation we'd had earlier, about love and relationships and what I'd said about how I'd cope if I no longer had David. It sounded callous to my ears now – to say that I'd bounce back, eventually, and life would go on. It sounded like my love for him was … finite. It didn't feel like that when we were together, and I could still conjure up in my chest the feeling of overwhelming elation I'd had when he'd told me he'd always felt the same about me as I had about him. From the very start. I hadn't dared hope that. Couldn't even have begun to believe it during those years I'd seen him from afar and daydreamed.

And now that it was all wonderfully real, to say that I'd survive without him seemed heartless.

But it was true. We *do* survive. We have to.

After another dozen shots – a man cutting bamboo with a huge machete, a striped lizard about as long as my foot and just a few inches away from it, and a teenage boy pulling a handcart piled high with coconuts (like something out of a tropical version of the framed Constable print that hung in the Thornhill library) – Will appeared at the end of the road.

When he was about ten feet away, it was clear he'd been crying. I opened my arms and he fell into them and I stroked his hair and told him it would be fine.

Eventually.

27

A Sore Point

We waved goodbye to Latif from the stone pier that led from the water to the very splendid-looking Guruvayur Hotel on its banks.

I'd never done this before – simply turn up at a place, on the hoof, without booking – but another couple of glasses of Latif's wine (a blend, it turned out, of Sauvignon Blanc and something called Black Muscat) had not completely drowned Will's sorrows but had at least thrown a bucket of cold water in their face.

'Right. This trip has been a total ball-ache so far. I need you to have some fun.'

'I always have fun when I'm with you.'

'Bollocks. It's been a shitshow from start to finish.' He glanced at Latif. 'Apart from this lovely trip on the river. But we can't sleep on this boat, can we? Latif – please take us to a very nice place. Money no object.'

So Latif had steered his lovely rice barge across country, through the region's maze-like network of rivers, curling away from the hills and back towards Kochi and the coast, and had dropped us here. Outside a hotel that looked like the kind of place Richard Branson might hang out in. Or own.

'Are you sure about this?'

'I've never been surer about anything.'

'It'll be a bloody fortune.' Twenty yards away, on a wide verandah, a couple of waiters in crisp white uniforms were delivering drinks to two affluent-looking middle-aged women in linen dresses and Joan Crawford hats. 'I'll pay my share.'

'You fucking well won't, so don't even start. I know you're Lady Muck these days, but this is *my* treat. Well, *treat* isn't really the word, is it, when I've dragged you half way round the world to witness a daft queen having his heart ripped out. *Reward. Thanks. Payment.* Whatever we call it, it's going on *my* credit card, not yours. Right?'

I kissed him on the cheek. 'Alright.'

The evening was delightfully cool and, after a shower and a change of clothes, Will and I were sipping dry martinis on the verandah. I hadn't asked for an account of his painful conversation with Kavi, but he felt he had a duty to fill me in.

'He still loves me.'

'Of course he does.'

'But family is hugely important to him. I've always known that. It's one of the things I love about him.'

'He's a good guy.'

'He is. The trouble is, she's dying. His mother.' Will teared up.

'Oh, god. I'm so sorry.'

'I know. And I so want to be there for him. And he wants that, too. Really. But he knows it can't be like that. He can't have what he wants. Because, here, he can't *be* what he is.'

'I get that. Crazy though it is. It's just the culture. And he has to accept that. For the sake of his family.'

'His family is pretty ... traditional. Asha was freaked out by me. I tried to ... pretend that I was just his friend. A pal. Someone he has a pint with, you know. Watches the cricket with. All that blokey bollocks. But she knows what her brother is – although she can't say it – and she'd got my card marked from the moment I opened my mouth. We danced around the truth together, but we both knew the score. She was pretty reluctant to give me the address. But I persuaded her.'

'How?'

'By crying like a demented Harry Hoofter all over her workplace. She gave me the address just to shut me up.'

I smiled. 'So ... what did he say?'

Will looked at the floor. 'He has to make a choice. Between what he wants, and what his family needs.'

'God. That's a hell of a sacrifice. And a very noble one.'

'He's a good guy.'

'And what about ... I can't say this without sounding like the world's most heartless bitch ... after his mum's gone. Can't he come back? Won't he?'

'His dad will need him. Asha works. And Kavi doesn't want her to give that up – that's the one thing he's put his foot down over, that his sister won't simply give up her career in hospitality and become her dad's carer – so he's stepping in. Turning his back on everything else – me included – so he can do the right thing by his family.'

'It's incredibly honourable. But also incredibly sad.'

'It's much, much worse for him.' Will downed his martini. 'So I should stop behaving like a stupid fairy and accept that life's pretty shit sometimes for me, but for others it is monumentally shit. But for the next seventy-two hours, it's going to be fucking wonderful.'

And he beckoned a waiter over and ordered two more martinis.

***

'Please take off clothes, mam.'

I was in the shiny Ayurvedic Massage Centre within the sumptuous grounds of the Guruvayar Hotel.

I pulled off my sandals and my turquoise linen skirt and my white linen blouse. Then, not without sheepishness, I slipped off my bra.

'Everything, mam.'

'My panties as well?'

She nodded. 'Yes. Panties, too.' She handed me what looked like a cross between a panty liner and a nappy. 'And please put this on.'

I had no way of knowing which way round it went and awkwardly applied it to my crotch, thankful that my pubic area had completely recovered from Kate's ministrations of a few months ago.

My masseuse giggled. 'Sorry, mam. Wrong way.' And she carefully removed it and, with great delicatesse, slipped it on the right way. Then she opened a door and ushered me into a stone-floored room with, in the centre, a wooden bedlike structure with a built-in metal slab (I had an image of a butcher's block and me as a side of beef) and, in the corner, a wooden cabinet about as tall as my waist. And a stool.

She invited me to sit on the stool. Then she left the room. I looked around and wondered what would happen next.

She returned with a large brass teapot. She lifted it high above my head and released a stream of hot fragrant oil that hit me squarely in the middle of the scalp and ran down the sides of my face. Then she pulled the hot oil through my hair until my whole head was completely saturated.

The following ten minutes were given over to the most vigorous head massage I've ever had. Well, okay – the only head massages I'd ever previously had were the pseudy, fakey ones you get at the hairdresser's. My stylist in Southsea – Gareth – had a nineteen-year-old assistant in a black beauty tunic who'd done a day's massage course at a college in Portsmouth and who, by virtue of a soft voice, a pretty face, and a couple of scented candles, always made you feel relaxed and pampered.

This was very different. Ayurvedic medicine (Google had told me the night before) is based on the theory that your body contains 108 vital points – called marmas – which, when stimulated, give your body's natural healing abilities a bit of a boot up the backside. There are six types of vital points in your head. And I can tell you that my masseuse didn't just track them down – she threw them into an interview room and treated them to a full-on inquisition, with all the desk-slamming, spotlight-in-the-eyes stuff you see in the crime dramas on the telly. Then she hauled them into a torture chamber and treated them to a spot of casual waterboarding.

After a ten-minute, full-on pasting by this woman's stainless steel fingertips, my head felt like it had come unscrewed.

Then this tiny lady with the sinewy forearms bade me lie down on the butcher's slab.

'Now you must relax,' she said, then she left the room.

It sounded like an instruction. Because I didn't want another head-pasting if I stepped out of line, I complied, meekly.

I took a deep breath, closed my eyes, and conjured up an image of the beach in Northumberland I always go to in my head when dark thoughts crowd in at night and sleep seems like it'll never come.

And a wonderful thing happened. My head suddenly felt like it was phenomenally, tinglingly alive. It also felt weightless, like it was floating a couple of inches above my shoulders. It was at once real and surreal, and slightly scary but also strangely uplifting. I lay there with a wonderfully disembodied head for several minutes.

Then my tiny torturess came back into the room, poured oil from the brass teapot all over my body, and went to work again, for about half an hour, on every inch of my pasty frame – kneading, pulling, squeezing, pummelling. At the end of which I felt fabulous. Clean, fresh, alive.

Then she walked over to the wooden cabinet and, in the manner of a bikini-clad 1980s game show hostess, gestured towards it as if it were a prize I might be lucky enough to win if I played my cards right.

Inside the cabinet was another stool, onto which I plonked my bottom. There was a hose feeding into the cabinet and, as she closed the cabinet door, I traced it with my eyes and saw that it led to a little mechanical contraption I assumed was a pump of some sort.

With the cabinet door closed, and just my head sticking out, I imagined I looked like a rather moist and dishevelled Debbie McGee in that moment before Paul Daniels saws her in half or makes her disappear.

The pump thing sprang to life and, within seconds, had filled the cabinet with hot, fragrant steam.

Right. This is a steam bath.

Wisps of the steam escaped upwards and curled round my nose and I tried to identify the scent.

'Is that turmeric?'

She nodded. 'Haldee. Yes.'

'You put the powder into water?' I had visions of my body looking like a generous helping of chicken tikka masala.

'Not powder. Oil.'

'Right.' The tikka masala image faded a little but didn't completely go away. I closed my eyes and once again strolled along my Northumbrian beach (which had now sprouted a stall selling Indian street food).

I must have dozed off because the next thing I knew, she was opening the cabinet door and gesturing for me to step out. I checked my legs for tikka masala and was relieved to see they looked every bit as pasty as usual, if now a little pink and sweaty. My arms looked the same.

My new guru smiled. 'Good?'

I took a second to check in with my body. 'Yes, actually. Very good.'

She seemed amused by my surprise. 'Yes. Of course. We do this for thousands of years. We know.'

'Yes.'

A country that devotes thousands of years to learning stuff that makes people feel good.

I was slowly falling in love with India.

My body had been a temple all day. So it seemed entirely necessary that I trashed it at night with a couple of pre-dinner cocktails.

Will had spent my ayurvedic hours doing yoga on some other part of the estate and I hadn't seen him since breakfast. But we'd texted at lunchtime ('Fucking knackered. And we've only done the gentle stuff. This afternoon we're doing the FLOW. Sounds intense. I'm shitting bricks.') and arranged to meet on the verandah at six. It was now gone half past and no Will. I'd need to call him. But first I called David.

Half six in the evening in India is eight in the morning in New York and David was just getting into the office. I told him about my day's exertions.

'And you enjoyed it?'

'Not at the time. It all felt like a bit of an assault. But it's left me feeling light. And sort of new.'

'Don't get too new. I really liked the old you.'

'Don't worry. We're back on the martinis. I say 'we' but I have no idea where Will's got to. I might have to drink his martini as well. Out of politeness to the barman.'

'I think you absolutely should. How is he? Will, not the barman.'

'He's alright. He was a bit of a mess yesterday – it's a very big deal, losing someone you love and who you've been with for years – but he gets it. And he's the epitome of a trouper, so he's putting a very brave face on.'

At that moment, Will appeared on the verandah with a face that looked anything but brave.

'And in fact, here he is, looking like a day of yoga has been excruciatingly painful.'

'Right. I'll let you go. Say hi to Will. And tell him to look after my very precious princess.'

'Princess of Thornhill. Hm. Quite like that title.'

'I think all that steam has gone to your head.'

'Never. Goodbye, my love.'

Will walked over to the table with the gait of a cowboy who's lost his horse and I couldn't resist a smile.

'Yoga sorted you out, then?'

'It did, yeah.'

'You look like you can hardly walk. I reckon you'll be pretty stiff in the morning.'

He lowered himself carefully into the wicker armchair opposite me.

'I'm always stiff in the morning.'

'I'm talking about your legs. Not your wedding tackle, smut boy.'

'My legs aren't stiff.'

'You could have fooled me. You're walking like the Lone Ranger after a long day in the saddle.'

'That's not from the yoga.'

'What's it from, then?'

Will looked sheepish. 'The yoga sort of bucked me up a bit – I mean, it was knackering at the time, but it left me feeling …'

'Light. New.'

'Yes. Exactly.'

'Me too. After the massage and steam thing.'

'And I decided this was the new me. A fresh start. So I decided to give myself a bit of a tidy-up.' I looked at his hair. 'No, not up there.' He looked at his trousers. 'Down there.'

I gave him a sidelong glance. 'Right. What did you do?'

'Well, I met this woman. In the yoga class. Leonora. Pushing sixty but looks fabulous. Great tits. Nearly as good as yours.'

'Stop flannelling and tell me what you've done.'

'She's from Guildford but she lives in Dubai – her husband's a lawyer for one of the sheikhs, so they're stinking rich – and she comes over here once a month with a bunch of girlfriends and they do the whole detox thing during the day, then live it up a bit at night. And while she's here, she hooks up with her lover, Ramon.'

'What?'

'He's a personal trainer on the estate. Thirty-five. Bloody gorgeous – she pointed him out at lunchtime. They're very discreet during the day. All very businesslike. Then, every night she's here, they go at it like rabbits.'

'Does her husband know?'

'Has no idea. But she goes back to Dubai feeling refreshed and satisfied but also proper sexed-up, so hubby gets a good seeing-to for a few days, and everyone's happy.'

'No. Couldn't do it.'

'I know what you mean. But it works for them.'

'No. She's lying to her husband.'

'Sort of.'

'Not sort of. Outright. I don't like her. Anyway, what's this got to do with your … tidy-up?'

'Well, one of the things she gets done while she's here is a pubic wax. The full Brazilian. Ramon likes … a clear runway. And her husband doesn't mind it, either.'

'Right.' I was really hating this Leonora woman.

'And they *will* do it for men. Here. But I didn't fancy putting … myself … in some other man's hands.'

'I get that.'

'So Leonora gave me this cream.'

'It's not Veet, is it?'

'How did you know?'

'You've put Veet on your nuts? Are you mad?!'

'It's actually fine on your nuts. Nice and warm, actually.'

'I'm sure it is. Women use Veet on their legs, you dingbat!'

'I didn't know that. Anyway, I sort of slapped it on a bit. And some of it went on … places it shouldn't have. Tender places. And I panicked and tried to wipe it off. But I'd got the cream all over my hands and the wiping just made it worse.'

'You are a monumental twonk.'

'I've had to go commando.'

'Will, I know we're very good friends, but …'

'Too much information?'

'It's *all* been too much information. And I want to throttle that Leonora bitch. Her and her bloody clear runway.'

'She's actually very nice.'

'She's actually an adulterous slag.'

'You're very … principled, aren't you?'

'I am a princess. Princesses need to be principled. It's in the job description.'

'Listen at you, Lady Bloody Muck.'

'Shut up and drink your martini. We're in India and I want to get shitfaced with my best friend.'

28

A Bit of a Blow

As he stood by the steps of his coach at Heathrow Central Bus Station, Will was beginning to look human again.

'Seven days jetting round the world with you has just about killed me.'

'It's your own fault for being such an impetuous old queen. Dragging us off to India at a bloody moment's notice.'

'How come you look so fresh? I feel like I've been dragged through a hedge backwards. About thirty-seven times. By an angry, homophobic bull.'

'I'm just naturally gorgeous.'

The truth was, I'd spent half an hour – mostly over Turkey, according to the screen in the toilet – with my head down an Air India pan, revisiting the six or seven very dry martinis the barman at the Guruvayar had forced me to throw down the night before. Then another ten minutes repairing the damage the experience had wrought on my face.

Such that quite a queue had formed by the time I opened the door. And the quiet desperation of standing with his legs crossed while some hungover old tart evacuates her stomach at length had given the face of the man at the front of the queue more than a hint of serial killer. I'd given him my best winning smile and blamed the in-flight biryani.

And now here I was saying goodbye to a best friend working hard not to look like he'd had his heart ripped out.

'You're a crafty cow, is what you are.' Then the mask of flippancy fell from Will's face and he stepped forward and gripped me in a tight embrace and I felt his chest heave with the tears he was working hard to contain.

'You *will* be fine. He loves you. You can take a lot of comfort from that. And he always will. But the world is full of lovely people and you'll find another one. Who also loves you. You know the saying, It's better to have loved and lost than never to have loved at all. I can't remember who said it …'

'Some clown who'd never had his heart trampled on.'

'It's true, though. We have to believe that. And if you've felt that once, you can feel it again. Trust me. I know whereof I speak.'

'Give it a rest with the bloody Shakespeare bollocks.'

I kissed him on the cheek. 'Just know that you'll be fine. And that you can call me whenever you need to. At any time. Day or night.'

'Thanks. I'm sorry.'

'Shut up. It's been great. We saw an elephant. Just there.'

'That *was* cool.'

'It was. Now go. And know I love you like a fat kid loves cake.'

And he climbed aboard the bus and with a hydraulic swish and a wave, he was gone.

***

When I dropped my bags in the hall, the house was deathly quiet.

Luther and Woodbine came over to greet me, Luther with his customary warm restraint and Woodbine with his manic enthusiasm. They followed me through to a kitchen that was deserted – Marius was an early riser and an early bedder – but full of gorgeous cooking aromas, emanating from a large casserole he'd loaded into the Aga's simmering oven to let it work its magic overnight.

I wanted to lift the lid and take a peek at tomorrow's delights but I knew he'd know I'd looked and I didn't fancy being hauled out of bed at dawn and marched out into the walled garden to face a Romanian firing squad.

The fridge always held plenty of delights, though, and I found a couple of roast chicken thighs that looked like leftovers from Miranda's previous day's labours and I checked in with my stomach to see if it was up for a snack after its inflight exertions. I decided to risk it, plonked one of the thighs onto a plate, and made my way along the corridor, across the hall and into the sitting room.

Where I found Miranda stretched out on one of the sofas, a gin at her elbow.

'Sorry, I didn't hear you come in. How was the flight?'

'Fine, mostly.' And I told the tale of my extended occupation of the bathroom. 'So things here have been fine?'

'Yeah, great. No problem. This week's clients seem like a very nice bunch, on the whole. One of them, a nice-enough guy who works in marketing for Bloomsbury Publishing – the Harry Potter people – keeps asking me about my personal life and I'm quite close to putting him in his place, but I don't want to make a fuss in front of the others.'

'Do you want me to have a word?'

'No. I'll handle it myself, if I have to.'

'So he fancies you?'

'I guess. Which is sort of nice – he's a perfectly nice-looking bloke – but it's a bit awkward and it feels unprofessional.'

'No, you're right. We can't have that. Is it harassment?'

'I'm not sure I'd say that. Don't worry. If he makes any more comments, I'll pull him to one side and shut it down with a verbal knee to the balls. He's only about twenty-seven.'

'You've still got it, then. Nice. How about Nat? Where is she, actually? I texted her at Heathrow but she hasn't come back to me.' Miranda looked at the floor and I knew something had happened. It always bloody well does. 'What's she been up to?'

'She's been cosying up to Robbie a fair bit.'

'I told her to back off. She was making those noises before I left. I thought she'd got the message.'

'I think she can't help herself. And he's clearly not keen.'

'I told her that. She'd frighten the bloody life out of him.'

'But he's been very polite about it.'

'Of course. He's an absolute gentleman. As I feckin' well told her.'

'But, at lunchtime, she was moping about the place looking like a wounded princess. Then later I saw her climb into a taxi – about sevenish – and go off somewhere. I don't know where.'

'Has she left? Did she have bags?'

'No. More like out for the evening.'

'Bugger!'

Then my phone buzzed into life and Nat's name flashed up. 'Where are you?'

A sibilant male voice replied. Cameron, the barman from The Queens, the pub outside Chipping Norton that was becoming a Thornhill local.

'Jen? We've got your friend Nat here. She's a bit the worse for wear.'

'Right. I'm on my way.'

Nat was sprawled at the far corner of the bar, cradling her head with the one arm she had on the bar and, with her other hand, waving a tall white drink with a slice of pineapple in it. She was holding forth to an uncomfortable-looking Arthur and Tom, in the manner of a local councillor just getting into her stride on election night.

'This, you see, is the whole problem. All the good men are either gay …' she waved her drink at an amused-looking Cameron, who was slipping her phone back into her handbag. '… or old enough to be my father. Not that age bothers me …' Arthur leaned back a couple of inches. '… in fact, my ex-husband, who was more than a little bit of a bastard, was almost twenty years older than me.'

I put my hand on her shoulder. 'Come on, Nat. Let's get you back to the house.'

She spun round, spilling some of her drink onto my shoes. She blinked hard, twice, and the expression *one over the eighteen* popped into my head.

'JEN! You're BACK!' And she threw her arms round my neck. How was INDIA?' She said the last word like it had about thirteen syllables.

'It's late, Nat. Let's get you home.'

Her face slid from elation to dejection in a nanosecond and she crumpled. 'Home. Where *is* home? Where's *my* home? Cowley? That's *not* my home. It can't be. It's got COW in the name. But that's what I am, isn't it? I'm a cow. A stupid cow. Who always picks the wrong men. They're either gay or they're ancient or they live with their mothers or they're fucking ARTISTS ...'

'You're not stupid. You're just a bit drunk.'

'DRUNK?! I've only had a couple of pina coladas.' Over her shoulder, Cameron held up seven fingers. 'And I haven't finished talking to these old men.' She spun round alarmingly quickly and waved her drink at Arthur and Tom. 'Forgive me. I didn't mean to offend you.'

Arthur, looking sober(ish) in comparison to Nat, leaned back on his stool another couple of inches. 'No offence taken, young lady.'

Nat spun round again to face me, her emotions melting. 'See. See, Jen. These lovely old men here are ... well, we're having a lovely conversation. Lovely.'

'I know. But it's late. These gentlemen are leaving now anyway ...' I glared at Arthur and Tom and they jumped to attention and nodded and drained their pints. '... and we can come back some other time and carry on your lovely conversation. Let's go.'

And with a firm, schoolmarmish hand, I pulled her upright, clamped her arm in mine, and steered her towards the car park and my waiting green Defender.

The road from Chipping Norton to Thornhill isn't exactly thronging with traffic. I'm guessing the police in this part of the world have very little to do other than watch out for the odd wayward airman from nearby Brize Norton who, turning his back on the generously subsidised bar at the airbase Mess, has chosen to break free and rub shoulders with the civilian riff-raff, believing that extra pint of Brakspear will slip under the radar.

So any chance to pounce on a misdemeanour is gratefully accepted.

And when we zigzagged past a police car stationed in a discreet layby on the B4477, with Nat visibly wrestling me for control of the radio, I knew we'd soon be seeing flashing lights.

The officer looked about twelve.

'I noticed you were driving … erratically.'

'My friend is a little frisky this evening, so I'm taking her home.'

Nat leered at the young lad in the uniform and tried her inebriated best to sound like a vixen. 'Frisky.'

The young bobby looked past her and spoke to me. 'What about you, madam? Have you been drinking?'

Nat answered for me. 'No, she hasn't! How dare you! She's a very …' Nat had a bash at framing the word *responsible* but the Ps and the Ss were tripping over each other. '… good … person. She would never, NEVER …'

'Just let your friend answer, madam.'

'I am NOT a madam. I am a MISS.'

'I need the driver to answer me.'

'No, I haven't been drinking. But I had a call from a friend asking me to come and get her …'

At which Nat glared at me, outraged. 'A call? From whooooom, may I ask?' I looked past her.

'… which I've done. She's a little reluctant, as you can see.'

The young officer walked round to my window and fitted a mouthpiece into the breathalyzer he was holding. 'I'd like you to breathe into this for me.'

Outrage again from Nat. 'How DARE you?!'

I held up my hand to placate her. 'It's fine. Yes, of course.'

But Nat was not for backing down. 'You don't have to do it, you know. They can't make you.'

The young officer was struggling to keep his patience in check. 'Your friend is right. But failure to co-operate with a preliminary breath alcohol test is an offence under section 6A of the Road Traffic Act 1988.'

'It's fine. I'm happy to take the test.' A wave of panic passed over me as I thought of the gallons of Indian martinis I'd imbibed over the previous week. I leaned forward to take the test, praying every single milligram of the alcohol that *had* been in my bloodstream several hours earlier was now part of the cloudscape above Turkey and none of it was still lurking inside my (suddenly rather queasy) system.

The officer was silent for several seconds, while he looked at his gizmo.

Then he turned unsmiling eyes on me. 'That's fine. Thank you. You're free to go.'

Nat leapt back onto her high horse. 'FREE?! Of course we're FREE! This isn't a police state!'

I glared at her. 'You need to shut up now. Okay?'

Nat crumpled in her seat and instantly became a chastised child. I turned back to the young officer.

'Thank you. Sorry to have bothered you.'

He smiled. 'No problem.'

29

Flaming Red Hair

'You don't have to go today.'

Nat was standing in the hall with her bags packed and a taxi at the door. 'I do. I've abused your kindness too much already. Again. I'm really sorry about last night.'

'It's fine. We all go a bit bonkers from time to time.'

'Come on. With me, bonkers goes with the territory.'

'You *are* a bit left-field sometimes. It keeps me on my toes. But, seriously, stay for a few more days.'

'No. Thanks. I'm ready to go now. Plus, there's a big exhibition on next week at the gallery and they need me now. You should come. Might be good for your business here.'

The exhibition was called *Lovers*.

The gallery was one of those modern joints with white walls and stripped floors and about five hundred cubic feet per tiny exhibit. No plush carpets or red velvet ropes or retired men in peaked caps stationed on chairs at each doorway.

Ursula Ward-Black was, the catalogue told me, 'one of the foremost female practitioners of Neo-avantgarde', an artist whose work is 'intensely subjective' (which sounded like shorthand for *Most people think this stuff is shit*). This 'major retrospective' had been mounted to coincide with the artist's sixtieth birthday.

Nat was looking sleek (and sober) in beige canvas slacks and a breast-hugging white linen blouse. She looked like an advert for the French Riviera.

She and her boss, Jocasta (why do these places never have a manager called *Sharon*?) were dancing attendance on a shapely vamp wearing half a dress and what looked like Bono's sunspecs – the latest round ones with the purple lenses. Their violet tones struck a discordant note butting up against a long fringe on a head of hair that was bright red. Not ginger or auburn or strawberry blonde. Actual red. Scarlet. The colour of the Swiss flag. Or Postman Pat's van.

The artist herself, I assumed.

If so, she was in very good nick for an old bird. I wondered what punishing dietary regime was responsible for the tight waist and the razor-sharp jawline. Maybe she was just getting all her vitamins. Or getting some she shouldn't.

Nat was clearly going to be far too busy ministering to the star attraction to spend any time with me and, as a networking opportunity, this seemed about as much use as sitting at the side of the A40 throwing business cards at the windscreens of speeding trucks.

But I was here now and I thought I might as well have a smoked salmon canapé and a gander at the world of the Neo-avantgarde.

I like to think of myself as broad-minded. Liberal. Open to new things.

I'm not.

Exhibit 34 – called 'Untitled' – seemed to consist of an old jam jar containing a clump of what looked disconcertingly like pubic hair.

A thin-waisted young man wearing a black roll-neck sweater (*Aren't you boiling?*) and an earnest expression appeared at my shoulder.

'It's about provocation.'
Don't you just love a mansplainer?
'Is it?'

'Yes. That's the whole thesis of the Neo-avantgarde.'

'Their *thesis*?'

'Yes. You see, they eschew traditional paradigms of newness. For them, it's not enough simply to hold our hands and drag us in front of something new.'

'I see.'

'No. They want to provoke us.'

I took a deep breath and held his eyes with a steady gaze.

'Are you yourself one of the exhibits?'

'Sorry?'

'Because that's what you're doing. Right now.'

'I don't …'

'They want to inspire anger, hatred, resentment.'

'Well …'

'Like you're doing. By assuming – based on what? That I'm a woman? That I'm middle-aged? That I look 'bourgeois'? – by assuming that I know nothing about the Neo-avantgarde movement. And that I need, or indeed welcome, your intervention. Your enlightenment. And I therefore conclude that you are yourself an exhibit. That you are intending to provoke a response.' I smiled a cherubic smile.

'Er, no. I simply thought …'

'That I'd find your insights fascinating.'

'I didn't mean to …'

'Insult me. Patronise me.'

'No. I mean, Yes. I didn't …'

'Think. You didn't think. Like a lot of men who are a bit clever, who've read a couple of books, and who've spent time in the company of dim, meek, easily impressed young women who treat their every word like manna from heaven, you see *every* woman as a willing audience. As a springboard for your fragile ego.'

I must have been raising my voice. Half a dozen heads were turned our way. A young woman with dyed black hair, a nose piercing, and an armful of tattoos was enjoying the show.

'So here's a new thesis for you. A young man with a penchant for patronising bollocks should take his Beat Generation wardrobe, his twenty-eight-inch waist, and his desperate need for affirmation, and shove them where the sun never shines.'

The poor lad looked like I'd hit him squarely in the face with a sledgehammer.

He glanced around the room, suddenly aware that he had, indeed, become an unintended exhibit and, robbed of the power of speech (what a new sensation *that* must have been), he turned on his heel and marched out of the room.

The pierced and tattooed young woman appeared at my side and leaned in, conspiratorial.

'That was fucking brilliant. Thank you.'

'What for?'

'For making my day. It's been worth putting up with a couple of hours of pretentious bollocks to witness two minutes of absolute bullshit-busting gold.' She held out her hand. 'I'm Sharon.'

I smiled at the name. 'Jennifer.'

'It's been an absolute pleasure, Jennifer.' She was about to walk away, then stopped herself.' Have you seen those bracelets dozy Christians wear? With WWJD printed on them? *What Would Jesus Do?* To prompt the God-botherers to think about to how to handle a situation?'

'No. I've never heard of them.'

'You should bring out your own range. *What Would Jennifer Do?* That's my new mantra. You're a fucking inspiration.' She stretched her head towards me, kissed me on the cheek, then headed for the door.

When I looked round, Nat was walking towards me, with Jocasta and the birthday girl. Nat swept her hand towards me.

'This is my friend, Jennifer.'

Bono's sister held out her hand and I shook it and she smiled a celebrity smile. 'Delighted to meet you. Do you know my work?'

'No.'

Jocasta looked mildly alarmed. Ursula herself looked a mixture of crestfallen and irritated. 'Oh. Never mind.'

'But I gather it's about provoking a response.'

'All art is. Or should be, I think.'

'*Any* response?'

'As artists, I don't think we can control how people will respond to our work. As long as they do respond. In some way.'

'They can't *not* respond, can they?'

'If the art is … valid, no, I don't think they can. They must respond.'

'What I mean is, let's say I paint a picture of kittens. And people – artsy, fashionable people – are, let's say, *bored* by it. Or they laugh at it. Or they look down their noses at it. That's a response. They're responding.'

'In a way.'

'Right. So, are only certain responses – to use your word – valid?'
Jocasta shuffled her feet and looked at Nat.

Ursula – give her her due – didn't bat an eyelid. Metaphorically. I couldn't see her actual eyelids behind the Bono specs and the red fringe. 'Well, I think it's more interesting if the response is … complex. Mature. Informed.'

'Isn't that a bit of a shame? If ordinary people can't respond? Or if their responses don't count?'

'What do you mean by *ordinary* people?'

'People who haven't been to university. People who watch *Pointless*. People who buy a framed Van Gogh print because the colour of the sunflowers matches their couch.'

A young man in a black T-shirt appeared in the corner of the room carrying a huge cake covered in burning candles and Jocasta scurried over to take charge of this point in the proceedings.

'Well, I think perhaps different forms of art appeal to different types of people.'

'And who is a jam jar full of pubic hair intended to appeal to? What *type* of person?'

Ursula let that question hang in the air for a couple of seconds. I was getting her back up now.

'Well, not the type of person *you* are, clearly.'

Jocasta had coached the assembled company into a halting rendition of *Happy Birthday* and Ursula turned away to accept their adoration.

This foremost female practitioner of the Neo-avantgarde bent down to blow out her sixty candles. Sixty very *long* candles.

It took the room a second or two to register the fact that Ursula's hair really was on fire. A stunned Jocasta hopped around on the spot for a second, frantically scanning the room for a solution to this burning emergency. A man in a voluminous scarf (*Aren't you boiling as well?*) started to unwind it from his neck.

But I beat him to it.

In situations like these, swift action is the only answer.

The clear glass jug on the table at my side probably contained two litres. By the time I'd finished, it contained about two *milli*litres. Quite a lot of the water had soaked into Ursula's hair and her skimpy dress. The rest was dripping from her scarlet fringe and from Bono's glasses and was running down the valley between her unreasonably perky breasts.

But I'd put her fire out. Well and truly.

30

Old Wounds

The odd weekend hospitality booking was now dovetailing nicely with the Monday-to-Friday cookery school side of the business.

For a couple of months we'd been marketing The Pavilion as a venue for parties and other gatherings and business was, encouragingly, beginning to take off.

So far, we'd hosted a fiftieth birthday party and some sort of awards ceremony for the Oxfordshire and Gloucestershire Young Farmers' Association (more tweed and check and corduroy than you can shake a stick at).

But our core Pavilion business was looking like it would be the hen party (although the classier gatherings were always quick to point out they preferred other labels: *ladies' night* and its American cousins *wedding shower* and *bachelorette party*).

And The Pavilion was big enough to offer overnight accommodation for smaller gatherings of a dozen or so, for the complete hen weekend package.

Most of the business came from Oxfordshire and Gloucestershire but smaller groups looking for accommodation were happy to travel from quite far afield.

So when we got a hen weekend booking from a Barbara Cooper from Portsmouth, my old stomping ground a couple of hours' drive away, I wasn't surprised in the least.

The ladies arrived around six on the Friday evening, in customary high spirits. Some of them were a little older than our standard hen weekend clients – around my age, I'd have said – but there were a few youngsters in the party to keep the energy levels high.

And from casual chat over a welcome glass of champagne, I gleaned this was Barbara's fourth go at matrimony. It didn't look like the patchy track record was doing her any harm, nor indeed did it appear to have taken the shine off the prospect of throwing on a nice frock and doing it all again. And her friends, all of whom wore gold bands, were clearly up for making this a weekend to remember.

The booking had been made sight unseen and Barbara was clearly delighted with the venue and the surroundings.

'Such a gorgeous place!'

'I'm glad you like it. We specialise in informal luxury.'

'That's exactly what I'd hoped for. It's nice to be comfortable but I hate those places where the staff hover, ready to top up your glass or whatever.'

'Well, rest assured – nobody here will hover. The Pavilion is yours for the weekend and nobody will disturb you. We'll welcome you into the dining room in the main house for breakfast and dinner. And you'll have exclusive access to the Orangery for afternoon tea if you wish – just let me know in the morning – and of course feel free to explore the estate.'

'Sounds wonderful.'

'Now you're all here, I'll just go through a few bits of safety information …'

'Oh, there's one still to arrive.'

'No problem.' I pointed to the phone by the sitting room door. 'Just buzz me when she's here and I'll …'

Barbara looked past me through the window. 'In fact, here she is.'

I turned. And the sight set my heart racing.

A red sports car.

Don't be silly. There are thousands of little red sports cars. What are the chances?

The driver's door opened and a pair of willowy legs stepped out onto the gravel. A size-ten figure. But no – the hair was different. It wasn't her.

Hang on. What had Will said? No longer blonde, but 'fairish.'

The size-ten figure approached the door and Barbara opened it and stepped outside to greet her good friend.

Bloody Bitch Bronwyn. BBB.

The bimbo who'd turned Pete's head. Who he'd sent secret texts to. Who I'd bawled down the phone at in the middle of the night, in a vodka-fuelled rant. Who he'd dumped me for later that night.

His cruel words were still burned into my memory.

Can you blame me? With your saggy arse and your roots showing and stinking of bloody vodka. You're pathetic.

I could still conjure up the image – my reflection in the hall mirror, the last drops of my dignity lying in the bottom of the glass I'd dropped on the floor.

And here she was. My guest.

How the hell was I going to play this?

The party tumbled back into the Pavilion's sitting room in a melée of hugs and kisses on the cheek. I stepped forward with my hand outstretched.

'Welcome to Thornhill.'

Bronwyn – BBB – smiled and took my hand. 'Thank you. What a lovely place!'

Barbara waved an arm around the room. 'Isn't it? Space. Luxury. Champagne. What's not to like!'

Bronwyn smiled at Barbara. 'Sounds perfect. Great choice.'

Well, if she recognised me, she was hiding it extremely well. Perhaps I was unrecognisable. Perhaps everything I'd gone through these past four years had made my transformation complete.

I pasted on as much business cool as I could muster and ran quickly through the safety brief before taking my leave.

'Well, I'll give you space to settle in. As I say, just pick up the phone if you need anything. Otherwise, we'll see you over at the house for dinner. Is eight o'clock still okay?'

Barbara consulted the party with her eyes and there were nods and murmurs of assent.

'Great. We'll see you then. And there's a second bottle of champagne in the fridge in your little kitchen.'

Over in the big kitchen, Miranda was prepping dinner for our hens (Marius had asked for a night off to try out a Krav Maga class in Witney). But her main job at the moment was trying to calm me down.

'It doesn't sound like she's made the connection. But even if she has, you have the upper hand here. Look at this place. You don't just run it, you bloody well *own* it! How big a trump card is *that*?!'

'You're right. You're right. I'm being stupid.'

'You are.'

'But she still got the guy.'

'No, she didn't. *You* got *the* guy. She got some washed-up, treacherous, paunchy old gardener.'

'Landscaper.'

'Whatever. He still digs dirt for a living. And you run half of Oxfordshire. And you're happy. With your life. With your man. You win.'

'I behaved badly. Very badly.'

'With very good reason. He was – probably still is – a complete shit. And the way he behaved was enough to send anyone a bit bonkers. We're all allowed – *you're* allowed – to go a bit mental from time to time. Relax.'

'I'll try.'

'Good. Now for God's sake stir this soup while I check my tarts.'

Dinner was a strange affair.

Superficially, everything passed off very well. Miranda's food – an autumn squash soup, nutty rose tarts with a spelt flour base, a melt-in-the-mouth slow-roasted lamb with cinnamon and baked fennel, and caramel apple crumble pots to finish – was consumed with relish and gusto and Delyth and I waited the table and made sure the wine kept flowing (with the main course, my mid-range Pomerol that the party ordered four of at £45 a pop).

But Bronwyn, seated next to uber-hen Barbara, seemed very subdued. Nobody else noticed – Barbara was far too busy giving chapter and verse on her outfit to anyone who would listen – but every time I glanced at Bronwyn, it was clear she wasn't really in the room.

At dessert, I was filling up her glass with a 2011 Château Monbazillac and she turned and held my gaze for three or four silent seconds. Not in an aggressive or threatening or confrontational way. If anything, the look was more one of sorrow. Melancholy.

I suggested coffee, cognac and Miranda's delicious armagnac truffles in the library, where Delyth had made a roaring log fire, and the party trooped through with delight – all laughter and sparkling eyes.

All except Bronwyn.

And when, after more cognacs and a few rounds of Who Am I with Post-It notes stuck on the forehead, the group staggered to their feet and thanked me for what I have to admit had been a fine evening indeed, Bronwyn hung back, glued to one of the leather Chesterfield couches.

I walked over with the decanter.

'More cognac?'

She looked up at me with glistening eyes.

'I didn't get it.'

'Sorry?'

'I didn't understand. The pain. *Your* pain. I understand it now.'

A tear rolled down her cheek. I sat down beside her.

'I didn't think you'd recognised me.'

She wiped her eyes. 'I didn't at first. You seem so … different. In a different world. This faraway world. Then it came to me. At dinner. You do a thing with your hair – tucking it behind your ear with one finger. And I remembered where I'd seen it before. And it all came back. What I'd done.' And the tears came again.

'It's fine. I'm fine. Really. All's fair and all that.'

She wiped mascara off her cheek. 'It's not, though. Fine. Or fair. It's shitty. I was shitty. Am shitty.'

'Well, it did feel very shitty at the time. But that was a different time. Very different. And I'm different. I'm over it.'

'I wish I had your strength. Because I'm not. Over it.'

'What do you mean?'

'It's my turn now. To be the Wronged Woman.' I must have looked blank. 'Because he's done it again. Moved on to a different model.' The floodgates opened and she buried her head in her hands.

Half an hour ago, I couldn't have imagined I'd be doing this, but I put my arm around her shoulders. Then she turned towards me, threw both her arms round my neck, buried her head in my shoulder, and sobbed.

We sat like that for perhaps thirty seconds, before she pulled away.

'I'm sorry.'

'Thank you. But it's okay.'

'You're amazing.'

'I'm really not. It took a long time to recover. But I have. And I had the support of very good friends.'

'Good. I'm glad.'

'How old is she? This one.'

'Oh, I don't think it's an age thing. She's actually a couple of years older than me – I've done the whole Facebook stalking thing; I'm such a cliché – but it's just …' Bronwyn's eyes began to fill with tears again but she mastered herself. 'I think he just likes a change.' She wiped her eyes.

'He's a child. A big kid.'

'I think that's part of it. He just wants to know that he's still attractive. Generally. He needs to prove it to himself. And his way of doing that is to …' She smiled a rueful smile. '… shop around.' She took a deep breath. 'God! I feel so stupid. And so shitty, to be talking about this to you, of all people.'

'It's fine. And you're not stupid. And neither am I. This is not on us. Either of us. It's on him.'

'Why do men do that? Behave like bastards.'

'Not all men do. But some men are definitely one-hundred-percent, cast-iron, gilt-edged wankers.'

'They are. Wankers.' Bronwyn's face took on a look of mischief. 'That's more or less the message his neighbours will see, next spring, when the crocuses I've planted come up.'

'How d'you mean?'

'I bought three hundred bulbs and one of those planters that cuts out discs of turf. And planted them in his front lawn. Stayed up all night doing it while he was away. And carefully arranged them so that, in a burst of springtime colour, they'll spell out the word TOSSER.'

I was impressed. 'That is one hell of a revenge.'

'Oh, it doesn't stop there.'

I was laughing now. 'Do tell.'?

'Did you know that homeless old guy who sits outside that pub …?'

'The Crown and Anchor?'

'That's the one. Well, he's going to be nice and warm this winter. In Pete's favourite leather jacket.'

'The Aeromarine? Made to measure. Vintage horsehide. Nine hundred quid.'

'Nine hundred and seventy. Yeah, that one. I gave it to that homeless guy.'

'Does Pete know?'

'Oh, he knows alright. Sees the bloke wearing it every Friday when he pops in for a pint. And that's not all he's wearing.'

'Bloody hell! What else?'

'Sunglasses.'

'The Ray Bans?'

'All six pairs. Practically a different one for each day of the week.'

'That is bloody marvellous.'

'I'm a total bitch.'

Should I say it?

'That's how I've always thought of you. Bloody Bitch Bronwyn.' I held her gaze. After three long seconds, she shook her head. 'I know. Quite right.' Her turn to look me in the eye. 'I'm sorry.'

'I know. Me too. I was a deranged cow.'

'Trust me. I know how that feels.'

'You will get over it. Believe me.'

Bronwyn took my hand in hers. 'Thank you. For everything. And sorry. Again. For everything.'

'It's forgotten. For me. And you will forget it, too. And, in the meantime, you'll have thoughts of his leather jacket to keep you warm.'

31

Womanhattan

When the Portsmouth hens shipped out on the Monday morning, I felt good.

We'd provided a top-notch luxury weekend for yet another group of very satisfied customers. But, much more importantly, I'd finally made my peace with Bronwyn.

Although the part of my life that had been Pete had been put to bed (an apt turn of phrase in the circumstances) some time ago, the Bronwyn element had occasionally gnawed away at me and had still held some power over me.

But now that power had been exploded.

I have no way of knowing how that meeting would have gone if she and Pete had still been an item, had lived happily ever after. If she hadn't, like me, been the Wronged Woman. The reject. That shared experience had given us something to bond over. Would she have had that perspective – the ability to see the situation from my point of view, and have the grace to apologise for it – without having gone through it herself?

I'll never know.

But it was over. There had been a resolution. A final line drawn under a very different – and distant – part of my life.

David was, as ever, philosophical about it.

'If she hadn't come into your life, you'd never have left him. And we may never have got together.'

'I'd have still bumped into you. And fancied you.'

'The first, yes. The second, maybe. But it wouldn't have gone anywhere.'

'I'm not so sure. The feelings were very strong.'

'But you're you. Good. Honourable. Noble. You wouldn't have allowed those feelings to develop. Not if you'd been in a happy relationship with Pete.'

'Maybe.'

'Definitely. This is you, remember. You do what is good. What is right.'

'Well, being with you is both good and right.'

'Well, that makes what I have to say very much easier.'

No. You're not going to, are you? Not over the phone.

'How do you fancy a trip to New York?'

Right. Phew. I knew you were too classy for a phone proposal. But is that what this trip is about?

'Well, yes. Of course. I'd be delighted. But it's not that long since you were here.'

'I know. But I've got a taste for it. For you. Have you got the time? I was thinking a week. Or, if that's too long, how about five days, four nights?'

'I think it'll be fine for a few days, anyway. But what about you? Can you spare that much time?'

'In principle, yes. There might be the odd morning or afternoon when I'll have to leave you to do your own thing. But we'd still have plenty of time together. Most of the time, in fact. Would that be okay?'

'It sounds great. But let me run it past Miranda.'

'If *you* don't go, *I'll* bloody well go.'

'But I'm only just back from a trip to India.'

'That was weeks ago. And anyway, I can handle the front of house cookery school stuff …'

'You don't mind?'

'Of course not. It just means a bit more prep in the mornings – half an hour – so I'm free to bring them over here at lunchtimes. And Marius is actually great with them. His no-nonsense Slavic drill-sergeant routine goes down quite well over lunch. Then they're ready for more of nice old me in the afternoon sessions. Just go. Or I will. And you'll be stuck here, doing *The Seven Classic Variations On The Basic Bechamel Sauce*.'

'If you're sure.'

'Of course I'm sure. I can even handle estate email if you want me to, to give you a proper break.'

'That would be wonderful.'

'Just bring me back something nice. Nothing fancy.' She winked. 'Bit of Tiffany or something.'

My recent Heathrow experience had put me off airports for life, and Gatwick wasn't exactly doing much to rekindle my childhood love affair with the glamorous world of air travel (an affair that had begun with a school trip to Rome when I was sixteen). Even in October, it was heaving.

After a three-hour delay I'd spent largely spraying myself with every female fragrance in the duty free shop, I finally settled into my seat smelling like an explosion in a perfume factory.

Compared to my recent trek to India, the six hours to New York seemed like a short hop. A fact I was thankful for given the company I was keeping in row 38 – on my left a Japanese businessman who established domination of the armrest before you could say charity scratchcard and, on my right, a One Direction reject who clearly saw little difference between the words *aeroplane* and *torture chamber*. His legs were going nineteen to the dozen, his skin was waxy, and he was riffling through the magazines and menus in his seat back looking for the sick bag.

'Are you okay?'

'Sorry. I just get a bit nervous on planes. I know people say you're more likely to die in a car crash … '

'One in a hundred for cars, I think, and …'

'Around one in ten thousand for planes. I know. I should be comforted. But that still seems like a scary statistic.'

'Haven't you got a book or something? To distract you?' I held up my latest Harry Bingham thriller.

One Direction shook his head. 'I can't concentrate. I've downloaded a few podcasts but I'm not sure that'll work either.' He smiled weakly. 'I'll try not to bother you.'

'What about alcohol? Does that relax you?'

'I hope so. I had four Jack and Cokes in the bar while we were waiting to get on.'

I smiled. 'Right. Fingers crossed.'

A couple of gins is actually my usual way of passing the decades we're all obliged to spend in an airport before every flight these days but, to be honest, my liver still hadn't recovered from Operation Indian Martini Bucket. I hardly been (much to Miranda's undisguised amazement) near the gin bottle since I'd got back.

An uneventful hour or so into the flight saw Master Styles dozing peacefully on my right, while the Japanese manspreader on my left remained buried in his newspaper, a publication in which columns of figures seemed to be the main feature of interest.

Then we hit a bit of turbulence and the airborne world shuddered.

Three things happened in quick succession – the seatbelt sign came on, a chunk of my chicken forestiere did a backflip out of its plastic coffin and landed on my jeans, and Harry Styles threw up on my trainers.

'Do I smell of vomit?'

'Were you sick on the plane?'

'The young lad next to me was. On me. Well, on my shoes.'

'No, you don't smell of vomit. You smell of perfume. A new one, isn't it?'

'It's a mixture. Of every one they had in the duty free shop. We were delayed. As you know. So that's what I did.'

'You used the time to smother yourself in perfume? Because you knew you'd need to mask the smell of vomit?'

'Is there a smell? Of vomit?'

'No.'

'Good.'

'Can I kiss you now?'

I was still plying the wet wipes on my trainers as our taxi hit the George Washington Bridge and I got my first view of the magnificent Manhattan skyline.

I turned to David and smiled and he squeezed my hand.

Suddenly, we were over the river and onto the tiny peninsula crammed with colossal towers, the streets like narrow canyons. Then, just a few minutes later, the taxi pulled up outside David's apartment block on Riverside Drive.

I'd imagined this – me being here – every single one of the hundreds of times we'd FaceTimed or Skyped or spoken on the phone. But the sights and the sounds you get on a screen do nothing to convey the energy you feel when you're standing on a New York sidewalk.

I closed my eyes and let the energy wash over me as the driver unloaded my little case.

David paid him then wrapped his arms round my shoulders and kissed my hair.

'Welcome to New York.'

32

Green Around The Gills

David dropped my case on a red and black Persian rug and I took in the gorgeous space of his open-plan apartment.

'It's even nicer than the picture I've been carrying around in my head. You don't get the full impact on a phone screen or a laptop. Can I see your balcony?'

'Of course.'

I walked towards French windows through which bright autumn sunlight was pouring into the room.

A room that suddenly started to swim before my eyes. I grabbed the back of a yellow velvet couch to steady myself.

David rushed forward. 'Are you okay?'

I suddenly felt as lousy as One Direction Boy had looked. My fear of heights wasn't tested very often – the last time had been a very trying ride on the London Eye when I'd been showing a sheikh the sights as one of my extracurricular duties in my capacity as his account manager at Artisan Wines – but it dawned on me that the city of the skyscraper was going to be a trial. If I let on to David, this whole trip would be a complete burst balloon. I was going to have to bluff it out.

'I don't know what's going on. Just felt a bit dizzy there. Probably just shattered – it's been an early start and I didn't really doze on the plane at all.'

'Have you eaten?'

'Yeah. I had a chicken thing in a sauce. I hope the bloody chicken wasn't off or something.'

'Do you feel sick?'

'A bit. Maybe that lad on the plane's given me his vomiting bug.'

'That was just airsickness, wasn't it?'

'I thought so.'

'Then it's not a bug. It's probably a combination of tiredness, jet lag, and hunger.'

'I do feel a bit peckish, actually.'

'Are you up for a bit of a walk?'

Not really. 'Sure.'

'My absolute favourite sandwich place is near Columbia University. Ten minutes.'

I just want to lie down. 'Sounds perfect.'

Columbia University looks like someone took a chunk of ancient Greece and dropped it into the middle of the world's busiest, modernest city. All the buildings look like temples and the place has lawns and fountains and mosaic pavements everywhere.

I sat on a stone bench with a watery October sun on my face while David ordered us his favourite New York sandwich from a van in the shape of a silver bullet. Down on terra firma, I checked in with my insides and was pleased and relieved to be feeling myself again.

'Pastrami and swiss cheese with mayo and mustard and arugula – that's rocket to you and me. On rye bread. Of course.'

'Of course. Pastrami on rye. Isn't that what Cagney and Lacey always had?'

'Who?'

'You never watched *Cagney and Lacey*?' I took a big bite and got mayonnaise on my nose.

'I've never even heard of it.'

I wiped my nose with my hand. 'It was my mum's favourite programme. Two women cops in New York. One's married with kids. And the other's a bit of a girl. I actually can't believe my mum let me watch it – the storylines were often full of pretty adult stuff and I was only about ten. But she was a bit of a feminist, my mum. On the quiet. Maybe she thought a show about two women being as tough and capable as the blokes would be a good life lesson.'

David was smiling. 'It's clearly a lesson you learned at a young age.' He reached over and wiped the remaining mayonnaise off my nose with a freshly laundered handkerchief.

'You feeling okay?'

I took a deep breath and looked at the blue sky and the beauty and the vibrancy all around me. 'I feel great. I was obviously just hungry.' I took another delicious bite.

'Then you've come to the right place. New Yorkers are very serious about their food. There's some sort of eatery about every fifty yards. And even pretty basic-looking places serve up the most delicious stuff.' He slapped his abdomen. 'As you can see, my time here is beginning to take its toll.'

'Stop it. You look as trim as ever.'

'Then looks are deceptive. I've had all my trousers taken out an inch since I got here. Every single pair.'

'One inch? Is that all? You're a complete amateur. Elastication is my middle name. If a garment does *not* have a bit of lycra in the waistband, I think very hard these days before committing to a purchase.'

'Shall we grow old and fat together?'

Is this it? Is this the proposal coming? 'I'd like that.'

'Then it's a deal.' And he leaned over and gave me another one of his searching kisses that summoned up thoughts of the bedroom. When we pulled apart, I blinked.

'Wow. Isn't it a little early in the day for that kind of stuff?'

'I just want you to be sure that I love you. Very, very much.'

'Well, I wasn't absolutely sure. But that kiss has convinced me.'

'Good. Now, what's the plan?'

'Plan?'

'What do you want to see?'

'You. As much as possible.'

'Along with me. Which bits of New York?'

'Your office. I'd like a clear picture of where you work. After that, I'm happy to be guided by you.'

'My office is much like any other. The grand tour will take all of five minutes. How about we do that early tomorrow morning, then get breakfast at my favourite place on Bryant Park?'

'Sounds ideal.'

'And now?'

'Are you in the mood for a "nap"?'

***

Bryant Park is an oasis just off Fifth Avenue, tucked between the Empire State Building and the Rockefeller Center. A very pleasant green space with a couple of classy food places and half a dozen basic, informal joints. We were breakfasting in basic. Just the way I like it.

I was bellying up to the biggest plate of blueberry pancakes I'd ever seen, complete with syrup, bacon on the side, and, in case I still had a single unexploded button left on my shirt, a couple of kilos of scrambled eggs.

'I'll need a lie-down after this.'

There was a distinct twinkle in David's hazel eyes. 'Another one?'

I slapped his leg. 'Simply so I can properly enjoy my food coma.'

'We need to walk it off. I think that's why New Yorkers are always in such a hurry. They're always trying to shift the few thousand calories of whatever mammoth meal they've just ingested.'

'There must be juice bars and muesli joints. Places where the willowy people go.'

'Like Lola Montgomery?'

'Yes. Like her. And like Madison.'

I dropped that pebble into the water and let it ripple for a couple of seconds.

Madison was David's intern. He'd introduced me to her during our earlier whistle-stop tour of his office. She was about a foot taller than me and a size eight. Toned, gym-girl arms. Flawless skin. Fabulous cheekbones. Firm and full breasts. Think Charlize Theron but twenty-two.

'I guess. Although she cleans her plate whenever we go out with clients. I think she just goes to the gym a lot. I bet you Lola does, too. It's a Hollywood thing, isn't it?'

'I suppose so.' *Are you changing the subject?*

'When are you seeing her?'

'Lola?'

'Yes. Haven't you arranged to meet up?'

'She's away. Filming in Atlanta. I emailed her with my dates but she's away for another three weeks. Some Netflix series.'

'That's a shame. I was hoping to meet her. Well, I was dreading it actually. Because I thought I'd have a bad case of starstruck idiot.'

'I know. I still can't really believe I'm texting and emailing this superstar like she was an old pal.'

'You made a big impression on her. As you do on everyone.' Another hand on the cheek and another searching kiss.

'That's enough, Mr Fruity. Show me the sights.'

***

The following three days were lived in a total whirl.

I can't tell you that we saw every one of the iconic landmarks that New York has to offer, but we racked up quite a list: Ground Zero and the new One World Trade Center (the hugely moving empty pools taking me right back to that day when I watched the news in horror); Katz Deli on the lower East Side, where Meg Ryan had her fake orgasm in *When Harry Met Sally* (and where I had the potato latkes with apple sauce and sour cream – I was enjoying some new and very weird food combinations); the oddly uplifting Statue of Liberty (I skilfully sidestepped a chance to, as it were, go up her) and the deeply affecting Ellis Island, on a breezy bright morning; and, on day three, a visit to the Top Of The Rock for the iconic view of the Empire State Building (a view I would have been perfectly happy to look at on a laptop screen, but I'd just decided to brass-neck it out).

'The problem with going up the Empire State is you don't see the Empire State, because you're on it. The Rockefeller Center is the better way to get the classic Manhattan view.'

'I am entirely in your hands.'

'That *is* where I enjoy you best.'

He leaned over and kissed me, in a lift with four other people.

I lowered my voice. 'When did you get so smutty?'

He leaned in to whisper. 'I can't help it if you're irresistible.'

When the lift doors opened and I got a glimpse of the observation deck, I went wobbly again. I had to steady myself with a hand on the wall.

'Are you okay?'

'Just went a bit woozy for a second.'

'Like when you walked over to the balcony in my apartment.'

'Yeah. Like that.'

'Have you always had a thing about heights?'

'I'm sorry. I'm not normally a big wuss.'

'Is it dizziness?'

'Yeah. And a bit of bubbliness in the stomach.' This latter was a strange variant on my usual acrophobia, which normally stuck to just making my head feel like a goldfish bowl someone was swinging around for the fun of it. In New York, my stomach seemed to be joining in the fun.

'Do you feel actually sick?'

'I'll be fine. I'm maybe just a bit worn out.'

'Sorry. I've been dragging you around for days. And keeping you up at night. You need some rest.'

'It's been great.'

'It's been pretty exhausting, though. I'll cancel the dinner tonight. And we can just stay in and I'll cook.'

That sounded absolutely perfect, but it was my last night and David had planned to make a big thing of it – dinner with half a dozen of his colleagues (including the lithe and luscious Madison) in a place called The Odeon, a cool but informal joint where writers and fashion models hang out and where you might have Al Pacino sitting at the next table.

'No. You've made big plans. And we can't cancel on your colleagues at the last minute. And you booked the table weeks ago.'

'That doesn't matter. I'll cancel it just like that if you want me to.'

'No. Thank you, though. I'm fine. I'll be fine.'

I'd actually been dreading the dinner, even without my touch of queasiness. The prospect of an evening in the company of the outrageously pert Madison had dragged all my old insecurities back from the depths and was now boiling them right at the surface. I was feeling pretty fragile in every sense.

The slinky lilac dress from LK Bennett in Cheltenham that usually makes me feel like a superstar was, this evening, looking like an old dish rag on an old sack of spuds. My hair wasn't behaving and I'd had to squeeze every last drop out of a bottle of Sheer Glow foundation to keep me looking just about on the right side of a bus pass.

'You look gorgeous tonight.'

'No I don't.' *Jesus. Don't snap at him. It's not his fault you look like Nora Batty's mum.*

'Trust me. I'm a man. I know about these things.' He gave me the full-on warm hazel eyes and I melted (as usual) and felt like a complete bitch.

'Thank you. I'm just not feeling … myself.'

'I'll call everyone and cancel right now.'

'No. Please don't. I couldn't stand to be the one who lets the whole side down. Who mucks everyone about.'

'I don't care about them.'

'Well, I do. That really wouldn't be fair. I'll be fine.' I took a deep breath and pasted on a smile. 'Besides, we might bump into Al Pacino.'

'Quite right. And you can add him to your list of Hollywood chums.' He looked me in the eyes. 'Are you sure you're up to this?'

'I'm sure. I'm fine. Thank you.'

The Odeon is a curious mix of America and France in the heart of the fashionable Tribeca district of Lower Manhattan, an area popular with artists and fashion designers and filmmakers. They hold an annual international film festival there. It's where Robert De Niro has his office.

The first thing I noticed was how busy the bistro was. Its tiny space was crammed with diners all having a very good time. There was a very appealing buzz about it. This was going to be an enjoyable evening.

Then the second thing I noticed was Madison's cleavage.

What magic do young women weave to get their smooth-skinned and perfectly formed breasts to sit beautifully inside a dress cut pretty much to the navel without the apparent support of a bra and have them held in a zone safe from wardrobe malfunctions while also allowing them to move with enough freedom to make them completely tantalising?

Every man in the entire place – even the gay ones – must have been salivating over the sight of these remarkable beauties. Jesus! She was almost working her magic on me. And the thought of what the sight must have been doing to David's blood pressure was making my own blood boil. Ridiculously.

Relax, you daft cow! The world is full of beautiful young people. Get over it!

'Hi Jennifer. Your dress is lovely. I love the colour.'

'Hi Madison. Thanks. You look gorgeous. Of course.'

Don't be a cow.

'Thank you. My mom hates this dress but it's one of my favourites.'

'You look stunning.'

Good. Keep it up.

'That's really kind. Thank you.'

We took our seats – Madison and her wonder puppies on my right and, on my left, Lisa Johnson, the head of David's legal team, one of those women who wears boxy suits with shoulder pads because she wants to look tough. David – not a fan of Lisa – sat down opposite me and threw me a smile of pure love that put me immediately at ease.

I don't remember much about the evening's conversations – Lisa pegged me from the off as someone she didn't really want to talk to but Madison, bless her gorgeous cotton socks, kept me involved in the banter with a curly-haired young man on her other side with a name like Brad or Chad or something who seemed like the joker of the pack and had a knack for making Madison throw her head back (thrusting her beauties heavenward) and bray like a donkey. The braying got louder with every joke and every cocktail.

In the lift on the way up to David's apartment, I started to feel queasy again.

You'll be fine as long as you stay away from the window.

'Did you have a good time?'

'I did, actually. I'm sorry about earlier.'

'No need to apologise for not feeling well.'

'It wasn't just that.' *Time to fess up. Honesty and all that.* 'To be frank, I wasn't looking forward to an evening with Madison.'

David looked genuinely nonplussed. 'Really? She's very nice.' Then he doubted himself. 'Isn't she? I've always thought so. Am I missing something?'

'No. She is. She was a real sweetheart tonight. With me. It's just ...'

'What?'

'She's so bloody gorgeous. God! That body! Every man in the office – in the entire city – must be walking around with a permanent erection. I practically fancy her myself.'

'Is that really it? What was making you off colour?'

'Not entirely.' My stomach lurched again. 'I did feel a bit dicky. I do again actually.'

The lift door pinged and David put his arm round me and guided me towards his front door. 'I'm sorry. What can I get you?' He buzzed the door open with his card.

I lay down on his yellow velvet couch and prayed my stomach would settle. 'Just some water, please.'

'Coming up.'

The ceiling came to a halt and my insides began slowly putting themselves back in their box. David returned with a glass of water and handed it to me.

'You really are very silly, you know.'

'I know.'

'I don't know what it will take for me to convince you how much – how very much – I love and cherish and admire and worship you. How I always have. And how no number of young girls wearing half a dress will deflect my mind from that steady course.'

'I'm sorry. We forty-something women are a very sensitive breed.'

He knelt down beside me. 'I get it. We forty-something men are exactly the same. Every time we're faced with a six-foot-five Adonis with golden hair and a visible six-pack throbbing away under a muscle T-shirt. But Madison is younger than Lottie. Besides, I can't stand to be around that laugh for more than five minutes at a time.'

I smiled. 'It's certainly not her best feature.'

'It's not. She's very pretty. Of course she is. But so are you. And I respond to your very many beautiful and desirable qualities in ways I may never be able to explain. But I'm willing to keep trying. For ever.'

And then he produced the most beautiful piece of jewellery I had ever seen. A perfectly proportioned aquamarine surrounded by small but exquisite diamonds in the most stunning setting. Tears leapt into my eyes.

'And I hope you'll be willing to let me keep trying. For ever.'

I took his face in my hands and kissed him, the tears rolling down my cheeks and onto his face.

'I will.'

***

'I'm really going to miss you.'

An airport concourse is never the best setting for a tearful goodbye and Newark Airport was no exception.

'Me too. It's been so lovely having you here for a few days.'

'Let's not leave it very long before your next trip to Thornhill.'

'We won't. I'm already looking at the diary. I'll fix something soon. Very soon.'

The ring was a novel feeling on my finger. I couldn't stop looking at it and touching it.

'It's so beautiful.'

'Then it's a perfect match for my beautiful fiancée.'

'We don't have to grow fat together, but we do need to grow old together. Promise me we will.'

'I can think of nobody I would rather grow old with. In fact, I can think of nobody else. Period. As they say here.'

'Promise me.'

'I promise you. Old. Together. But a good few years of young together first. Of exploring new places together. Of trying weird food in strange restaurants together. Of walking your dogs together. Of curling up on the Thornhill sofa together. For as long as we both shall live.'

'Then dying together. In a waterskiing accident in California when we're eighty-five. Or being eaten by a lion on safari in Kenya. Or after a cream-tea overload in a coffee shop in Stow.'

'It's a bit too soon to think about dying.'

'I just couldn't bear it. To be without you. I used to think I could. I said that to Will. To comfort him after Kavi. That we just go on. Because we have to. But I can't think that now. I would be an empty person.' The tears rose up in my eyes and David wiped them away.

'Hey. Stop being so morbid. This is a beginning. For us. The end is a very long way away. Let's enjoy now. Several decades of now.'

I coaxed my trembling lips into a smile and David stroked my cheek and my hair.

'I love you very much, Jennifer Brown.'

'It's a good job.'

'It's the best job I've ever had. And a job I'm going to enjoy doing for a very long time to come.'

33

A Testing Time

'It's so beautiful.' Miranda wiped her hands on a dishtowel and took my hand in hers. 'It's such a lovely size and shape. Classic.'

'It's an antique. A bit like his fiancée.'

'Shut up, you cheeky cow. You're three years younger than me. And you look bloody ten years younger.'

'That's total balls. But it's very nice of you to say it.'

'So, it was brilliant?'

'It was a wonderful trip, actually. I was a bit off-colour for part of the time. My usual acrophobia, mostly.'

'Right. All those skyscrapers wouldn't have done you any favours, then.'

'No. But it was a bit different this time. My guts were all over the place as well.'

'Oh, I'm sorry.' She scraped finely chopped onions from a board into a pan of butter and oil and they started to sizzle. 'What's going on there, d'you think?'

'I don't know. It was probably just jet lag. I was fine in India, though.'

'I think going forwards is easier on your body than going backwards. In time, I mean. I read that somewhere.'

'Yeah, maybe.'

'Have you been alright since you got back?'

'Okay, yeah. Just … wiped out. I'm not sleeping that great.'

'Tell me about it! That feckin' cock!'

Jon Bon Jovi – Robbie's new rooster – was letting the whole estate know he was the new main man in the neighbourhood. At around six in the morning. Miranda had bought industrial-strength earplugs and issued them to all the cookery school guests, along with sleep masks, and nobody was complaining, thankfully.

But I was finding it near-on impossible to get back to sleep. It sounded like she was in the same boat.

'And I feel like a nap in the afternoons. Like my mum used to have. I'm turning into a bloody old woman.'

'Maybe you should see a doctor.'

'I don't think there's anything really wrong.'

'There might be something, though. A vitamin deficiency or something. Can't hurt to get it checked out.'

'Maybe.'

Ridiculously, I hadn't even registered with a GP since moving into Thornhill.

After phoning half a dozen practices in Oxfordshire and being told they weren't accepting new patients, I finally struck gold with a group practice just over the border into Gloucestershire, in Eastleach, a couple of miles along the road from The Queens near Chipping Norton.

A nurse with Alan Rickman's nose took my blood pressure, measured my heart rate, and put a clip on the end of my finger.

'What's that for?'

'It measures the amount of oxygen in your blood. It lets us rule out serious conditions. Heart and lungs. Things that could be dragging you down. Yours looks fine, though. Did you bring a water sample?'

'Water?'

'Urine.'

Did you think the word 'urine' would offend me? 'Oh, yes.' I fished the little bottle out of my bag and handed it over.

'Thanks. And, if you roll up your sleeve, I'll take a blood sample.'

After this comprehensive round of pricking and pumping and clipping, she dispatched me back to the waiting room. Forewarned there'd be a wait of around an hour for the results, I pulled Harry Bingham out of my bag and settled down for a bit of me-time.

When I opened my eyes, the receptionist was shaking my shoulder gently.

'I called your name three times. You didn't even hear the buzzer on the screen.'

'I'm really sorry.'

'It's fine.'

A little boy of about six was sitting on the floor by his very young mum, playing with a toy plane. He looked up at me and smiled. 'You were snoring.'

His mum opened her eyes wide. 'Archie! That's not nice.'

'Oh, it's fine.' I smiled at the boy. 'Old people snore sometimes. Sorry.'

The boy looked puzzled. 'You're not old.'

I could have kissed him. 'Well, that is the nicest thing anybody has said to me today. Thank you.'

Doctor Imran Korai waved me towards a chair. 'How are you feeling?'

'I just feel a bit … strange. I've been a bit queasy now and then. And I'm pretty tired a lot of the time. Which isn't really me. I usually have a lot of energy.'

'Well, I'm pleased to tell you that there are no major issues with your health. Which is very good news for someone in your condition.'

'My condition?'

'Yes. You're pregnant.'

34

Being Positive

I spent the rest of the day feeling like I was living someone else's life. Like I'd seen a friend post about their pregnancy on Facebook. Like I was on the outside looking in.

I wanted my mum to be around so I could talk to her about it. She'd have known the right things to say.

Then it hit me. How much my mum – the mum I had before dementia and death took her away – would have loved her grandchild. She'd died without ever having that joy.

As dusk gathered, I sat in the walled garden, on George's bench, and let the tears run down my cheeks. Woodbine looked up at me, puzzled, and Luther came and sat by my side and leaned his weight against me. Which only made the tears flow more.

I cried on and on into the night, a hundred thousand tears, mostly for my mum, for her life, for her loss, for *my* loss. For all the times I hadn't visited her when, with a bit more effort, I might have squeezed it in, even when work took me away. For all the times I'd been a bit sharp with her, or impatient, or thoughtless. For all the times I should have thanked her for being such a kind and caring mother.

And now, in something like six months' time, I'd be a mother myself.

Older parents have more life experience to give a child. I'd heard people say that. In your forties, you've generally got things sorted: career, partner, roof over your head. So there are fewer distractions.

You can give yourself totally to this new life. To this person who has come from your body. Is part of you.

This was good.

Wasn't it?

I lay awake and looked at the crack in my bedroom ceiling (why hadn't I got round to fixing that?) and tried to feel calm. Things would be fine. This *was* very good news. I was living in a gorgeous house – think of all the space a young child would have to run around in! – and things were beginning to look fairly secure on the money side. And I was having a baby with the man who'd been the focus of my daydreams for so long. A man who'd just asked me to marry him. It could hardly have worked out better.

Then I panicked.

What if this wasn't at all what David wanted? What if children with me had never been on his radar? He'd been through all that already, years ago. With Lottie and with Mark. It's true he seemed besotted with Lottie's little boy, Hugo. But grandchildren are different. You don't have to be there for the whole show. You drop in and out and just do the fun things.

And we'd never talked about having children together.

I don't think either of us had ever imagined it would happen.

It suddenly seemed a matter of great urgency that I discussed it with him (*What's to discuss – you're bloody pregnant!*) and I snatched up my phone and scrolled to my favourites.

Then I looked at the time. Just after one in the morning in New York. No. I didn't want him all bleary when I told him this important news.

But I had to tell someone.

'I know you said *I* should call *you* anytime, day or night. But I don't remember making the same offer. Unlike you, I *need* my beauty sleep.'

'Will …'

He could hear the seriousness in my voice and he snapped out of his jester routine.

'What is it? Are you okay?'

'I'm pregnant.'

He took a second to decide what the right response was. Then he screamed down the phone like the big fat drama queen he was.

'That is fucking brilliant! I'm going to be an uncle. Uncle Will. And if it's a girl … Do you know yet? If it's a girl or a boy? Doesn't matter. I'll take it – him, her – to all the best boutiques. I'll be their style guru. The Style Counsellor. They'll be the coolest kid on the block. Too cool for school. In fact, I'll teach them how to bunk off. We'll have shopping days in Brighton. No, London. Lunch out. When they're like just five or six. And by the time they're ten, they'll know it all. The best fashions. The best music. How to do your own henna tattoo. And later, piercings and proper …'

'Will.'

'And hair! God! The. Absolute. Coolest …'

'WILL!'

'What?'

'I haven't told David.'

'What?'

'I only found out yesterday. And I've been lying awake all night, wondering what to do.'

'What d'you mean, "what to do"?'

'How to tell him.'

'He'll be delighted.' A second of thought. 'Won't he?'

'I don't know. We've never talked about it.'

Will pulled on the cap and bells again. 'Of course he will, you daft cow. You'll make an adorable mother – you're kind, patient, considerate …'

I smiled. 'God. You make me sound like a Labrador.'

'It's that golden hair. And it's about bloody time! I mean, come on. You can't leave it much longer, can you?'

'I'm forty-three. Not bloody eighty-three. But that's not the point. The point is … what if this is not good news for David? What if he doesn't want kids?'

'Look. This man worships you – you know he does. And if this is something that makes you happy, then it will make *him* happy.'

'Do you think?'

'I don't know David very well. But I think I know him well enough to know that …'

'What?'

'He just wants to see you happy.'

Marius laid a plate of sourdough toast in front of me and slid two beautifully poached eggs onto the plate. 'Eat. Nothing that is wrong cannot be fixed by food.' He passed me the pepper grinder.

'How do you know something's wrong?'

He smiled. 'Please. Do I look like I have a zip at the back?'

I didn't really see the analogy but I caught his drift.

'Well, it's just a personal thing I need to deal with.'

Marius held up his hands like I'd got him at gunpoint. 'Sorry. Don't mean to stick my nose in.'

'No, it's fine. The eggs look great. Thank you.'

Miranda wheeled into the kitchen looking for a belt of Marius's coffee and he lifted the pot and walked over to fill up her Thermos cup and bend her ear. 'Jennifer has troubles. Maybe a woman can help.'

Miranda glanced at her watch and I held up my hand.

'It's fine. Don't keep your guests waiting.'

'Where will you be at lunchtime?'

'Come and find me in the library. If you have time.'

'I'll make time. But I have to dash now. Sorry.' And she disappeared in a whirlwind. I looked at the kitchen clock. 8.46 am in Oxfordshire was 3.46 am in New York.

No. You can't do that.

A flushed Miranda skipped into the library at just after one and plopped herself into George's armchair.

'What's going on?'

I looked up from my laptop. 'I'm pregnant.'

As Will had done, Miranda took a second to consider her response. Unlike Will, she exercised restraint. And made it about me, not her.

'And you're not happy about that?'

'No. I mean, I'm not *not* happy. I'm just not … sure.'

'And how does David feel about it?'

I took off my glasses. 'I haven't told him yet.'

'Right. Because …?'

'Because I'm not sure *he'll* be happy.'

I glanced at the clock on my laptop screen. 1.14 pm in Oxfordshire was 8.14 am in New York. He'd just be walking across Bryant Park. Maybe just arriving at the office. A good time to catch him.

Maybe.

Miranda was considering what advice she could offer me. 'Well, you can't *not* tell him, can you?'

'No. At some point, I do need to tell him.'

'But not now?'

'I wish I could know how he was going to react.'

'What are you worried about? What are the potential pitfalls?'

I smiled. For her, this was like a business decision. Miranda's pragmatic, contractual approach.

'That he doesn't want this. He is, essentially, retiring in a year's time. And I think he's looking forward to a life of ease. I mean, not daytime telly and cardigans and dominoes in the pub.'

'He's not even fifty!'

'I know. He's got loads of energy. And he'll help out here. Help me run this place and stuff. But a baby? I don't know. I don't know that he wants that. He certainly won't be expecting it.'

'He's got kids of his own, though. And a grandchild.'

'That's just it. He's done all that. The nappies and the sleepless nights. And the mess everywhere. And the carrying bottle steamers and buggies with you whenever you go any bloody where for longer than eight hours. I mean, *I'm* ready for that.'

'Are you?'

'Yes. I think so.'

'Well, isn't that all you need to know? Really. If *you're* up for this. If this is what *you* want. And if it is, then it'll be what David wants, too.'

'That's what Will said. That David just wants me to be happy. Can someone be like that, though? Completely selfless.'

'I don't think it *is* that. I think your happiness makes him happy. So telling him your good news will be good news for him, too.'

I took a deep breath.

'You're right. I'm just going to tell him.'

35

The World Stops

D avid died that day.

Was already dead, in fact, when Miranda and I were having our heart-to-heart in the Thornhill library.

He'd skipped up the subway steps at 42nd Street and Times Square at just before eight o'clock, Madison said. That's what she'd been told by Ramon, the guy who runs the news stand where David always stopped to pick up his copy of the *New York Times*. He'd seemed bright, cheerful. Just his usual self, the newspaper guy said.

Madison's voice wobbled. 'Ramon asked him, How's your beautiful fiancée? And David said, She's beautiful! And Ramon laughed and David turned to walk away and ...' Madison's tears choked her speech. And she sniffled, and then sobbed. Heavy, body-wracking sobs. 'God! I'm sorry! I can't believe it! He just fell. Dropped. And that was it.'

The ambulance had taken him to the emergency room at Mount Sinai Beth Israel hospital in Lower Manhattan, where they'd carried out resus, even though the paramedics had known at the scene that he'd gone.

The doctor I spoke to on the phone sounded French. He pronounced the name 'David' like it rhymed with 'avid.' Although they wouldn't know for sure until the autopsy, he said the cause of death was most likely an ischaemic stroke. A blood clot that had been developing in a different part of David's body for months had suddenly decided to move into one of the arteries that leads to the brain. And it had simply and suddenly blocked all blood and oxygen.

'It would have been instant and completely without pain,' the doctor said. 'One second, he was alive and happy and smiling. The next second, everything stopped.'

***

The hours that followed are just a series of blurry snapshots.

Miranda crying with me in the kitchen, her red curls in my face; Marius stroking my hair, a dishtowel falling from his shoulder onto the tiled floor; Delyth looking blankly at me as I staggered across the hall to the taxi outside; then, later, Lottie's beautiful skin drained of its golden colour when she saw my face and knew – sensed – the very bad news I was about to give her; baby Hugo, now toddling, biting his mummy's jeans as she sat crumpled on the hall chair, staring at the floor, tears dripping from the end of her nose.

***

The thing nobody tells you about death is the intrusion of the mundane into the boiling cauldron of emotion. Somehow, you have to find the strength to lock your feelings in a box for several hours at a time and do some serious admin.

And, although I was David's fiancée, there were others to factor into the equation: a daughter, a son, a mother.

It emerged from Patricia's meeting with the family solicitor that David had, after our first long weekend together at Thornhill, made a couple of 'minor changes' to his will (that was lawyerspeak for 'changes that have nothing to do with money'). One of those changes had been his wishes regarding funeral arrangements – he was to be buried in the little graveyard overlooking the lake at Thornhill, following a service conducted in the Thornhill chapel.

I was shocked and deeply touched when Patricia called me to explain. Months before the proposal in New York, he'd made up his mind. He'd seen his future here, with me.

A future we would now never enjoy.

I'd expected Patricia would be miffed – possibly even obstructive – about these arrangements. I imagined there was a family plot in Highgate Cemetery, perhaps comfortably close to George Eliot and a safe distance from Karl Marx, and that this expression of wishes was putting a major spanner in the family works.

But, over the phone, David's mother could not have been warmer or more accepting. There was still a hint of the matriarch, as befitted the difference in our ages and the long place she'd occupied in his life.

'With your agreement, I'll make the arrangements to have David flown home – to London, I mean – and then taken onwards to Oxfordshire.'

'Yes. Of course. Thank you.'

'And please know I am ready to assist with funeral arrangements if you wish to involve me.'

'Thank you. I will.'

***

This service at the Thornhill chapel wasn't the one I'd been planning in my head, off and on, since David had handed me the gorgeous piece of jewellery I was now fiddling with in the chapel's tiny vestibule.

This wasn't the Harwood family reunion I'd wanted. This wasn't the way I'd wanted to get to know David's mother, Patricia, see again Lottie's husband, Sandy, and finally meet David's son, Mark.

But sometimes we don't get what we want.

Spectacularly not.

Looking at Mark was like looking at a younger David but less elegant and less well-groomed. He shook my hand warmly, his eyes every bit as misty as mine.

'Dad loved you very much. We Skyped every week and the conversations were always mostly about you – how lucky he felt to be with someone so lovely. How strongly he felt that being with you was meant to be.'

'Thank you.' I could barely get the words out. 'I felt exactly the same.'

We – the family and the loved ones – filed grimly into the chapel to join the rest of the congregation, which was a little abuzz with the presence of Hollywood glamour. Lola Montgomery was trying her best to blend in but she was still casting an involuntary spell over the assembly. From her discreet spot about six rows back she reached up and squeezed my hand as the family and I made our way forward and settled ourselves on the front pew, a mere couple of feet from the altar.

When Clifford Carmichael – David had left the choice of vicar up to me – got to the line from Isaiah about the grass withering and the flowers wilting and I couldn't hold my tears in any longer, Patricia put her hand on mine and squeezed it, her own emotions held masterfully in check, as seems so often to be the way with people of a certain class.

And I felt myself go again when Jonathan stepped forward to deliver a short reading – a Yeats poem that had apparently been one of David's favourites. I had never heard it before. But its lines will be forever etched on my soul.

When you are old and grey and full of sleep,
And nodding by the fire, take down this book,
And slowly read, and dream of the soft look
Your eyes had once, and of their shadows deep;

How many loved your moments of glad grace,
And loved your beauty with love false or true.

Then Jonathan lifted his liquid eyes from the text and looked straight into mine, his voice quivering as he read on:

But one man loved the pilgrim soul in you,
And loved the sorrows of your changing face;

And bending down beside the glowing bars,
Murmur, a little sadly, how Love fled
And paced upon the mountains overhead
And hid his face amid a crowd of stars.

Not even Patricia could contain her tears.

In the churchyard, a few leaves still clung stubbornly to the oak tree that had been planted by Edmund's grandfather, as a bitter November wind prompted me to pull the collar of my astrakhan coat closer around my neck. Edmund himself, resplendent in full regimental uniform and greatcoat, looked like the cold wasn't laying a glove on him, and I thought, *You'll outlive us all, you old bugger.*

It was good to see Veronica again. And Rosemary, bless her bloody cotton socks, had made the ridiculous journey from Boston – six-and-a-half-hour flight, schlep across London, train from Paddington to Oxford, taxi from Oxford – without telling anyone, not even Veronica, who'd phoned her with the news. Lola had made a similar journey from Estonia, where she'd just finished filming a Russian Revolution epic (with bits of Tallinn standing in for St Petersburg).

Bob and Brenda, too, had dropped everything and pointed the orange Allegro northwards, Brenda looking like a minor royal in a turquoise coat and a fur hat of the kind you see Princess Margaret wearing in newsreel films from the 60s.

And a few of my good friends from the Intext days – Helen, Marilyn (whose biker chic had turned a few heads in the chapel), and my best mucker Will, of course – had made long and inconvenient journeys on what was the coldest day of the year so far.

And it was always nice to see Kate, and the memory of the last time I'd seen her, and of the state my nether regions had been in as a result, brought a smile to my face on a day that offered very few reasons to smile.

When the Orangery started to empty as people drifted away, and Patricia, Lottie, Sandy and Mark came over to say their goodbyes and issue an invitation to spend the weekend in London – soon – I held Lottie back while Patricia and the others went to get their coats.

She held me close and I put my tear-stained face on her immaculate shoulder. When I pulled away, she could see again that I wanted to tell her something.

'What is it?'

This just wasn't the way I'd imagined I'd be breaking this news. 'I'm pregnant.'

Her beautiful face managed to express both genuine joy and deep sorrow at the same time.

'And did he …?'

I shook my head. 'No. I only found out the day before he … ' I wiped my eyes. 'And, stupidly – very, very stupidly – I held onto that news overnight. I was worried how he'd react. By the following afternoon, though, I'd decided just to tell him. But by then, of course …' I looked at her beautiful face and her features started to swim and she stepped forward to hug me. 'And now I can't make that right. I can never make that right.'

She pulled me in close and stroked my hair. 'You can't do that. Blame yourself. You wanted time to think. And that's perfectly fine. Normal. And you could never have imagined this would happen.'

I pulled away and wiped my eyes. 'How do you think he'd have taken it?'

Lottie smiled and, with all the diplomacy that comes so naturally to the blue-blooded, gave me the perfect answer.

'I think he would have taken it precisely the way you'd have expected him to.' She lifted my hand and kissed it. 'I hope you know I will always be here. For you.' She glanced at my abdomen. 'For both of you. This is a very good thing.'

'Thank you.'

'When are you due?'

'April.'

'A spring baby. How wonderful. I will tell, or not tell, the rest of the family according to your wishes. You are in charge.'

'David's mother should know. That she's having another grandchild.'

'Yes. She should. But *when* she knows is when you're ready to tell her.'

I looked her in the eye. 'I hope you know I think you're wonderful.'

She kissed me on the cheek. 'You've stolen my line. Dad knew a wonderful woman when he saw her.'

36

I Feel

Sleep became my enemy.

Whenever I drifted off, I entered a world that didn't exist. A world of relaxation, of happiness, of plans, of looking forward. Then, when I woke, I died all over again. David died all over again. And then came the hammer blow to the chest, the stomach-wrenching pain, the darkness in my head.

So, for reasons of self-preservation, I stopped sleeping.

'You can't go on like this.' Miranda was right. I had a lot more than myself to preserve, after all. 'You need to rest. The baby needs you to rest. To be strong and healthy.'

The health visitor agreed. 'Your blood pressure's a bit high. Which is hardly surprising. It's not a major cause for concern. Yet. But it'll become one if you don't find a way to sleep. And the baby's life will be at risk. Would you like me to investigate counselling? Or therapy?'

'A psychiatrist, you mean?'

'It doesn't have to be. But someone you can talk to. Who will listen. To help you … let things go.'

'I think I've let things go too much already. I need to pull myself together.'

'You need to go easy on yourself. And give yourself the chance to rest. Mentally. They're linked a lot more closely than we think. Body and brain. You need to let your brain rest so your body gets

243

the strength it needs. For the baby's sake. It might help to make this about the baby. Not about you.' Then she smiled, this very wise and sensitive young woman. 'God. I sound like my mother. "It's not all about you, Gemma"'

'You're right. There are bigger things at stake.'

'Yes. Treat yourself as a way of treating the baby.'

I ordered a diffuser for essential oils and a couple of oil mixtures designed to promote sleep. I removed all electronics – phone included – from my bedroom. I started taking melatonin supplements. I bought myself a sleep mask. I found a yoga group online and re-discovered the pleasure of stretching and relaxing that I'd enjoyed so much before Pete's sneery mockery had prompted me to pack it in. And, gradually, I learned to rest.

And by the time Christmas came, and I was five months gone, I felt like I'd turned a corner.

Brenda called me and asked if I'd like to spend Christmas with them and suggested Bob drove up to fetch me. But the more time I spent brushing leaves off David's headstone, and arranging sprigs of holly and mistletoe in the little brass pot at the foot of his grave, the less I felt like leaving Thornhill. It'd feel like I was abandoning him.

So I invited them up to spend Christmas with me. Marius was heading back to Romania for two weeks (for what sounded like a full-on marathon food-shovelling contest with his seven brothers and sisters) and Miranda was doing what she always did during the festive season – cooking a Christmas dinner for Mad Mary (and trying to keep her out of jail) and the couple of dozen homeless people who pitched up at the cafeteria of the community college where she used to work and which, thanks to an initiative steered by Miranda herself, had been, for several years now, throwing open its doors on Christmas Day. Delyth, by contrast, was allowing herself no more than two days off.

'I've had enough by the twenty-seventh, to be honest. I like Christmas Day, and I really like Boxing Day, but after that it all goes a bit flat. Plus we need to keep things ship-shape here ready for guests coming back first week in Jan.'

So, for a couple of days anyway, apart from the dogs, I'd have been on my lonesome. Bob and Brenda were the best idea I'd had in a long time.

Then Jonathan called.

'What are you doing on Boxing Day?'

'What's happened to Provence?'

My effortlessly suave former boss at Intext owned – in keeping with his persona as International Man Of Cosmopolitan Smoothery – a house in the hills north of Avignon, not far from the gorgeous vineyards of top Rhone appellations Vacqueyras and Gigondas, to which he usually decanted himself and the leggy Steph for a midwinter month or so.

'Well, things have been a bit … fluid.'

'How d'you mean?'

'I'll tell you some other time. So, Boxing Day?'

'Well …' And I went on to explain about Bob and Brenda.

'Okay. Well, I wouldn't want to intrude.'

'You wouldn't be intruding. It would be lovely to see you. Before he left, Marius prepared a goose and about thirty side dishes, and all I have to do is heat them up. Plus we need reinforcements to help us get through it all.'

'Sounds perfect. If you're sure I wouldn't be in the way.'

'I'm sure.'

Jonathan's white Morgan Roadster pulled up on the Thornhill gravel on Boxing Day morning just as Bob and Brenda were dropping soluble paracetamol into glasses of water and trying to turn the volume down on their groaning.

Whilst I'd been on spring water with elderflower and ginger cordial, my elderly aunt and uncle, continuing a pattern established over the very boozy weekend of the Summer Gala, had washed their food down with dangerous amounts of alcohol, some of it of frankly reckless potency, including a bottle of navy-strength gin that was, according to Bob, 'perfect for them cocktails you like, Brenda.' I'd checked the label and discovered it came in at a head-splitting sixty-two percent ABV.

Then, just to make their hangovers more interesting, they'd followed that (and the breakfast champagne and the bottles of Paulus and Monbazillac they'd knocked back during the meal) with a couple of glasses of Mirabelle, the plum brandy which is a speciality of the Lorraine region of France and to which I'd been introduced by Philippe during my time working at Château Paulus.

And now here was Jonathan with flowers and chocolates. And half a dozen bottles of top-notch wine they couldn't say no to.

But Bob and Brenda rallied like the old troupers they were, with Brenda only occasionally overstepping the mark to comment on Jonathan's physique. To which Jonathan, like the sweet, charming gentleman he always was, responded with just the right amount of slightly saucy banter. And he gamely joined in when, after dessert and more Monbazillac, Brenda jumped up from the couch and suggested charades.

After Bob had dragged a sleepy Brenda upstairs for the night, Jonathan put another log on the fire and sat next to me on the couch.

'Thank you.'

'You're very welcome. It's been lovely to see you. So … fluid?'

'Sorry?'

'That's the word you used when I asked you about Provence. You said you and Steph weren't going because things had been "fluid".'

'Right.' The normally surefooted Jonathan suddenly looked off balance.

'You don't have to tell me anything.'

'No. I want to. I need to, actually.'

'No, really. You don't. Not on my account. Your relationship is your private business.'

'That's just it. There isn't one. A relationship. Not any longer.'

'Ah. I'm sorry.'

'Oh, don't be. Really. It's been a mess from day one. Thanks largely to me. To my failure to commit. And, appearances notwithstanding, Steph's not stupid.' In spite of myself, I smiled. And so did he. 'Alright, she's never been the sharpest tool in the toolbox.' Jonathan's leggy girlfriend with the Hollywood smile and the surgically enhanced breasts had once memorably professed an interest in horticulture in one breath and in the next breath registered surprise to learn that holly grew on trees. 'But she could always see me for who I am.' He held my gaze. 'Or who I was.'

'Steph is a very attractive woman. And you make – made – a very handsome couple indeed. But I could see that she was craving a commitment you weren't ready to give her.'

'No.'

'But it sounds like you're ready now. So you just need to tell her that.'

'That's not what I'm trying to say. I have absolutely no desire to commit myself to Steph.'

'Okay.'

Jonathan reached out and took my hand. 'You know I adore you. You know I always have.'

Where is this going? 'And you know I have tremendous affection for you. I consider you one of my closest friends. You've been hugely supportive to me over the years. Incredibly generous. But …'

'I am ready to be whatever you want me to be. To make any commitment you want. Or need.' He glanced at my five-month-old bump.

For all his debonair, rakish, Casanova ways, at heart Jonathan was an old-fashioned knight in shining armour. A modern-day Galahad. His deep sense of chivalric duty moistened my eyes.

'Only you would offer to make such a sweet and honourable gesture, Jonathan. And I am deeply touched by your willingness to tie yourself to me for the rest of your life …'

'I will do it in a heartbeat if that's what you want.'

'I know you will. But it's not what I want. And it's not what *you* want. I am incredibly touched by your very strong sense of friendship, but we can't let this … tragedy … decide the future for you and for me.'

'I just want to help you.'

'I know. And you have. And you will. I promise I will always turn to you. For support.'

'Please do.'

'But this I'll do on my own. I'll manage. I'll be fine.'

'You are incredibly strong, I know, but …'

'I am. Strong enough. For me. And for him.'

'It's a boy?'

'Yes.' I'd known since the twenty-week scan, a couple of weeks before. 'So this little chap will get to know his Uncle Jonathan very well. That much I promise you.'

'I am ready to promise more.'

'I know. And thank you. But more I don't need.'

'You are a rare and wonderful woman.'

'And you are a very kind and noble friend.'

37

Patricia

A new year seemed like a good moment to make a resolution.
So I sat at the little walnut writing desk in my bedroom and took out a card with a William Morris design and wrote a note to Patricia. I had a phone number and an email address. But some things need to be done right.

The following weekend, Patricia's green Land Rover Discovery Sport pulled up on the Thornhill gravel and she climbed out, looking every inch like an old school friend of Princess Anne's, in pink tweed stand-collar jacket and navy slacks. Like Cécile, my old boss at Artisan Wines, David's mother managed to look like the clothes she wore had been designed specially for her.

I opened the front door as she reached the top of the steps. She dropped her leather travel bag and took a step towards me.

This was the first time the two of us had ever been alone in each other's company – no gathering around us to offer distractions or pretexts to excuse ourselves – and it was clear we were both unsure how well this was going to go.

I decided the best policy was to take charge – this was my turf, after all – and I took two steps towards her, took both her hands in mine, and leaned in for a peck on the cheek. She squeezed my hands in a way that took me back to the chapel and David's funeral and that memory made my knees wobble for a second. But Patricia's heartfelt smile helped me recover myself.

'Thank you very much for this very kind invitation.'

'It's very good of you to come.'

'I am absolutely delighted to be here. And to have the chance to spend some time with you.' She glanced down at a bump that was growing bigger by the day. 'And to lend a hand, if you need me to. How are you feeling?'

'Pretty well, thank you. I get a bit tired in the afternoons.'

'I remember that feeling very well. With both of mine.'

And it hit me again. The feeling I'd had looking at Edmund during George's funeral. The pain you must feel as a parent surviving a child.

'Come in. Let's get you comfortable and settled.'

Robbie appeared, always ready to play a kind of butler role when he knew that a visitor needed – or expected – special treatment. He whisked Patricia's bag upstairs and I ushered her through to the sitting room, which she'd never seen before. Although it was only ten in the morning, Delyth had got a gorgeous roaring fire going to make sure we'd be comfortable.

'What a splendid room!'

'Thank you. There are several lovely rooms in this house – we're very lucky – but this is one of my favourites.'

'You are indeed very lucky to have such a beautiful home. It's a rare gift to bestow on someone. The previous owner clearly admired you very much. And he wasn't the only one, of course.'

I had feared that the warmth and compassion Patricia had shown me at the funeral might have been specific to the occasion but the smile behind her words radiated affection. Then the smile died and she suddenly looked stricken.

'I have always considered myself to be a Christian. A believer in whatever plan God has in store for me. And a believer in the redemptive power that resides in the fact of Jesus Christ and his coming into the world.' Tears rose in her eyes. 'But I'm not sure I shall ever forgive God for taking David so young. Which I realise is a terribly blasphemous thing to say. But the death of a loved one is perhaps the most serious test of faith.'

'Yes.'

'And I know I am not alone in mourning David. And it is terribly selfish of me to imagine that my own grief outweighs that of other very important people in his life. So please forgive me.'

'Not at all. I can't imagine the grief of a mother for her child.'

Patricia looked me in the eye. 'It is my most sincere wish that you will never experience such grief. What you are feeling already is punishment enough.'

We two sat in silence for several seconds before I remembered I was the hostess.

'Where are my manners? You've had a long drive. Can I make you some tea?'

'That would be lovely. But the drive was fine.'

I stood to make my way to the kitchen and Patricia stood, too. 'I'm not going to let you wait on me.'

'I don't mind.'

'Nonsense. Let us surviving women make the tea together. Where's the kitchen?'

I guided her through the hall and down the corridor to Marius's domain. 'So the traffic wasn't too bad?'

'Well, getting out of London was a nightmare, of course. They're digging up Richmond Road again so I had to go through Kensington and you're practically faster walking. But I like driving. Always have. As a child, I used to sit in the passenger seat beside my mother – who also loved to drive – and I'd imagine what it would be like to be a grown-up and just jump into a car and have it take you anywhere. The power. The freedom. And as you get older, of course, you realise that adult life is restricted in ways your childish self could never have imagined. More so than your life as a child, in many ways.'

I pushed the kitchen door open and let Patricia walk through ahead of me. Marius was stirring something in the red Le Creuset pot and, turning to see Patricia, he lay his dish towel on the worktop and sort of stood to attention in a way that made me chuckle.

Patricia, sensing his unease, walked over and held out her hand. 'Hello. I'm Patricia.' Marius looked at her hand for a second, possibly weighing up whether this was some sort of British class-system test and whether taking this aristocratic hand might see him hauled off to the Tower and flogged. In the end, he decided to risk it.

'Hello. Pleased to meet you. My name is Marius.' It sounded like a speech he'd been learning at evening class.

'Marius. What a fabulous name! Are your parents fans of Roman military history?'

'Er …' I'd never seen Marius look so flustered. He was like a schoolboy thrust onto the stage in a bad play for which he hadn't learned the words. 'I don't know.'

'I thought you might have been named after the Roman general, Gaius Marius. He reformed the structure of the Roman army. It was he who, essentially, made it the all-conquering military force it was to become.'

Marius's sense of panic intensified, as if he thought he ought to be taking notes for a forthcoming test. Patricia touched his forearm gently and smiled.

'Forgive me. My late husband was a military historian with a great admiration for the Romans. I've forgotten most of what he used to talk to me about but the name Marius has stuck. I've always thought it a strong name. Impressive.'

Marius's blood pressure dropped a couple of notches and his face regained a little of its natural colour. 'Thank you.'

Patricia turned to me. 'Now, where's your kettle?'

After a copious brunch of smoked salmon and smashed avocado with poached eggs ('How very fashionable,' pronounced Patricia. 'Very

Chelsea.'), followed by tea and scones (the announcement 'Delightfully fluffy. Well done, you!' bringing a charming flush to Marius's cheeks), the two of us walked round the estate in crisp January sunshine, Patricia rhapsodising over its 'elegant prospects' and 'generous proportions'.

Then we reached the chapel and its little graveyard.

Patricia knelt down and stroked the headstone and looked around her. 'It really is a beautiful spot. He chose very wisely.' Then a glance at me. 'In many ways.' She stood and wiped her eyes. 'He was such a good man. Such integrity. They say a child's character is fifty percent genetics and fifty percent upbringing. In other words, the parents are one hundred percent responsible. If that's the case, I am very happy to take the credit.' She smiled a rueful smile. 'And yet I have no idea where we went wrong with Giles. He is a very disappointing human being. So either we were rather inconsistent in our parenting. Or the theory is poppycock.'

The rest of the weekend passed off very companionably. Marius laid on a delicious Sunday lunch of slow-roasted pork with fennel and white wine, which we walked off with Miranda and followed the walk with a tour of the Shooting Lodge and an exposition of the whole cookery school enterprise – Miranda seemed very keen to impress Patricia and it seemed to work.

'What a fabulous venture. You have the perfect location, excellent facilities, and the success you're already enjoying is testament to your business acumen.'

Miranda flushed with pride but was keen to deflect it towards me. 'It was all Jennifer's idea.'

'That's not strictly true.'

'It absolutely is. I said I wanted to open a cookery school. But you were the one who saw the potential of running it here. And the one who's made the whole thing happen.'

'The clients respond to you as much as they do to the venue. Without your skill and charm, it would be nothing.'

Patricia smiled through our mutual backslappery. 'Well, it's clear you are an excellent partnership with a winning formula. Congratulations.'

Evening came and Patricia threw her bag onto the back seat of the Land Rover.

'Thank you for all this. For letting me in.'

'I wouldn't want it any other way.'

'You're very kind. And I'm very grateful. I will not interfere – I know you will already have in mind a 'birthing partner' or whatever the term is – but please do call me for other things. Even just for a chat. It can be tough with a new baby and when you're … ' Her voice faltered for a split second before she mastered herself. '… on your own, there's nobody to lean on, to complain to, to cry at. So please know that I can be that person if you need me.'

'I will. I do. Thank you. I want to involve you. And not just because that's what David would have wanted.'

Patricia leaned in and kissed me on the cheek. Then she climbed into her car and swept away.

38

Express Delivery

At the thirty-week mark, I got an email from Oxford Health inviting me to attend Bump and Baby classes at a centre in Chipping Norton.

As I pulled the old green Defender onto the health centre car park, a couple in their twenties were walking into the building, the woman waddling in that backward-leaning way that suggests the baby is an elephant and is also about three minutes away from being born. Then the young dad-to-be said something and the woman threw her head back and laughed.

Their fresh-faced good humour suddenly made me feel like the oldest new mum in the world. And the loneliest.

My first class kicked off with a childbirth video that looked like it'd been made around 1973 with decidedly amateur actors on a budget of about six quid. There was lots of comedy screaming, close-ups of her fingernails digging into his arm, and some fabulously hammy reaction shots of him wincing in pain.

Throughout the film, a couple about my age – expecting their fourth child – kept chipping in with reassuring chat about shredded nipples and vaginal tears, much to the horror of a very young mum – no older than seventeen – on my other side, seemingly attending the class on her own, too, poor love.

Then we moved on to birth positions, pain-relief choices, and the chances of 'going to the toilet' during labour. The seventeen-year-old looked aghast.

'So, on top of all this, I'm going to shit myself?'

In the evening, sitting in George's armchair with my feet up on an elaborately carved footstool Edmund had brought back from Aden in the fifties, I recounted the experience to Will on FaceTime as I sipped from a glass of AromaSeed Spice, a zero-alcohol drink designed to taste like gin which Miranda had seen on Facebook and which, sweetheart that she was, she'd ordered in for me.

'Then we passed round a cantaloupe melon and a doughnut pillow and all had goes at shoving the melon through the hole.'

'Jesus! It all sounds a bit primary school.'

'Very much so. Even the seventeen-year-old rolled her eyes.'

'I can imagine. So when's the next one? And are you even going to bother?'

'They're every week, from now until the birth. But I'm not sure I can stick it for another ten weeks. I'll see how the next couple of weeks goes. The health visitor comes in once a week anyway and does all her checks, so that's the main thing. I don't think sitting in the health centre chatting to a bunch of strangers is going to prepare me for anything, really. I'll deal with it when it happens.'

'You're like bloody Superwoman. Or that no-nonsense ballsy one with the sword and the sexy leather bodice.'

'What *are* you talking about?'

'Xena, Warrior Princess. Did you never watch it? It was a nineties thing. Starred Lucy Lawless.'

'Sounds like some bloody awful porn video.'

'She was brilliant. Travelled the world sorting out bad guys and taking absolutely no shit from anyone. That's you.'

'Well, I *am* pretty badass as I waddle from the couch to the kitchen and back.'

'Are you at the waddling stage?'

'I'm getting there. This bump is growing by the hour. If it keeps growing like this for another ten weeks, they'll need to take me to the hospital in a furniture van.'

'And it's definitely not twins?'

'Definitely not. I've had a couple of scans and, despite outward appearances, there's only one baby.'

'Which will be so big you'll just pop him out, put a school uniform on him, and send him straight into Year 2.'

'That's what it feels like. Never mind a cantaloupe – I should be practising with a bloody water melon. Or a yoga ball.'

'You will be wonderful.' Then a change of tone from Will. 'How are you? Really?'

I took a deep breath and felt a lump in my throat almost as big as my bump.

'I'm okay. I'm feeling good physically. I'm sleeping well, eating well, my blood pressure's behaving …'

'You know what I mean, though.'

'Yes. I know what you mean. Well, the truth is I'm … angry. A lot of the time. Angry at everything and everyone. At people whose fiancés *haven't* dropped dead. At David for having a stroke. At the bloody blood clot that killed him. At why it couldn't have been happy to just bugger up his kidneys or something, instead of his fucking BRAIN!' I was waving my glass around and sloshing non-gin on the library carpet. 'Jesus! I'm throwing gin on the floor.'

'You're drinking gin?!'

'No. It's fake gin. Zero alcohol. Full of botanicals.'

'Is it hitting the spot?'

'Not really. It's about as much like gin as I am like Kate Moss.'

'Skinny cow. Who needs all that elfin cheekbone crap when you have gorgeous curves?'

'Well, I've certainly got curves. I'm not sure they're gorgeous, but they're unmissable.'

'Shut up. You're glowing even more than usual. You're like a sunset on a golden pond.'

'You're so full of bullshit.'

'I know. It's why you love me. Listen …'

'What?'

'I want you to promise me something.'

'What?'

'That you'll call me if you want me. You know, if you want someone to be with you.'

'At the birth, you mean?'

'Yes. Or before. Or after. Or all three. I know you've got Miranda.'

'I can't ask her. The baby might come – probably will come – right in the middle of a cookery course. She couldn't just drop everything and leave half a dozen guests twiddling their thumbs.'

'So, who else is there?'

'I don't know. I haven't really thought about it. I'm sure I'll manage on my own.'

'I don't want you to have to just *manage*.'

'I'm fine. I'm a good manager. It's what I do.'

***

At week thirty-four, two things happened. My ankles doubled in size.

And Will turned up.

'What the hell are *you* doing here?'

'Shut up and sit down.'

'What? How have you …?'

'I've been saving my leave. I haven't had a day off since India. When you trailed half way round the world to look after me. So now it's my turn. So sit down and I'll put the kettle on.'

'I don't want tea.'

'It's not *for* tea. It's for the baby. Towels and boiling water. That's what they're always fetching on *Call the Midwife*.'

'The baby isn't due for another six weeks. And, anyway, since when do you watch *Call The Midwife*?'

'Since my best pal told me she was pregnant. You've got to do your homework.'

'It's a bloody telly programme. It's not real. And it's set in the bloody sixties.'

'I know. But that's not the only homework I've been doing.'

'What do you mean?'

Will unzipped his bag and pulled out a copy of Miriam Stoppard's *Pregnancy and Birth Book*. 'It's the complete practical guide for all parents-to-be.'

I pulled him in close and stroked his cheek and he kissed my hair and held me for several seconds before pulling away.

'Right. Enough of this soppy stuff. Where do you keep your towels?'

For the six days that followed, Will fussed around me like a mother hen. He made tea. He rubbed a blend of almond oil and ginger into my swollen ankles. And when I'd been sitting at a laptop for an hour, he came over and switched it off and told me to put my feet up. He was a very kind and sweet house-elf.

On day seven, my backache switched up a gear and I went to bed with a hot pad under it and my feet on a rolled-up bath sheet.

At quarter past three in the morning, the backache was joined by a new tightness across my stomach. Was this it? If so, it was five weeks early. Five.

Relax. It's the middle of the night. You can't wake Will now. And there's no need.

I flicked through my own book, published a couple of decades after Will's. Braxton Hicks contractions. Not exactly painless, but not really painful either.

I noted the time of the tightening then lay down and tried to get back to sleep. This stuff can go on for days, my book said. The message was clear: don't panic.

Fifty minutes later, I had another contraction. A bit beefier, this one. And there was blood on my bedsheet. A 'show', the book said.

Sounds like something they'd have said in the bloody Middle Ages.

Just a small amount of blood, so no big deal. Nothing serious. 'If you're bleeding, call your midwife or maternity unit straight away.' But, no, this wasn't 'bleeding'. This was just the bloody, mucusy plug that comes away in the 'latent' stage of labour.

The real thing could be days away, yet. Relax.

I pulled off the sheet and pulled on a clean one and laid over it two of the massive absorbent pads that Miranda had ordered a box of.

After just nineteen minutes, another contraction. A belter. Proper pain. And a gushing sensation between my legs.

Your waters have broken. All over your clean sheet.

I took a big glug from one of the dozen or so bottles of isotonic sports drink Will had brought back from Sainsbury's in Witney.

Six minutes later, another contraction took my breath away.

Time to wake Will.

'I thought the baby wasn't due for another month.'

'I know. But it's not an exact science. It's about as predictable as a pizza delivery.'

'Right.' Will leapt out of bed and pulled on his silver satin pyjama top. 'What should I do?'

I smiled. 'Call the midwife.'

'Seriously?'

Another contraction – after only three minutes – cut the legs from under me and I dropped to my knees. 'Yes. Seriously.'

Will snatched up his mobile and tapped furiously at the screen. 'Fucking hell. No service. Fuck! Why do you have to live in the fucking back of fucking beyond?'

'Use mine. By my bed.'

He sprinted out of the room and, half sprawled on his bedroom carpet, I leaned my aching back against the side of his bed.

He hopped back into the room seconds later. 'You've got no battery, you fucking dozy cow! How can you *not* keep your phone on charge at a time like this?!'

'I didn't know it was going to *be* a time like this. Relax. Use the landline in the library. The number's by the phone.'

'Jesus. It's like living in the fucking dark ages.'

'Stop moaning, you bloody drama queen, and get a fucking move on.'

He hopped out of the room and I heard him leaping down the stairs three at a time.

Please God, don't let him break his bloody neck.

From half of Thornhill Hall away, I couldn't make out Will's words on the phone. But I heard their volume.

He bounded up the stairs and burst into the room.

'Thirty fucking minutes!'

'It's fine.' Another contraction ripped across my body.

'Why can't you live in a normal place? Why do you have to live somewhere gorgeous and rural and a million fucking miles from fucking anywhere?!'

'Calm down.'

'How the fuck am I meant to calm down?!'

'Aaaaargh!'

My scream snapped Will out of his self-absorption. With my back still leaning against the side of his bed, I opened my legs and gripped his wrist with the nails of my left hand.

'I need you to do as I say.'

'What's happening?'

'THIS BABY IS COMING NOW!'

'Oh shit!'

'So you need to relax. And you need to help me to relax. Okay?' I opened my eyes wide and glared at him. 'I need you now.'

Will slapped his cheek four or five times, like machine-gun fire. 'Okay. I'm here. Do you want me to get some towels?'

'Forget the FUCKING TOWELS!'

'Forget the towels. Right.'

'Rub my back. At the bottom. Firmly but slowly.'

Will reached in behind my sprawling torso and started rubbing.

'Harder than that.'

'Okay.'

Firmer pressure. Some small relief. Good.

I started to do the breathing I'd seen people do in countless birth scenes in TV dramas. 'Right. I need you to look between my legs and tell me what you can see.'

Will's eyes started to roll in his head and I slapped his arm.

'You cannot fucking faint! Not now. Get your shit together!'

Will slapped his face again, hard. 'I'm here.' He looked me in the eyes. 'I'm going in.'

'It's not Operation Desert Storm. I just need you to look and tell me what you can see.' It felt like I had the cantaloupe firmly in place now.

'Your … erm … it's very … erm … open. And the baby's head looks like it's halfway out already.'

I held onto the frame of the bed with both arms and pushed down through my abdomen and into my groin.

'The head's out. Completely. And one shoulder. Jesus!'

I breathed. One big breath. Then several short breaths as I steeled myself for another body-wrenching push.

Then the world went quiet. My heart slowed. My body seemed to relax.

I saw David's face. His hazel eyes. His smile. Felt his lips on mine. His hand on my cheek.

Will looked up from between my legs. 'Just one more push and I think we'll be there.'

I closed my eyes, heard David's velvet vowels – 'I love you, Jennifer Brown' – and pushed with all the strength in my body.

I heard myself scream like my life depended on it.

The next sound I heard was the voice of my son.

He screamed his way into the world with what sounded like a very fine pair of lungs indeed.

Will, his eyes and cheeks red with tears, lifted my baby like he was a moist and bloody unexploded bomb and laid him in my arms, the umbilical cord tight between my legs.

I washed the head of my child with my own tears and William David Brown cried for all he was worth as I covered his tiny, furry, bloody head with a dozen kisses.

I looked up to see Miranda ushering two green-suited paramedics into the room. They knelt down beside me and opened their bags.

Miranda sat down beside me and kissed my head and put her arm round Will as the paramedics dealt with the cord and wrapped a blanket round little William.

'He looks fine. You've done really well. Congratulations. What a team!'

I felt elated. 'Thank you.' Then exhausted. 'God. I'm done in.'

'I'm not surprised.'

Will kissed my cheek. 'You are fucking brilliant.'

'I'm sorry for being bossy.'

'I'm sorry for being a big girl's blouse.'

'You were here. That means everything.'

Will glanced at his phone on the bedside cabinet and his eyes filled with tears again.

'What is it?'

'Today is March the first.' His lips trembled. 'Saint David's Day.'

39

We Are Family

One week later, I had to practically kick Will out.

'But who's going to make you tea and rub your feet?'

'My feet are fine. And I'm perfectly capable of making it to the kitchen to flick the kettle on. I've got Miranda and Marius fussing over me like mother hens and you've given up enough of your time already. You need to get back to work.'

'Oh, bollocks to work. Some things are more important.'

'Of course they are. And you're a darling for giving me so much of yourself, but I need to get used to it being just me and William. You know?'

'I know. I'm being selfish. I just love being around you and this little handsome bundle of cuteness.' He leant his head down to the baby sling and kissed William's fluffy head and my darling little boy blinked his hazel eyes and smiled.

'And it's been wonderful having you here. You've been so brilliant. But I just need to learn to do this on my own.'

'I know.'

The truth was, having Will around was starting to get to me. In practical terms, he was a wonder – endless cups of tea, non-stop laundry support when William threw up every six minutes on a muslin square, and deep-tissue foot rubs whether I wanted them or not.

But, emotionally, he was draining.

Every time he looked at little William, his eyes filled with tears and I knew what he was thinking – how can a world be so cruel? How can it take away this sweet little child's daddy? How can it do this to my friend?

I was having to work hard myself to keep these feelings under control. And I was just about managing it. But looking at Will's face was making it a harder trick to pull off.

So I have to tell you it came as something of a relief to be waving Will off a few days later.

'You will still FaceTime me, won't you?'

'Of course.'

He stroked William's head. 'I'm having bloody withdrawal symptoms already.'

'Go. I promise I'll call you. Tonight.'

'Promise?'

'Yes!'

***

I managed a day of solitude and independence.

One day.

Before Bob and Brenda's orange Allegro spluttered its way up the Thornhill drive and Bob staggered up the steps with about six years' worth of nappies.

'You know there's only *one* child, right?'

Bob rolled his eyes. 'That's what I said to Brenda. She told me to shut my face and load them into the car.'

'I did *not* say that. I said you were miles from the nearest supermarket and you had plenty of storage in this big house and why make life harder than it needs to be.'

'Well, you're both very kind. Thank you. Even if you *are* only here to drink my gin.'

Bob held up a Morrison's bag. 'We stopped off on the way. A litre of Hendrick's for twenty-three quid! A *litre!*'

'You always could spot a bargain.'

'I know. That's how I managed to bag Brenda.'

Brenda countered with a dig in his ribs. 'He only talks like that when you're around.'

'She's right. I know she won't stab me if there are witnesses.'

'Well, these nappies will come in very handy.' I helped Bob lug them into the hall and we dumped them there and wandered through to the sitting room and flopped into chairs. 'But my eco-warrior friend Helen would disown me if she knew I was using disposable ones.'

It was Brenda's turn for eye-rolling. 'They do my head in, that lot. I mean, who's got the time for all that rinsing and washing and drying these days. Why make life harder for yourself?'

Bob winked at me. 'You just like making *my* life harder.'

'Well, you deserve it. Bloody tattoos at your age.'

I stared at Bob, wide-eyed, and he stared back. 'It's your fault.'

I was shocked. 'Me? I haven't got any tattoos.'

'No, I mean being around you.'

'What do you mean? That I lead you astray?'

'No. It's just … well, it's been … sort of …' My uncle suddenly looked like he was going to cry. '… liberating.'

I leaned over and wrapped my arms around him.

Brenda was looking a bit misty, too. 'He's right. Daft sod though he is. And it's … well, it's just made us feel like living our lives and doing things we like. And about family and how important it is. And we feel bad for not being around for quite a lot of your life.'

I went over and kissed her on the cheek. 'Most of that is my fault. I didn't get in touch for years and years. And then only when I wanted something from you. I still feel bad about that. I'm sorry. It was … shitty.'

Brenda stroked my hair. 'Not at all. We knew you were stuck. We knew it was a great opportunity. But you needed a bit of support. And it made us feel good that we could help a bit.'

'You helped a lot. I couldn't have taken that opportunity without you. And without that, there wouldn't have been this. You're right. Family is very important.' I took both Brenda's hands in mine.

She wiped her eyes. 'Right. Enough soppy stuff. Where's my gorgeous little great nephew?'

I whipped out my phone and showed them the video from my BabyCam. 'Sleeping like a cherub.'

'Oh, goodness. He looks like a little king.'

Bob was interested in the technology. 'How do you do that?'

'There's a camera on the cot. Via the app it sends live video footage to my phone. Or you can switch the video off and just use audio, like an old-fashioned baby monitor. But I never do. I like watching him too much.'

Brenda was gaga. 'I'm not surprised. He's just beautiful. Can we see him. For real?'

'I'll take you up.'

'Great.' Then a glance at Bob. 'You can stay here and ogle your tattoo.'

I held up my hand. 'Hang on. Nobody's going anywhere until I've seen Uncle Bob's ink.'

Bob looked a bit sheepish. Then he pulled off his jacket and rolled up his sleeve. On the inside of his forearm, about four inches long, was a beautiful stylised tree – its branches all swirls and whorls – with the word 'family' sort of woven into it. Bob smiled a boyish smile and his eyes filled again.

Brenda smiled and shook her head. 'Bloody idiot.'

This March weekend did what March so often does in this part of the world and pulled on its full Spring glad rags, which gave me and Bob and Brenda the chance to take William round the estate and fill his lungs with fresh Oxfordshire air and his eyes with the sights and sounds of new life.

We sat on the bench overlooking the lake – the one on which Lola Montgomery had opened up to me, kick-starting our friendship – and Bob, with the theme of family clearly still very much on his mind, asked me about Andrew, the half-brother we'd talked about the weekend of the Summer Gala, when I'd pressed my old aunt and uncle to come clean about a hard time early in my parents' marriage that had always been hushed up.

'Have you ever tried to look him up?'

I smiled. 'I've looked him up, yes. In the sense that I know where he is. And how to get in touch. But I haven't. Yet. There just hasn't been the space in my head. You know …'

Brenda put her hand on my arm. 'Of course.'

In fact, I'd done dozens of hours of online research, which had all proved pretty inconclusive. There are thousands of Andrew Barkers online and the few details I'd got hadn't helped me narrow it down terribly much.

Then I'd signed up with FindMyFamily and, with only a few names and dates and my dad's military service number, they'd thrown up a handful of possibilities with, remarkably, photos to go with them. The first couple had been non-starters but I'd hit the jackpot with the third.

It was like looking at my dad as a younger man. Skin a shade darker but the same deep brown eyes. Same chubby cheeks. Same smile.

I'd found him.

'He's a dentist. Andrew Barker DDS. Doctor of Dental Surgery. He lives in Dublin.'

Bob smiled. 'That's great. What are you going to do?'

'I want to meet him. When things have settled down here a bit and I'm in a proper routine with William – that might take a few weeks – but I *am* going to look him up. Make contact.'

Brenda smiled. 'Good for you.'

'It's the right thing to do. I hope.'

'I'm sure it is.'

'I've been thinking – since I found him – about what his life must have been like as a child. After my dad came back here and after I was born. Thinking about how I had a dad – *our* dad – here with me. To take me to the park and play with me on the beach and read me stories in bed. And he didn't have that. And that makes me feel bad.'

'It's not your fault.'

'I know. But I want him to know how I feel. I want to tell him. In person.'

'You have a very good heart, Jennifer Brown.'

***

In the couple of weeks following Bob and Brenda's visit, I got used to my new life as a mum. A single mum.

Miranda was as busy as ever with the cookery school but, whenever she sensed things were getting on top of me – usually by looking at the bags under my eyes from another night with about two hours' sleep – she took William from me for an hour after dinner and ordered me to take a nap.

And Marius took to plying me with nutrient-rich dishes ('To keep you as strong as a cow'), particularly his version of chicken soup, which contained about six kilos of chicken and five types of lentils and was a concoction so rich in protein and carbs a racehorse would have needed a lie-down after just one bowl.

Things were settling down.

40

Not Half

The first of May found me sitting in the lounge of a chain hotel in Warwick – the kind of place that thinks complimentary notepaper that looks like it's been made from beaten eggs will mask the fact that they haven't hoovered under the radiator by the desk for about six months.

Sitting. And sweating.

For two reasons.

Firstly, I'd never left William overnight before. Bob and Brenda had motored up to Thornhill to be on babysitting duty – any excuse to see their gorgeous great-nephew – but they'd never had children (only canaries). Still, Miranda had assured me she'd be around the whole twenty-four hours, as a kind of unobtrusive backstop. And though she'd never had children either, she'd been managing Mad Mary for the past twenty years and, frankly, there is no more severe test of life skills.

And, secondly, I was about to meet my half-brother. For the first time.

A couple of weeks earlier, while William was having an uncharacteristically long lie-in, and before fear and common sense could stop me, I'd sent an email to the address at Andrew's dental practice that the FindMyFamily people had given me. Then I'd sat back and waited.

I'd only had to wait half a day. Just after lunch, I got a reply.

He was delighted I'd made contact. Was thrilled to learn he had a sister. Was regularly over to the UK for conferences. In fact, had a conference coming up in Warwick in a couple of weeks' time. Could we meet? If it wasn't too soon? He'd understand if I needed time.

If the events of the past several months had taught me anything, it's that you never know how much time you'll have. So, that thing you want to do – feel you need to do – do it. Act now.

And the very warm smile on the very familiarly shaped face of the man who walked towards me with both arms outstretched was a clear sign that this had been the right thing to do.

'I cannot tell you how delighted I am to meet you.' His voice had a softness that reminded me at once of my dad and, very powerfully and strangely, of David.

'I'm sorry it's taken me so long to find you.'

'Oh, please don't apologise.' A very pleasant Irish lilt. 'I, too, could have dug a bit deeper. But I didn't. Out of fear, probably.'

'You knew about me?'

'Not exactly. I knew there was another life, somewhere. My mother was always – she left us seven years ago, after a long and very cruel illness – she was always very reticent about the past. She was a very strong woman, and unsentimental. She didn't see any merit in looking at the past and she refused to do it, choosing only to look forward. And I get that, now, at my age. But, as a younger man, I did wonder. It was a mystery. And you've been kind enough and brave enough to solve it, for both of us.'

'That's a lovely thing to say. Thank you.'

'Well, when you got in touch, I just knew this would be a good thing. Any man my mother would let into her life had to be a very fine individual indeed – she was a remarkable person – so I reckoned that any child he brought into the world, and raised, would have to be a person very much worth knowing.' He held both my hands and smiled into my moist eyes. 'And, I have to say, it is very clear to me that that is most definitely the case.'

I stepped forward and wrapped my arms around him and we stood together – we two siblings separated by love and bitterness and tragedy – for several seconds, dripping tears onto each other's shoulders, in the foyer of a Warwick hotel that really needed to fire its cleaning staff.

In the hours that followed, over a long lunch, then over several coffees, and later a very smooth Irish whiskey, we learned about each other's lives and personalities and how they converged in many ways.

I had a fear of heights and so did he. I hated dried fruit, so did he. I was a natural peacemaker but, pushed into a corner, would come out fighting. That was him to a tee, he said.

He told me about his family – his wife Maggie ('your sister-in-law'), his daughter Kathleen and son Michael ('your niece and nephew').

And I told him about William. And about the joy and then the tragedy of David, and the complicated family dynamic that had left me with. And about my life before – about Pete, and how awfully that episode had ended, and about the very good friends who'd helped me and supported me and saved me, and about the luck that had sustained me, about the various jobs I'd had and the strange and wonderful people I'd met along the way, about the challenges and the trials and the hardships and the opportunities and the whole crazy, messy beauty of it all.

Andrew smiled. 'What a remarkable life you've had so far. It's a terrific story, and you tell it very well. Have you ever thought of writing it down?'

'How do you mean?'

'I think it would resonate with a lot of people. You know, as a book or something. It's a very uplifting story. It's not all sweetness and light – far from it – but it's real. Authentic. And that's what a lot of people want, I think. Authentic stories about real life. It's just a thought. I'm not a writer or anything. But I read quite a lot. And I'd read that. I think a lot of people would.'

The cogs were turning in my brain. 'Well, no, I've never thought about it. I'm not a writer, either.'

'You tell a good story.'

'But this is just a chat, over whiskey. It's not the same as being a writer. I don't think that's something I could do.'

'Why not? You've done a lot of other things. Why not writing?'

'I just don't think I'm a writer.'

'Maybe you're right.' Andrew lifted his glass. 'Then again, maybe you *are* a writer and you just don't know it yet.'

41

A Bittersweet Symphony

Miranda was all for it. 'It's a terrific idea. He sounds like a very astute chap, that brother of yours.'

'A *brother*. It sounds crazy when I say it. But that's how he referred to himself, and to me. Brother and sister. Not *half*-brother and *half*-sister. And I've got a sister-in-law. And a niece and a nephew. It's just lovely.'

'I'm so pleased for you. He sounds like a great guy. And, as I say, a very canny one. So?'

'So, what?'

'So when are you going to start writing?'

***

A couple of weeks later, after an exhausting day of trying William on solids – a roasted banana and rosemary puree that Miranda had found a recipe for – I finally got him down to sleep at around eight.

I poured myself a large glass of the Paulus I still had a case and a half of in the cellar and, with the BabyCam open and my phone propped up against a fruit bowl on the library table, I pulled out my laptop.

After staring at a blank screen for a good thirty minutes, I began to type.

Without having the slightest idea where it was going, I rattled off twenty-two pages that first evening and flopped onto my bed at just gone one in the morning.

I couldn't sleep. My head was full of ideas and snapshots and questions. How should I structure it? Who should I include? Should I only tell the good, happy bits? No – that would be a lie. And this needed to be true. 'Authentic' was the word Andrew had used.

But I needed my sleep. So I grabbed a notepad from the writing desk by the window and decided it should live at my bedside, so I could empty my mind and let slumber take hold. I scribbled down a few notes. Then I plugged my earphones in and turned on the sound of rain on a tent that always gets me off to sleep.

It didn't work.

I jumped out of bed and fired up the laptop.

I typed on through the night, through Jon Bon Jovi heralding the dawn with his head-splitting crowing, through Marius sliding his bread into the Aga at his usual 6.30 – regular as clockwork – and even through a gurgling William on my lap clapping his hands and drooling all over my spacebar.

In the kitchen, Miranda looked concerned. 'God, you look like you've been up all night.'

I poured myself a mug of Marius's coffee and it tasted like a kick in the pants. 'That's because I have.'

Miranda looked at William bobbing sweetly back and forth in his bouncer chair. 'You bad boy, keeping mummy awake all night. It's a good job you're gorgeous or she'd have strangled you by now.'

I took another belt of coffee. 'No, he's been fine. Slept right through until seven.'

Miranda looked puzzled. 'So what have you been doing all night?'

I smiled over my coffee mug. 'Discovering I'm a writer.'

***

Eighteen months later …

Thirty-nine cookery courses, six film location gigs, and about sixteen thousand cups of coffee later, I had a manuscript.

One hundred and seventy-four rough pages.

Actually, not that rough. I'd been through the whole thing six times – fixing typing errors, looking up bits of grammar I wasn't sure of, checking dates, changing names – and I was actually pretty pleased with the result.

But what did *I* know?

Nothing.

Better ask someone who knows something.

Nick Boyd laughed out loud when I handed him a second lemon drizzle cake.

'I could get used to this. It's very kind, but you didn't have to bring another cake.'

'Well, you didn't have to agree to read my manuscript. And offer to maybe, possibly, perhaps, perchance, haply … I can't think of any more synonyms … show it to your agent.'

'Ah. So the cake is a bribe.'

'A shameless bribe, yes.'

'Well, I'm a writer so, by definition, I have no morals. I am very happy to accept your bribe. The last bribe was delicious.'

'Oh, that wasn't a bribe. But I suppose it was a sort of calling card.'

He ushered me towards a large armchair and sat down opposite me, my three and a half kilos of ditzy storytelling in his lap.

'Well, if you write anywhere near as well as you bake, I'm in for a treat.'

I looked at the pile of paper sitting on his jeans and all my confidence and self-belief suddenly evaporated. 'Er … it's very different from your own work. Of course.'

'I'm sure it is. I *hope* it is.'

'It's a very different kind of writing.'

'In my view, there are only two kinds of writing – good and bad.'

'That's what I'm worried about. You will be honest, won't you? That's what I need. To know honestly if it's any good. If I can really do this.'

Nick Boyd, author of eight best-selling psychological thrillers, winner of International Thriller Writer Awards in 2009 and 2013, and owner of a very comfortable former rectory and a very shiny Porsche, looked me in the eye.

'Are you sure you want the truth? Even if my true assessment is that your writing isn't very good?'

I took a couple of deep breaths. 'Yes. I've had plenty of knocks over the years. Kicks in the teeth. Rugs pulled from under me. Hammer blows to the heart. If the truth is I'm not a writer, and my stuff's only fit for lighting the fire with, I can handle it. I *will* handle it. Goodness knows there's enough going on in my life to keep me busy and happy and fulfilled. I don't *need* this. I just fancy it.'

Nick hadn't taken his eyes off me. He smiled. 'That's the best way to be. Realistic. Pragmatic.' He patted the pile of paper on his knee. 'You didn't have to print it out. You could have just emailed me the file.'

'But then you'd have nothing to light the fire with.'

I promised myself I wouldn't fret. Or sweat. Or check my emails every six seconds.

I was doing all three.

When a week had gone by and I'd heard nothing, I wrote him a long and grovelling email begging his forgiveness for imposing my pile of llama poop on him and assuring him he didn't need to respond and apologising for even approaching him in the first place and couldn't we just forget I'd ever turned up on his doorstep with my fucking stupid manuscript and my shitty lemon drizzle cake?

Then I pressed Delete.

Four days later, I got an email.

Hi Jennifer

Sorry not to have got back to you sooner. I'd forgotten I was delivering a workshop at the Aldeburgh Festival last week and I had a bit of work to do to prepare for that.

Anyway, I finished your manuscript last night …

My heart had jumped onto my tongue. I wasn't sure I had the courage to read on.

… and I have to tell you I think you've got something really rather good here. It reads very well. It's full of humour and emotion and wonderfully drawn characters. The pace is good. You balance the rough with the smooth very nicely. I think, commercially, it's very strong.

With your permission, I'd like to show it to Amanda, my agent. If you're happy for me to do that, would you email me the file – I don't think my carrier pigeon is strong enough to lug the paper copy all the way to Holland Park.

I stood up and walked over to the library window. Two collared doves were strolling round the lawn, near George's bench.

with your permission … if you're happy …

I leapt back to the library table and fired back a reply.
Play it cool. Don't be a gushy schoolgirl.

Hi Nick

It's so kind of you to take the time to go through the manuscript, particularly when you had such a busy week last week.

Thank you for your kind words. I'd be delighted for you to show the work to Amanda. I've attached the full manuscript here.

Best wishes

Jennifer

And then, although it wasn't even lunchtime, I poured myself a gin.

***

One hundred and twenty-three. Zara, the manager at Waterstones in Piccadilly, had counted them.

'It's a very respectable crowd for the launch of a first book. There were only forty-six at the last Maggie Swinton launch. You should be pleased.'

I wasn't pleased – I was absolutely ecstatic. In another world. A world where a pile of books on a table in one of the most prominent stores in the capital had my name on the cover. Where its windows had posters with my name and face on them. Where online bookclubs and book bloggers had interviewed me. Where there were now over a hundred five-star reviews on Amazon. Where I'd received cards and flowers and lovely emails from friends across the years and across nations – from Philippe and Madeleine who'd trained me in Bordeaux, from Harry and Sheikh Saeed who'd been my top clients at Artisan Wines, from Rosemary in Boston, from Viv and Roger who'd been my guardian angels after the awful breakup with Pete, from Helen and Paul, who'd helped me get my life back together, from Hilary, Rose and Trisha – the old HRTs from Intext – from Larry, who'd treated me to a very rocky couple of weeks in Sydney when I was trying to find myself, from Karen, the old English-teacher friend I'd spent a disastrous week in Spain with, from Lola Montgomery, the Hollywood star who'd become a friend, from Leon, my mum's former live-in carer, from Madison in the New York office that had been the workplace of my darling David.

And assembled here, in front of the little stage erected in this room, gathered to cheer me on, so many of the people whose lives were intertwined with mine – Veronica, Miranda, Jonathan, Nat, Cécile, Edmund and Nutella, Marius, Kate, Robbie, Delyth, Bob and Brenda. And Andrew, my new brother.

And sitting very proudly on the front row, Patricia and, next to her, Lottie, with four-year-old Hugo on one knee and, on the other, my two-year-old son William, with every passing day looking more like the father he would never know.

I looked down at my black dress and the delicate Peace Rose I'd pinned to it and remembered that glorious summer evening with David and the overwhelming happiness I'd felt at that moment.

There's nowhere else I'd rather be right now, in the whole world, than here with you.

But we're on a journey. And mine had been a journey without a map – maybe there *is* no map – and a journey full of twists and bends and junctions and holdups and breakdowns and vast open roads, at once terrifying and exhilarating.

I was pulled back into the room by the sight of my outrageous and fabulous and ridiculous best friend Will, chief cheerleader of them all, clapping for all he was worth, resplendent in orange linen suit and red velvet fedora, like the love child of Zandra Rhodes and Quentin Crisp.

I looked out at the whole glorious assembly and started to shake. Not with nerves but with the sudden and powerful realisation of how lucky I was. To have people. To have funny and sad and desperate and strange and tragic and uplifting stories to tell.

To have life.

I took a deep breath and walked out onto the stage.

About The Author

Author Angie Langley was born in Somerset and has lived in the south west of England all her life. Nowadays home is a 17th century thatched cottage on the banks of the River Avon in Wiltshire. A tiny piece of heaven and a true writer's paradise. Angie's books are based on life experiences, inspired by the highs and lows of a distant past that has given her the strength to tackle each day with a smile. Lighthearted and poignant she tells her story with honesty and bags of humour focusing on everyday situations many women will relate to. Angie would like to thank you for buying her books and would be delighted to hear from you, so do please follow her via visiting her website: **www.jenniferbrownsjourney.co.uk**

Other titles available to buy in the Jennifer Brown series.

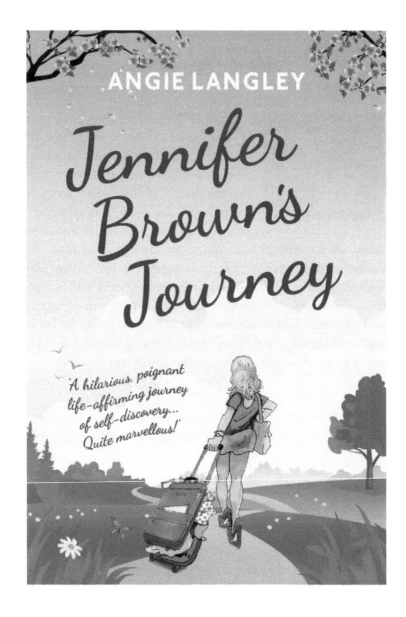

ANGIE LANGLEY

Jennifer Brown's Journey

'A hilarious, poignant
life-affirming journey
of self-discovery...
Quite marvellous!'

Other titles available to buy in the Jennifer Brown series.

ANGIE LANGLEY

Jennifer
Brown
Moving On

"An uproariously human Everywoman
who's fast becoming chicklit's
most engaging heroine"